MESA VERDE VICTIM

Praise for the National Park Mystery Series

"Graham's winning fourth National Park mystery uses Yosemite as a backdrop for a host of shady dealings and dangerous power struggles. This zippy tale uses lush descriptions of natural beauty and twisted false leads to create an exciting, rewarding puzzle."
—*PUBLISHERS WEEKLY*

"As always, the highlight of Graham's National Park Mystery Series is his extensive knowledge of the parks system, its lands, and its people."
—*KIRKUS REVIEWS*

"Intriguing . . . Graham has a true talent for describing the Rockies' flora and fauna, allowing his readers to feel almost as if they were trekking the park themselves."
—*MYSTERY SCENE MAGAZINE*

"Graham has crafted a multilevel mystery that plumbs the emotions of greed and jealousy."
—*DURANGO HERALD*

"Graham has created a beautifully balanced book, incorporating intense action scenes, depth of characterization, realistic landscapes, and historical perspective."
—*REVIEWING THE EVIDENCE*

"Masterfully plotted in confident prose, *Arches Enemy* is not only an adventurous and fascinating mystery you can't put down, it delivers important insight on ancestral cultures and their sacred lands. Scott Graham proves yet again that he is one of the finest."
—CHRISTINE CARBO, author of
A Sharp Solitude: A Glacier Mystery

"A winning blend of archaeology and intrigue, Graham's series turns our national parks into places of equal parts beauty, mystery, and danger."
—EMILY LITTLEJOHN, author of
Shatter the Night: A Detective Gemma Monroe Mystery

"One part mystery, one part mysticism, one part mayhem—
and all parts thrilling."
—CRAIG JOHNSON, *New York Times* bestselling author of
Land of Wolves: A Longmire Mystery

"Filled with murder and mayhem, jealousy and good detective work—
an exciting, nonstop read."
—ANNE HILLERMAN, *New York Times* bestselling author of
The Tale Teller: A Leaphorn, Chee & Manuelito Novel

"Only the best novelists have the gift of propelling readers into the
middle of artfully crafted adventures, and with *Yosemite Fall*, Scott
Graham once again proves he belongs in the very first rank."
—JEFF GUINN, *New York Times* bestselling author
of *The Road to Jonestown*

"Engrossing . . . a glorious portrait of one of the most compelling
landscapes on earth. Graham clearly knows the territory.
A topnotch read."
—WILLIAM KENT KRUEGER,
New York Times bestselling author of *This Tender Land*

"What an extraordinary ride! You know when a reader says they
couldn't put the book down? *Yellowstone Standoff* is one of those rare
books . . . a tour de force."
—WIN BLEVINS, *New York Times* bestselling author of *Going Home*

"*Yellowstone Standoff* takes man versus nature—and man tangled up
with nature—right to the brink of wild suspense."
—MARK STEVENS, Colorado Book Award-winning
author of *Lake of Fire: An Allison Coil Mystery*

"One of the most engaging mysteries I've read in a long while . . .
delivers it all and then some."
—MARGARET COEL, *New York Times* bestselling
author of *Winter's Child: A Wind River Mystery*

"Get ready for leave-you-breathless high country southwestern adventure."
—MICHAEL McGARRITY, *New York Times* bestselling
author of *Residue: A Kevin Kerney Mystery*

MESA VERDE VICTIM

A National Park Mystery
by Scott Graham

TORREY HOUSE PRESS

SALT LAKE CITY • TORREY

This is a work of fiction set in a real place. All characters in this novel are fictitious. Any resemblance to actual events or persons, living or dead, is entirely coincidental.

First Torrey House Press Edition, June 2020
Copyright © 2020 by Scott Graham

Published by Torrey House Press
Salt Lake City, Utah
www.torreyhouse.org

International Standard Book Number: 978-1-948814-23-2
E-book ISBN: 978-1-948814-24-9
Library of Congress Control Number: 2019952009

Cover design by Kathleen Metcalf
Cover art "Intersecting Planes" by David Jonason,
    www.davidjonason.com
Interior design by Rachel Davis
Distributed to the trade by Consortium Book Sales and Distribution

Torrey House Press offices in Salt Lake City sit on the homelands of Ute, Goshute, Shoshone, and Paiute nations. Offices in Torrey are in homelands of Paiute, Ute, and Navajo nations.

ABOUT THE COVER

Acclaimed Southwest landscape artist David Jonason painted the Mesa Verde scene that appears on the cover of *Mesa Verde Victim*.

Combining a keenly observant eye and inspiration drawn from a number of twentieth-century art movements, including Cubism, Futurism, Precisionism, and Art Deco, David Jonason achieves a uniquely personal vision through his vivid, dreamlike oil paintings of the American Southwest. Jonason connects on canvas the traditional arts and crafts of the Southwest's native tribes with the intricate patterns in nature known as fractals. "For me as a painter," he says, "it's a reductive and simplifying process of finding the natural geometries in nature, just as Navajo weavers and Pueblo potters portray the natural world through geometric series of zigzags, curves, and other patterns."

"Intersecting Planes" is used by permission of The Jonason Studio, www.davidjonason.com.

To the many archaeologists working to preserve Ancestral Puebloan history across the Southwest, with gratitude

PROLOGUE

Mesa Verde, Colorado
September 1891

Joey Cannon sliced through the roof of the hidden vault with the blade of his shovel. At first sight, the concealed chamber looked coffin-sized.

The sixteen-year-old stood on the uncovered mud-and-thatch roof of the buried vault. He was neck deep in the crater he'd dug over the last several hours, having deepened and widened the cavity by turns, tossing shovelfuls of soil and pebbles over his shoulder in dusty arcs. It was long past nightfall, his kerosene lantern low on fuel and sputtering. Sweat streamed in runnels down his back. His palms were blistered, the muscles of his arms and shoulders crying out for relief.

He had until midnight, not a second longer, to unearth the rumored cache. If, after centuries in hiding, the artifacts waited as Gustaf Nordenskiöld insisted, and if Joey reached them in time, he was to wrap them in cloth, stow them in his saddlebags, and set off for the train station thirty miles to the east, descending the rocky trail from the dig site, changing horses at the Mancos livery in the pre-dawn darkness, and galloping over Mancos Divide to reach Durango by mid-morning. There, he would add the treasures to the boxcar already loaded with objects gathered from Mesa Verde by Gustaf over the last two months. Joey would collect the reward pledged by the Swedish explorer-scientist, and the train would chuff away to Denver, the artifacts bound ultimately for Stockholm.

Joey paused to wipe his brow with the sleeve of his coarse work shirt. The pungent scent of piñon and juniper wafted off the clifftop above. The hour was late, the minutes ticking past. He tucked the tail of his shirt into his canvas work pants and straightened his suspenders, thumbing them over his shoulders. He took a bite of dried meat from the strip of jerky in his pocket, resettled his bandanna over his nose, and resumed the process of breaking into the vault, bent on discovering the hidden cache in time—and thereby setting a new course for his life.

He'd toiled since childhood on his family's root-vegetable farm. The small plot of land on the banks of the Mancos River was to him a place of endless tedium. Plant, irrigate, weed, repeat, year after monotonous year, with little opportunity for formal schooling. For as long as he could remember, he'd lived with the desire to pursue a genuine education, something, anything, beyond the bits of writing he managed for himself at night, by lantern light, after evening chores and before he fell exhausted into the narrow bed in the loft he shared with his younger brother Carl.

Local girls ignored him, batting their eyes instead at the wealthy sons of ranchers and store owners. Soon enough, however, the girls would know their mistake. The money he'd already earned from Gustaf plus the sizable bonus the Swede promised for the secret cache of artifacts would enable Joey to buy a ticket to Denver and find a job in the big city, there to pursue the studies the money would afford him.

Brown-haired, mustachioed Gustaf, in his early twenties, had stopped by the Cannon farm several weeks ago. Seated on his gleaming roan, the Swede had inquired of Joey's father in stilted English as to the availability of a laborer unafraid of hard work. Joey's father offered up his oldest son for a share of Joey's earnings. As Joey loped away on Gustaf's extra mount toward the green mesa looming two thousand feet above the Cannon farm, he directed a triumphant glance back at his siblings, chief among them Carl, a year younger and equally determined to escape the hardscrabble life he shared with Joey in the Mancos Valley.

In Gustaf's employ, Joey worked his way across the plateau with the three other members of the Swede's hired excavation team, moving from one ancient, abandoned, stone-and-mortar housing complex to the next. Prehistoric people had constructed the multistory dwellings deep in the plateau's canyons over many centuries, until the people had deserted the mesa en masse for unknown reasons, leaving an abundance of their worldly goods behind. With his fellow workers, Joey collected and packaged in straw-filled crates the ancient people's abandoned possessions—finely crafted clay pots and mugs; clothing and jewelry, including beaded turquoise necklaces, deerskin blankets, and turkey-feather shawls; projectile points, knife blades, and hide scrapers flaked from obsidian; and spiritual fetishes and children's toys fashioned from wood and clay to resemble rabbits, ravens, great horned owls, and bighorn sheep. Joey and the other hired hands also removed human remains interred in midden piles below the abandoned complexes—perfectly preserved skulls and full skeletons of adults, and the corpses of infants wrapped in blankets and tucked in reed baskets.

Gustaf rode back and forth between the plateau and his suite in Durango's Strater Hotel, assessing the team's progress during his visits to the remote canyons that cut straight down into the top of the sandstone plateau, and communicating by letter and telegram while in Durango with his primary financier, his father, the famed baron and noted Arctic explorer Adolf Eric Nordenskiöld.

At the height of the collection process, Gustaf was detained in his room at the Strater, accused by local authorities of the theft and attempted removal of cultural items from the United States. But the young Swede's wealth and connections resulted in his release after only a few hours. His succinct telegram home, the contents of which he shared with Joey, said it all: "Much Trouble Some Expense No Danger."

Brief though it was, Gustaf's detainment spurred him to move up the departure date for his return to Europe—and to single out Joey for the solitary mission in the heretofore unexplored canyon on the far west side of the plateau, culminating in tonight's hurried dig.

Midnight was less than an hour away when Joey broke through a layer of dried mud and intertwined sticks with the tip of his shovel, punching into the chamber at the bottom of the depression he'd dug over the preceding hours. He twisted the shovel, ripping apart the thatched twigs to create a blade-wide opening through the roof of the vault beneath his feet. He squatted and reached through the opening into the concealed chamber, his arm disappearing to his elbow. Sweeping his hand back and forth, he captured only air in his extended fingers. He lay on his stomach and extended the full length of his arm through the opening. He grinned as he swung his arm through the stale air of the vault. This had to be the secret chamber Gustaf sought.

Joey's fingers struck something stone-like standing upright in the hidden space. The unseen artifact toppled over with a quiet *clink*.

He withdrew his arm. The stale odor of must seeped from the vault. Thatched willow branches, sheered by his shovel blade, formed a ragged edge around the mouth of the opening. He gripped the thatched branches and tugged. A portion of plaited sticks and dried mud the size of a dinner plate came away in his hands. He tore off additional chunks of sticks and mud.

He directed his lantern through the enlarged opening and

into the chamber. The toppled artifact lay on the dusty floor of the vault beneath him, amid a dozen more of the objects lined upright on the bottom of the small room. He drew an exhilarated breath. The reward and the new life it promised him were nearly within his grasp.

He placed his lamp in the dirt at the bottom of the depression and swung his feet into the opening to the chamber, preparing to shimmy into the secret vault. Clods of dirt rolled past him, tumbling down the side of the cavity he'd dug into the floor of the alcove, and the sharpened blade of an ax struck the top of his head. The ax cleaved his skull, parting bone and brain matter in a powerful, deadly blow.

Joey's killer slid to the bottom of the depression and withdrew the blade of the ax from Joey's head with a slippery *snick*. Joey's body slumped sideways and lay twitching. The man tugged Joey's feet from the chamber opening and dropped into the hidden vault in Joey's place, crouching with his leather satchel over his shoulder and Joey's flickering lantern in his hand.

The lantern illuminated the low-roofed vault lined with the priceless artifacts sought by Gustaf—and others. The man filled his satchel with the objects and hoisted himself out of the chamber. He lifted Joey's inert body to a sitting position and shoved. The teenager's corpse slithered through the opening and flopped backward to the floor of the chamber with a muted *thump*.

The man wedged the plate-sized portions of sticks and mud back over the opening, resealing the secret vault. He climbed out of the neck-deep depression and set about refilling it with Joey's shovel. Dirt and pebbles poured down the sides of the cavity and gathered atop the closed chamber. The stick-and-mud thatching, back in place over the opening to the vault, disappeared beneath the cascading debris as the man transformed the chamber, shovelful by shovelful, into Joey's unmarked grave.

PART ONE

"People here have begun to oppose my excavation and work in a way that makes it desirable for me to soon leave this area."

—Gustaf Nordenskiöld,
after his 1891 detention on charges of trespassing
and cultural theft in the Mesa Verde region

1

"I hate this, I hate this, I hate this!" Rosie Ortega screeched. She squeezed her eyes shut, her hands gripping the rope affixed to the seat harness belted around her plump waist as she descended on auto-belay to the base of the indoor rock-climbing wall.

Chuck Bender wrapped her in a bear hug. "You did fine up there," he assured her.

"No, I didn't," she cried, stomping her foot on the padded gym floor. Tears pooled in her eyes. She wriggled from Chuck's grasp and tore at the climbing rope knotted at her waist. "I barely got off the ground."

Other climbers in the gym averted their gazes as Chuck helped twelve-year-old Rosie free herself from the rope.

"Carm's so good," she blubbered, her lower lip trembling. She pressed her knuckles to her walnut-brown eyes. "I *hate* her," she said to the floor.

"I heard that," fourteen-year-old Carmelita called from where she clung to molded-resin holds thirty feet overhead, working an inverted route extending across the ceiling from the top of the wall.

Chuck craned his head at her. "Your sister didn't mean it."

"Yes, I did," Rosie declared, looking up. "Well, the good part, anyway."

"That much would be right," Chuck told her. He massaged the back of her neck below her mane of curly black hair billowing from the bottom of her climbing helmet. "Your sister *is* good at this sport. Which is a problem for me, too."

Rosie's watery eyes widened. "For you?"

"I've always been a rock climber for the fun of it. Nowadays, though, climbing is a big-time sport, with everybody making it into a massive competition. And, like you said, it just so happens Carm's pretty good at it."

"Because she's so skinny," Rosie pouted.

"Just because," Chuck said. "But you and I have to remember we're climbing for fun when we're messing around down low on the wall."

She stomped her foot again. "I want to do something else for fun. Something that's just for me."

"Hmm." Chuck cocked his head at her and closed one eye. "I kinda like that idea. Maybe you and I can come up with something different for you to do while Carm's spending all her free time here at the gym, zipping around the ceiling like a spider monkey."

"I'm *not* a monkey," Carmelita exclaimed from above. Her dark ponytail hung long and straight down toward the floor from the back of her helmet. "That's racist."

Chuck grinned up at her. "I said you *climb* like one. Sheesh."

Carmelita lost her grip and fell a few feet from the ceiling before her rope caught her. "You're so culturally inappropriate," she admonished Chuck as she swung back and forth beneath the holds.

She shook out her chalked hands while the auto-belay engaged and the rope automatically unspooled, lowering her to the ground.

Chuck fixed her with a teasing smile. "Let me get this straight. You're labeling me a culturally inappropriate white man even though I married a Latina woman and have been stepfather to her two hotshot Latina daughters for the last five years?"

"O ... M ... G," Carmelita announced breathily. "I can't believe you just called Rosie and me 'hot.' That's so totally and completely *wrong*."

"I didn't say 'hot.' I said 'hotshot.'"

The corner of Carmelita's mouth twisted. "It still has the word 'hot' in it."

Chuck sighed but maintained his grin. "The two of you are handsome. How's that?"

"Better. Still judgmental, though."

"I'm just trying to let you know how proud I am of you." He spread his hands. "But I can't win, can I?"

"Nope."

He glanced at the clock mounted on the wall above the climbing gym's front desk. "It's about time to head for home. *Mamá* will be coming off her shift in a little while. I need to get started on a culturally inappropriate dinner for us." He dipped his graying head at Carmelita and smiled. "How about tacos?"

She groaned. "You're awful."

"*Grrracias,*" he said, giving the *r* an extra-hard trill.

"You're . . . you're . . . incorrigible." She added a matching trill to the double *r* of the English word, offering up the slightest of smiles.

Chuck put his chalked hands to his stomach, leaving matching white prints on his blue T-shirt. "Got me." He pointed at her shiny black climbing tights. "The way you use such big words, you're getting to be too smart for your britches, you know that?"

Carmelita's skin-hugging tights rose to her waist. Her burgundy top featured the Durango Climbing Team logo across its snug chest. The top was sleeveless and cut high across her midriff, baring her flat stomach and the smooth skin of her shoulders.

"That's my plan for world domination—using my prodigious intelligence to rule the planet," she said.

"Ooo, scary," said Chuck. "But I imagine you'll hold off taking over the world until later this afternoon, after your all-important run, right?" He reached behind her head and gave her ponytail a yank.

"Hey," she protested, ducking away. "You'll get my hair all chalky."

"*Lo siento,*" he apologized. "What are you up to now, twenty miles a day?"

"Five. Well, sometimes seven. All on dirt trails to protect my knees. Coach Tania says the climbing-running combo is good—upper body, lower body."

"Sounds like you're totally dialed in, as per usual. All that's left, it would seem, is for you to take over the world and dial things in for everybody else on the planet, too."

Chuck crossed the room to his soft-sided gear duffle. The navy bag rested on the floor next to Rosie's purple duffle and Carmelita's burgundy climbing-team bag. He toweled the chalk off his hands, pulled his fleece top over his head, and changed from climbing shoes into sneakers. He retrieved his phone from the bag. Its screen lit up with text messages the instant he turned it on.

WHAT IS HAPPENING AT YOUR PLACE??? read the most recent text, from Beatrice Roberts, the elderly widow who lived next door to the house Chuck had picked up in Durango's historic Grid district a decade ago, several years before marrying Janelle Ortega, the then-single mother to Carmelita and Rosie, after a whirlwind romance.

He scanned the other texts in backward time order.

The second-most recent: *If this is the phone of Chuck Bender, please contact the Durango Police Department immediately.*

Again, minutes earlier: *If this is the phone of Chuck Bender, please contact the Durango Police Department immediately.*

Ten minutes before that, an initial message from Beatrice: *Chuck are you there? Do you know anything about the sirens?*

Shoving his phone into the pocket of his climbing sweats and waving for the girls to follow, Chuck sprinted for the parking lot.

* * *

He sped south on Main Avenue minutes later, hands locked on the wheel of his big, blocky, Bender Archaeological crew-cab pickup truck. Carmelita sat opposite him in the front seat. Rosie hunched forward on the rear bench seat behind Carmelita, peering past her sister's shoulder. It was midday, the second Saturday in October, the cloudless sky brilliant blue, the temperature edging into the low seventies, the leaves on the cottonwoods lining the primary thoroughfare through town golden yellow.

"What's going on?" Carmelita demanded as Chuck blasted through a caution light well above the speed limit.

"We're about to find out," he said through gritted teeth.

Turning off Main into the Grid neighborhood, he slung the pickup around tight corners, left, right, left again.

"Whoo-hoo!" Rosie cheered from the rear seat, flopping from side to side with the swerving truck.

Chuck slid around a final corner and roared onto their block. Several black-and-white Durango Police Department sport-utility vehicles crowded the street ahead. The police SUVs were parked at haphazard angles in front of the house, their bar lights flashing.

Chuck slammed the truck to a stop in the middle of the street, hopped out, and ran for the house.

Janelle had left home at five that morning for a fill-in paramedic shift with the Durango Fire and Rescue Department, taking the place of a full-timer who needed the day off. Her shift wasn't over yet—but what if she'd returned home for some unknown reason while he and the girls were at the climbing gym?

He charged up the sidewalk. A twenty-something police officer in uniform blues, brass badge gleaming on her chest, stepped off the covered front porch of the house. The officer's skin was the color of mocha, her dark brown eyes lined with black makeup.

"Slow down," she warned Chuck, raising her left hand as she crossed the front yard. Her right hand hovered above the pistol holstered at her waist.

Inscribed on a tag beneath her badge, her last name, Anand, identified her as East Indian, an anomaly among Durango's mostly white citizenry interspersed with Latinos and Native Americans.

"This is my house," Chuck said as he reached her on the sidewalk, aiming his chin at the one-and-a-half-story brick Victorian behind the young police officer. His throat was tight, his breath constricted. "My wife."

"You're Mr. Bender?"

"Yes."

"ID."

"What?"

"I need to see some identification."

He slapped his hands to the side pockets of his sweats. "I left my wallet in my bag in the truck."

"You'll have to go get it."

"Not a chance." Chuck shoved his way past the officer.

"Oh, no, you don't," she said, following him.

He yanked his phone from his pocket. Its screen glowed with the texts from the police department. He waved it behind him at her as he walked. "I came as soon as I saw these."

She huffed as she trailed him across the front yard. When he neared the porch, she said, "Not that way. Around back."

Changing course, Chuck put his shoulder to the faded wooden gate at the side of the house, slamming it open and striding along the narrow passage beside the head-high wooden fence separating the house from Beatrice's house next door.

"What can you tell me?" Chuck demanded over his shoulder to the officer.

"I'm on perimeter." She jogged to keep up. "You'll have to talk to the others."

They reached the back of the house. A single-car garage filled one corner of the compact backyard. In the other corner, the branches of an apple tree extended over a fallow, raised-bed garden.

Between the garage and garden bed, the gate that led through the back fence to the rear alley stood open. On the cracked asphalt of the alleyway, framed by the open gate and covered by a white sheet, lay what was, based on its shape, clearly a human body.

Chuck came up short in the middle of the yard, staring through the gate.

The body lay on its back. Red stains spotted the sheet, which stretched over the human form from head to toe. A sizable stomach pressed the sheet upward at the middle.

Chuck quaked at the sight of the corpse, his legs growing weak with a combination of relief and horror. The dead body was not Janelle; it did not have her slender frame. But who was it?

He resumed walking toward the back gate, his eyes locked on the body. A uniformed police officer stepped from the alley into the yard and swung the gate closed behind her, blocking his view.

The officer was Sandra Kingsley. Like Chuck, she was in her mid-forties. She was tall and willowy, her sandy brown hair falling from her Durango Police Department ball cap to her chin in a blunt-cut bob. "It's okay, Chuck," she said, stopping in front of him. "It's not her."

SCOTT GRAHAM

"Who is it, then?"

She hesitated. "I can't say."

"But you know," he said in response to her hesitation.

She tipped her head forward, the brim of her cap momentarily hiding her luminous, green eyes.

"I know who it is, too, don't I?" Chuck asked.

She nodded again, a quick dip of her dimpled chin. Her gaze moved past him to the house, where another officer exited the back door. The officer was even younger than Officer Anand. Peach fuzz covered his upper lip and acne pocked his cheeks. A shock of auburn hair showed beneath the visor of his ball cap.

The boyish officer descended the three wooden steps from the rear of the house, the screen door swinging shut behind him. He hustled across the backyard and through the rear gate.

Sandra said to Chuck, "It appears everything started in your house."

"In my . . . in our . . . ?"

"In your study, to be exact. It's a mess in there." She fixed him with unblinking eyes. "Did you have anything in there someone might have wanted?"

He glanced past her in the direction of the body in the alley beyond the fence. "I'm an archaeologist. What could I possibly have that would be cause for that?"

"You've made some big discoveries over the years, headline-making stuff. Everybody in town knows it."

"I never keep anything of value in my house, ever."

"It would seem someone thought otherwise."

"Can I see?"

She pursed her lips, frowning. "You can't go inside, but I guess you could peek in the window. Maybe you'll spot something."

Chuck climbed the steps to the back door. Gripping the doorframe, he leaned sideways and peered through the window into the small room at the back of the house that served as his office. Inside the room, his scarred oak desk was swept clean. Spiral notebooks, photographs, a desk lamp, notecards, and pens and pencils that normally sat on the desktop or filled the desk drawers were scattered across the hardwood floor, along with his laptop and monitor.

Opposite the desk, the drawers to his two file cabinets were pulled open, their contents strewn on the floor with his desk items. A framed picture of Janelle and the girls had been lifted from the wall and lay on the floor as well.

Chuck cursed. He pushed himself upright from the window. "You're right," he said with a shake of his head as he returned to Sandra in the yard. "It's a mess in there."

"Somebody was looking for something."

"Obviously."

"And . . . ?"

"I have no idea. My laptop is still there. You'd think they'd at least have taken that."

"Think harder. It would appear somebody thought something in your study was worth killing over."

He pivoted at the cry of "Chuck!" from Janelle.

She rounded the rear corner of the house and rushed to him.

"Thank God, you're okay," Chuck said to her as they embraced.

She stepped back. She wore her Durango Fire and Rescue uniform—navy shirt and black cargo pants with large side pockets. Her smooth, olive face was lightly made up. Her black hair, long and straight like Carmelita's, was corralled in a bun at the back of her neck. Her cheeks were drawn and sallow. A sheen of perspiration shone on her forehead.

"Carm and Rosie are out front," she said. "The officer wouldn't let them come back here with me."

Chuck's eyes strayed to the rear fence. "For good reason."

She followed his look. "I heard he's in the alley."

"*He?*"

Sandra ticked a forefinger back and forth in warning, but Janelle continued nonetheless.

"It's all over the police radios," she said to Chuck. "That's why Mark—" her shift supervisor, Mark Chapman "—sent me home."

"I'm glad he did."

With the girls growing older and increasingly independent, Janelle had been accepting every offer of fill-in shifts that came her way, seeking to impress Mark and the other Durango Fire and Rescue supervisors enough to win the next full-time position that opened up with the department.

She took one of Chuck's hands in hers. Her voice shook. "It's Barney, Chuck. They're saying it's Barney."

"*Barney?* That's insane. Are you sure?"

Barney Keller was a senior archaeologist for Southwest Archaeology Enterprises, one of several firms in town that, like Chuck's one-man company, performed site surveys as well as full-on digs throughout the archaeologically rich Four Corners region surrounding Durango, where Colorado, New Mexico, Arizona, and Utah met.

Chuck had worked with Barney on a number of combined-firm contracts over the years. But Barney was more than just an occasional work partner to Chuck. He was one of Chuck's few close friends, a harmless teddy bear of a guy, jovial and kindhearted. In the years since Chuck had become husband to Janelle and stepdad to Carmelita and Rosie, he credited Barney's wise counsel with helping him tamp down the hot-headedness he'd displayed all too often during his many years as a bachelor. Barney and his wife, Audrey, had raised a son, Jason, in Durango. Jason was in his mid-twenties now, living in Denver.

"Barney doesn't have an enemy in the world," Chuck said.

"He couldn't," Janelle agreed. "Plus . . ." Her voice trailed off. She let go of Chuck's hand and shot a sidelong glance at Sandra before looking away.

Chuck knew what Janelle was thinking. "Plus, Clarence," he finished for her. He turned to Sandra. "Assuming that really is Barney Keller out there, I want you to know two things. First, to repeat: no one would ever want to hurt Barney. Everybody loves him, me included."

He paused.

"Second?" Sandra urged.

"Second is that Clarence Ortega, Janelle's brother, has been doing a lot of work with Barney over the last few weeks."

Chuck whirled to Janelle. Clarence's rotund frame matched that of the corpse beneath the sheet in the back alley. "Have you talked to him? Is he okay?"

Janelle tapped her phone, stowed in the side pocket of her pants. "I called him. He's at his apartment. He's fine."

Chuck pivoted to Sandra. "Barney's company, Southwest Archaeology Enterprises, has won just about every contract in the area the last few months. They've taken on a number of new workers as a result. Clarence is one of them."

"I'm sorry I can't confirm what your wife has heard," Sandra said to Chuck. "But any information her brother can provide will be helpful."

"Which means," Janelle said, leaning toward Sandra, "you haven't arrested anyone yet."

Sandra lowered her head, an almost imperceptible dip of her chin, but kept her gaze on Chuck. "I can't officially comment."

Janelle's jaw muscles tightened. "Of course, you can't." She clapped a hand to her mouth, her eyes growing big and round. "I just remembered," she said. "Barney's wife, Audrey."

She reached for her phone.

Sandra lifted her hand to Janelle and said to Chuck, "We'll get someone over to the house. It's better to tell her in person." She lowered her hand. "We'll need to do a round of questions with you and your wife before—"

"This might help, Kingsley," a police officer broke in as he entered the yard from the back alley. The officer closed the gate behind him. He was in his thirties, as fit and trim as Chuck but broader at the shoulders. Unlike Chuck's clean-shaven face, a clipped brown mustache covered the officer's upper lip. Prominent cheekbones and a squared-off jaw gave him a boxy look.

The police officer carried a ziplock evidence bag. He raised the clear plastic bag as he stopped at Sandra's side, facing Chuck and Janelle. A three-inch-by-five-inch picture postcard, bent and crumpled, rested in the bottom of the bag. The officer flipped the bag so the creased front of the postcard faced outward. Fresh splotches of blood, bright red in the afternoon sunlight, stained the front of the card.

Chuck gawked at the card, his mouth falling open.

"I take it you recognize this," the officer said, his eyes on Chuck.

"It's from my study."

"Any idea why a murder victim would be clutching it in his hands?"

"None whatsoever."

"What's it a picture of?"

Chuck pointed at the front of the card. "You mean, *who*."

2

Half an hour later, their house declared off limits to them as the investigation into Barney's murder got underway, Chuck, Janelle, Carmelita, and Rosie crowded into the cramped living room of Clarence's one-bedroom apartment, on the ground level of a two-story complex facing busy College Avenue on the edge of the Grid.

"Please, sit," Clarence said, sweeping crumbs off the sagging sofa and worn easy chair that filled the small front room.

Janelle settled on the couch between Carmelita and Rosie. She gathered the girls close, her arms around their shoulders, the sofa slumping beneath their weight.

Chuck perched on the edge of the torn, vinyl recliner in the corner of the room. Outside the front window of the apartment, a length of rusted, wrought-iron railing separated the narrow entryway from the courtyard of the complex. Clarence stood with his back to the window. He wore a flannel shirt over a black T-shirt. Stud earrings glittered in his lobes. His dark hair, as long and silky as his sister's, cascaded down his back nearly to his broad hips. He snugged the waistline of his faded jeans to the base of his protruding belly.

"Speak," he said, his eyes alight.

Janelle filled him in, her sentences clipped, as if reporting by radio from the scene of a Durango Fire and Rescue call. She concluded, "The police asked us a few questions and asked us to leave. They wouldn't let us inside. I don't know when we'll be allowed back."

Clarence swept his hand through the air, taking in his tiny apartment. "My castle is your castle, for as long as you need it." He blinked back tears. "Barney? Are you sure?"

Chuck gripped his legs with his hands, his fingers digging into his sweats. "Sandra did everything but say it flat out."

Janelle nodded in confirmation. "Before I got off my shift, a couple of officers said his name over the police radio. They referred to him only as 'the victim' after that."

Rosie sniffled. "I'm scared."

Janelle pressed Rosie's head to her shoulder. "It's okay. We're safe. We're all together now."

"Sandra?" Clarence asked Chuck.

"Kingsley," he admitted.

"She's . . . ?"

"Yes," Chuck said, the word short and sharp. "She or someone else from the department will be here soon. They'll be asking you for a list of everyone you've worked with lately."

Clarence hugged himself around his broad middle. "Me?"

"I told her what you'd told me—that you'd worked with Barney more than anyone else at Southwest Archaeology Enterprises."

A cloud passed across Clarence's eyes. "Barney," he moaned. "There isn't . . . wasn't . . . a nicer guy in the whole world."

Chuck nodded, a grim up-and-down movement of his chin. "Whoever did it got away—for now, at least." He smacked his fist into his palm. "I want to get them. For Barney. For Audrey and Jason. And for us, too." Reaching from the chair, he caressed Rosie's shoulder. "You have every right to be scared, *pequeña*. They broke in to our house. They killed a friend of ours in our back alley."

Clarence frowned. "I'm still not sure why you're saying the police are going to come here to talk to me so fast."

"They're putting together a list of persons of interest. Sandra said someone from the department will be over here as soon as they've got the scene secured."

Janelle leaned toward Chuck from between the girls. "You really think they'll consider Clarence a person of interest?"

"They'll consider everyone who's been working with Barney a person of interest." Chuck looked at Clarence. "Where have you been today?"

Clarence loosened his arms from around his stomach. "Right here, earning me a few extra bucks. The dig they've got me on in Cortez is shut down for the weekend."

"That's the one for the new subdivision on the edge of town, right?"

"Sí."

A land swap between the neighboring town of Cortez and Canyons of the Ancients National Monument had provided additional development acreage for the growing municipality. Southwest Archaeology Enterprises had won the contract to perform the required archaeological survey on the swapped land.

"I've been working on the project online today," Clarence continued. "Cataloging."

"Have you done any emailing?"

"A few back-and-forths with Michaela."

Michaela McDermott was the owner of Southwest Archaeology Enterprises.

"During the last few hours?"

"All day, off and on, since breakfast."

Chuck shifted in his seat to face Janelle. "Clarence's alibi should be solid. The time stamps for the emails on his computer will take care of it."

Rosie lifted her head from her mother's shoulder. "I liked Barney. He came to my concert."

Janelle rested her nose in the thick nest of Rosie's curls. "I remember that," she said into Rosie's hair. "He came to your school choir recital. Audrey came, too."

With Jason grown and gone from Durango, Audrey and Barney included the school events of the children of friends on their social calendar.

Janelle raised her head from Rosie's hair. "Audrey's probably all alone at their house," she said to Chuck. "We should get over there."

"Maybe she'll know something."

"If she's even capable of talking."

Clarence put a hand to his round belly. "What about me?"

Chuck rose from his chair. "You need to stick around. The police will be here soon. No use looking like you're trying to hide from them."

"What'd they ask you?"

"About what you'd expect. How well we knew Barney. Any idea why someone would break in to our house." Chuck didn't mention the postcard; he was still processing that piece of information himself. "They're going to want the names of people you know who've been working with him."

"The names of other archaeologists?"

"Barney's death has archaeology written all over it."

Clarence's eyebrows rose high on his forehead. "That's what I can't figure out. The murder of an archaeologist for archaeological reasons? Are you kidding me?"

"Not *just* for archaeological reasons. For money, if I were to bet."

"You really think . . . ?"

"You know as well as I do how bad things are getting these days, all around the world, including right here in the US."

"You really believe they'd come here, to Durango? You think somebody killed Barney because of some black-market deal gone wrong?"

"I think something along those lines is a strong possibility."

"Barney seemed like a totally straight-arrow dude to me. I don't see him being involved in anything illegal."

"Neither do I, to be honest. But I can't think of anything else at this point."

"On account of the break-in?"

Chuck nodded.

"How do you suppose that plays into it?"

"I don't have any idea. Not yet, anyway. It's too soon. You just have to tell the cops everything you know, anything you can think of."

Clarence rolled his shoulders. "When Michaela first hired me, she teamed me with Barney so I could learn from the 'old pro,' as she called him. But I've worked with plenty of other Southwest Archaeology people over the last few weeks, too. She's got four or five digs going right now. She's been sending me wherever she needs me from week to week, even from day to day sometimes."

Janelle leaned forward. "Like my part-time gig with Durango Fire and Rescue," she said with a nod. "I never know when I'm going to get a shift, from which substation."

"*Exactamente*," Clarence said to her. "Except, unlike you, I've been getting full-time hours from Southwest Archaeology. It's boom times for SAE."

Chuck caught Clarence's eye. "How many of Michaela's archaeologists do you figure you've worked with?"

"Six at least. Maybe more."

"But with Barney most of all, in Cortez."

"That's right." Clarence shook his head, the silver studs in his ears reflecting the sunlight streaming through the window. "The whole thing with him being murdered, it's . . . it's mind blowing."

"We don't have any choice but to wrap our minds around

it, though. Somebody just killed him, in broad daylight, behind our house."

"Who found him?"

"Neighbors, according to the police."

"What was the cause?"

"No one's saying yet." Chuck pictured the bloodstained sheet covering Barney's body in the alley. "Someone covered him up—whoever found him, I guess. From what I saw, it looked like a knifing."

"Eww," said Rosie.

Janelle looked at Chuck. "I'm still trying to figure out the card from your files." She turned to Clarence. "Barney was holding it when he . . . when he died."

Clarence's eyes flashed from Janelle to Chuck. "Card? You didn't say anything about that."

"I was getting there," Chuck said.

Carmelita's brow furrowed. "What was on it?"

"It was an old postcard," he explained to her, "from way before you were born. It had a picture on it of one of the most incredible archaeological discoveries in the history of North America. Hardly anyone remembers the discovery nowadays, though."

"How come?"

"Social consciousness, I guess you could say. On account of how we've learned to be more respectful of indigenous people in general, and Ancestral Puebloans in particular."

Rosie sat up straight, waving her hand wildly in the air. "The Ancestral Puebloans!" she exclaimed. "We've been studying them in school."

"As you've been learning," Chuck said to her with a nod, "Mesa Verde, west of here, was the center of their civilization a thousand years ago. After they abandoned the region, their stone villages in the canyons there survived because they were built under overhanging cliffs, out of the weather."

"That's why it's a national park."

"You got it. Most of the places Ancestral Puebloans lived were out in the open, so their houses and villages wore away over the centuries and were covered up by dirt and plants. But there were a few other places besides Mesa Verde where Ancestral Puebloans lived under cliffs—one of which was just a few miles north of Durango."

"Whoa," Rosie said. "Right here, where we live."

Janelle tapped the face of her wristwatch with her fingertip, her eyes on Chuck. "We need to get over to Audrey's."

He turned to the girls. "Your Uncle Clarence knows the story of the postcard."

Clarence inclined his head. "Falls Creek."

Chuck nodded. "The classic Anthro 101 case study." He turned to Carmelita and Rosie. "I'll finish telling you about it on the way across town."

A Durango police SUV approached Clarence's apartment complex as Chuck drove the big Bender Archaeological pickup out of the parking lot. Janelle sat opposite him in the passenger seat, the girls in back. He resumed the story of the postcard as he steered the truck away from Clarence's building.

"Archaeologists excavated the Falls Creek site north of Durango in the 1930s. By then, the villages under the Mesa Verde cliffs had been cleaned out, starting with Gustaf Nordenskiöld from Sweden in 1891. He shipped artifacts and human remains from Mesa Verde to Scandinavia, where they were held up until just a little while ago. After Nordenskiöld finished his excavations, other early archaeologists swooped in. So did looters. When the easy-to-get artifacts were gone from Mesa Verde, archaeologists and looters turned their attention to lesser-known Ancestral Puebloan sites to keep on learning or stealing whatever they could."

Carmelita caught Chuck's eye in the rearview mirror. "Like Falls Creek?"

"Yep."

Rosie rubbed her hands together. "And that's when they made their big postcard discovery, isn't it?"

"That's right," Chuck told her. "The first thing we archaeologists do when we're studying a site is survey it and collect any artifacts left above ground. Next, we dig into the site layer by layer, cataloguing new items we unearth as we go. That's called stratification. It lets us learn what was going on at a site decade by decade, sometimes even year by year. Stratification is something Nordenskiöld, the archaeologist from Sweden, actually helped invent. Around here, early archaeologists were particularly interested in the trash heaps, called midden piles, Ancestral Puebloans left at the foot of their villages."

They crossed Main Avenue and entered the Crestview neighborhood on the west side of town.

"By the time of the Falls Creek excavation," Chuck said, "archaeologists knew Ancestral Puebloans had used their middens as cemeteries, burying human remains right along with their trash. That might seem odd to us, but it was perfectly normal for them. Every now and then, archaeologists came across protected, crypt-like spaces containing human remains in the middle of the trash heaps. The corpses in those spaces often were adorned with personal possessions—turkey-feather shrouds, fur cloaks and blankets, necklaces and bracelets, even toys left with the bodies of children."

"What about Falls Creek?" Rosie asked. "You said they dug up one of the most amazingly amazing discoveries ever in the whole world there."

"They did." Chuck turned onto the quiet street leading to the home of Barney and Audrey. "Except, they made the discovery above ground, with no digging into a midden pile required."

Rosie bounced up and down in her seat. "What'd they find?" she asked breathlessly.

Chuck widened his eyes at her in the mirror. "Mummies."

3

Chuck rolled the truck to a stop behind a Durango police SUV already parked in front of the home of Barney and Audrey. The house was a 1950s rancher in a line of similar single-story homes, all with attached one-car garages and postage-stamp-sized front yards. The houses backed up to Overend Park, the sprawling forest park, webbed with trails, that skirted the west side of town.

Chuck turned to the girls in the back seat. "They found a bunch of mummified human remains at Falls Creek."

"The postcard has a picture of *mummies* on it?" Rosie asked.

"Actually, the card has a picture on it of one mummified person in particular."

Carmelita unbuckled her seatbelt and scooted forward. She folded her forearms on the top of the front seat and rested her chin on them. "Like from Egypt?"

"Exactly like that," Chuck said. "The air is so dry here in the Four Corners that the body was almost perfectly preserved, the same way the desert dryness in Egypt preserved the mummies there."

"And they made a picture postcard of it?"

"Of *her*, yes. Lots of them, in fact. They named her Esther and took her around the country on a big tour, like a carnival attraction. After that, they put her in a glass case in the Mesa Verde National Park Museum so everybody who visited the park could look at her."

"That's so gross."

"The whole thing is pretty awful by today's standards," Chuck agreed.

"But you had one of the postcards of the mummy in your files."

"There's an argument for keeping things like the postcard around to remind ourselves not to do anything like that ever again. In Esther's case, it took a lot of years, but they finally stopped displaying her, and they stopped selling the postcards of her, too. Eventually, her body was returned to where it was found."

"And after that, everybody forgot about her?"

"Mostly, yes. She's at peace now. At least, that's how I feel about her. But she'll always be at risk. Her corpse is one of the most perfectly preserved examples of mummified human remains ever found on this continent. She's worth a lot of money to grave robbers if they ever were to find out where she was reburied. They'd love to dig her up and sell her into some rich person's private collection. But she was a real, live human being. She deserves our respect, even our reverence, instead."

Janelle reached past Carmelita and put her hand on Chuck's arm. "Just like Barney was a real, live person," she reminded him.

Chuck killed the engine. In the sudden quiet, he stared out the window at the home of Barney and Audrey. How could Barney possibly be dead? And why had he been clutching a picture postcard of Esther, taken from Chuck's study, when he died?

Janelle climbed out of the truck. "*Vamanos*," she said to Chuck through the open passenger door. "You're the one who said we have to move fast, for Barney's sake." She tipped her head in the direction of the house. "And for Audrey."

Chuck clung to the steering wheel. "This just makes it so real."

"It *is* real."

He turned to the girls. "Audrey needs us right now, okay?"

Carmelita lifted her chin from her arms and looked at him with steady eyes. "I'm ready."

"So am I," said Rosie.

Sandra Kingsley answered when they rang the front doorbell. She stepped back from the open door, a clipboard in her hand, her eyes sweeping past Janelle and the girls and settling on Chuck.

"I'm glad you're here," she said, addressing only him. "I need to get moving, but I didn't want to leave her alone." She raised the clipboard. "She gave me a few more names in addition to the ones you provided. I need to start making some calls."

"How is she?" Janelle asked.

Sandra gave Janelle the briefest of glances. "She's in shock, as you'd expect." She returned her gaze to Chuck. "She called her son. He's on his way, driving from Denver, which will take a while. I'm sure others will be here soon, but you're the first."

Janelle addressed Sandra, her voice cool. "Thank you for the update."

Sandra slipped past Janelle, Chuck, and the girls without answering. Leaving the porch, she headed down the walkway to her car.

"And so it continues," Janelle said beneath her breath, watching the officer depart. She turned to the front of the house, squared her shoulders, and said to Chuck, "Ready?"

Audrey sat on a brick-red leather sofa in the front living room. A pair of matching recliners on either side of the sofa faced a flat-screen television affixed to the wall. A glass-topped coffee table with shiny brass legs sat between the couch and television set, and a woodstove squatted in one corner of the room. An arched opening lined with adobe brick led to a hallway and on to the kitchen and dining area at the back of the house.

Audrey looked up from the couch as Chuck entered the room with Janelle and the girls. She was a stout woman, with a double chin and gelatinous cheeks. She wore dark slacks and a knit sweater. Her dusky blond hair draped limply to her shoulders, and tears streaked the thick makeup on her face. She took shallow breaths, nearly panting.

Audrey had cheered louder than any other spectator at the Four Corners Open, Carmelita's most recent sport climbing competition at the rock gym last month, and had embraced Carmelita in a smothering bear hug after her victory. At Rosie's end-of-the-school-year choir concert in May, Audrey had cheered just as loudly for Rosie's brief, off-key solo. Now, however, Audrey sat in silence, her hands pressed into her lap.

Janelle knelt at Audrey's side, between the couch and coffee table. "Audrey," she said softly. "We're so very sorry."

Audrey tugged her hands from between her legs and clasped Janelle's hands in hers, squeezing them until her knuckles turned white. "Jason is on his way," she said. Then, a single, grief-stricken word: "Barney."

"We're here with you now, for as long as you need us," Janelle assured her.

Audrey shook her head vehemently, several hard twists in quick succession. "I won't cry," she said. "That just won't do. There'll be plenty of time for that later." Her eyes burned with sudden fury. "Right now, I just want to get the motherfucker who did this to my Barney."

Rosie, standing next to Chuck, inhaled sharply and grabbed Chuck's hand.

Carmelita walked to the opposite side of Audrey from her mother and laid her hand on Audrey's shoulder. "I'm sorry, too," she said.

Audrey grasped Carmelita's hand, attaching herself to both Janelle and Carmelita. "You're a sweetheart," she said to Carmelita. She looked up from the couch at Rosie. "I'm sorry, dear. I shouldn't have said that bad word. But I've never . . . I'm not . . ."

"That's okay," Janelle soothed. "We gave the police every name we could think of, too."

"They broke into your house," Audrey said, her voice trembling. "That's what the police said."

"That's where Barney was when . . . that's where it happened." Janelle paused. "What was he doing there? He didn't call. We . . . Chuck . . . didn't know he was going to be there."

"That's just it," Audrey said. "I haven't the faintest idea. That's what I wanted to ask you, in fact." Her voice steadied. "He went out for coffee, his regular afternoon jolt. He said he'd be back in a jiff. That's how he put it—in a jiff." She plucked her hands from Janelle and Carmelita and covered her mouth with them, her eyes filling with tears. "Oh, dear. Maybe I will have to cry after all."

"Cry as much as you need to." Janelle rose from the floor to sit beside Audrey on the couch. "But, if you can, what did the police officer say to you?"

Audrey resettled her hands in her lap, her eyes on the coffee table. "She barely told me anything about what happened. Just that there'd been a break-in at your house and that Barney was . . . he was . . ." She rubbed her nose with the back of her hand. "She wanted names. I gave her all I could." She turned to Janelle. "Including Clarence's, of course. Maybe he knows something that will help. He was friends with Barney. He's friends with everybody, just like my . . . my . . ." She blinked.

Tears coursed down her cheeks. Again, she took Janelle's hands in hers. "Barney thought the world of Clarence. Every time he said your brother's name, he just smiled and smiled."

"What about the others?"

"No one else was as friendly with Barney as Clarence. I'm sure it was the competition between all of them for work hours. Or maybe it was just the opposite—too much work for everybody these last few months. One or the other. That's how it always is with SAE, feast or famine. Not enough hours, then way too many. For years, I told Barney he should find something dependable to do, like me at the hospital. I've never once regretted being a nurse. I've got my regular hours, and I make decent money, too. But he loved what he did. He said he couldn't imagine giving it up. He said he felt like a kid at Christmas every time he showed up at a new dig site. He promised me he'd find something that paid better and had predictable hours if the work ever got old. But it never did, not for him."

She released Janelle's hands, dug a tissue from the pocket of her sweater, and swabbed her nose with it. Tucking the tissue in her sleeve at the wrist, she lowered her face into her hands and sobbed, shoulders heaving.

Rosie looked at Janelle with frightened eyes.

Janelle mouthed, "It's okay," to her.

Chuck's phone buzzed in his pocket. Audrey lifted her face from her hands as he checked its screen. He held his phone up. "If you'll excuse me, I'll take this outside."

"Jesus Christ, Chuck," Samuel Horvat said over the phone as Chuck stepped onto the front porch and closed the door behind him. "What in God's name?"

Like Barney, Samuel was another of Michaela McDermott's longtime archaeologists. Chuck had worked with him on many occasions over the years. His name was one of those Chuck had given to Sandra, along with the names of several other Southwest Archaeology Enterprises employees.

Chuck rested a hand on the porch railing, his phone to his ear. "What have you heard?"

"That there was a break-in at your place, and that somebody killed Barney."

"Bad news travels fast."

"I can't believe—" There was a break in the call, dropping Samuel's next words, before he finished with, "—to me, anyway."

"I lost that," Chuck said. "Where are you?"

Samuel spoke slowly, enunciating each word. "Mesa Verde . . . western edge of Chapin Mesa . . . spotty signal . . . texts, a whole bunch of them." A soft *hiss* filled the line. "I'm so sorry, Chuck," Samuel said over the hissing noise. "I loved Barney. I know you did, too."

"We all did."

A middle-aged woman walked past the house on the sidewalk. A white poodle strained at the end of a neon-pink leash in front of her. A mountain biker in skintight shorts pedaled down the street, hunched over her handlebars.

"Why are you calling me?" Chuck asked.

The sound of Samuel taking a deep breath joined the hissing on the line. "You have to see something. You have to come out here, Chuck. *Right now.*"

Chuck ended the call and reentered the house, finding Janelle and the girls alone in the living room.

"Audrey went to the bathroom," Janelle explained from the couch. She pointed at Chuck's phone, still clutched in his hand. "Who was that?"

"Samuel Horvat." He paused. "I need to go to Mesa Verde."

"You *what*?"

"He said there's something he wants to show me."

Janelle's mouth formed a hard, straight line. "You honestly think, with what's just happened, that you're going to leave us here in town and head all the way out there?"

"He already knew about Barney and the break-in. Whatever he wants me to see is related to Barney's . . . to the murder. He said he doesn't dare send pictures over the phone, that I have to see it for myself."

"That's nuts, Chuck."

"You and I agreed on the need to move fast."

"We agreed on the need for the *police* to move fast. There's a big difference."

Audrey appeared in the arched opening at the back of the living room. "Who won't send pictures of what?" she asked, her words muffled as she blotted her nose with a tissue.

"That was Samuel Horvat who called," Chuck told her. "He's out on Wetherill Mesa, on the west side of Mesa Verde National Park."

She lowered the tissue. "Barney spent a lot of time in the park over the years. He always loved being there. He said it was the center of his universe."

"It's the center of my universe, too. Samuel's on a dig out there. I hadn't heard of it, which means it's been kept pretty quiet—no press releases or tours or the usual public-relations stuff. His phone has been lighting up with texts since . . . since . . . for the last couple of hours." He held Audrey's gaze. "He said there's something out there he wants me to see."

"Then go," Audrey said. "*Go.*"

Chuck tucked his phone in his pocket and turned to Janelle with beseeching eyes.

Before she could respond, Rosie said, "I want to go along."

Janelle shook her head. "No. No way."

"But I *do*," Rosie insisted to her mother. "I want to help. And

I want to see whatever archaeology stuff there is to see."

Audrey squeezed the tissue in her hand. "You sound just like my Barney." She dropped her chin to her chest and released a harsh cry from deep in her throat. She raised her eyes to Janelle. "I know Samuel. I trust him. You have to let them go, right now, this minute. And while they're gone, you can do something for me."

"Anything," Janelle said. "Just name it."

"The officer, Sandra, said she'd let me know when I could see Barney's . . . his . . . the body. She said it wouldn't be for a while. But I can't just sit here in the meantime waiting for Jason to get here from Denver. I have to see where it happened. If nothing else, I have to check on Barney's car, and I don't want to go alone."

"His car?" Janelle asked.

Chuck tilted his head to one side, squinting. The location of Barney's car, presumably parked somewhere in the Grid, might well be informative. Had Barney parked well away from the house, attempting to keep his car's location secret, before sneaking in the back gate and breaking into Chuck's study? Or had he parked somewhere near the house, making no attempt to hide his car, and entered via the front door after knocking and finding no one home? That is, had Barney been complicit in the break-in? Or had he happened upon the crime while it was in progress and died trying to stop it?

"Yes, his car," Audrey responded to Janelle. "I want to find it, and I want to go to your house, too."

"Everything's closed off in all directions."

"Then we'll get as close as we can. We can take my car."

Carmelita stood up from the couch. "I'll go with you," she said to Audrey. She looked at Janelle. "With both of you."

Rosie turned to Chuck. "And I'll go with you."

Janelle frowned at him. "Do you really think—?"

"We'll be fine," he assured her. "Whoever did it is on the run, trying to get as far away from here as they can, as fast as they can."

"You sound awfully sure of yourself."

"Because I am," he said, injecting all the assurance he could muster into his voice.

4

Rosie sat with Chuck in the front passenger seat of the truck. The crew cab's diesel engine roared as he accelerated up the highway, climbing Mancos Divide. They were twenty miles west of Durango, on their way to Mesa Verde. It was mid-afternoon, barely three hours since he'd checked his phone at the climbing gym and sped home to find Barney's body in the alley. The sun was still high in the sky, the temperature a few ticks warmer than it had been at midday.

"Will we get to do any archaeology when we get there?" Rosie asked.

"I doubt it."

"Awww."

Rosie's sixth-grade class was a few weeks into the semester-long course on local archaeology offered each fall to Durango's middle schoolers. She tended to be less than enthusiastic about academics in general, but the archaeology curriculum had captivated her so far. After school each day, she excitedly told Chuck and Janelle everything she'd learned in class about the many ancient archaeological wonders of the Four Corners area.

Chuck glanced across the seat at her as he drove. In the aftermath of the break-in and Barney's murder, he was more comforted than he'd have imagined by her presence in the truck with him.

"Well," he revised, "we might get to do a little digging when we get there. We'll see."

"Goody."

They reached the top of the divide and began the curving descent to the entrance of the national park at the foot of the towering Mesa Verde plateau. Chuck leaned back in his seat and sighed heavily.

"You're sad, aren't you?" Rosie said.

"Really sad," he admitted. "Barney was a good friend of mine, and a good person. I worked with him for a lot of years."

"Uncle Clarence worked with him, too, didn't he?"

"A whole bunch the last few months."

"Will the police think Uncle Clarence did it?"

"Clarence was in his apartment, working, when Barney was . . . when it happened."

"But Uncle Clarence was alone. He said so."

"He was sending out emails. They'll show he was there."

"He could send emails from anywhere with his laptop. From his phone, even."

Chuck tightened his grip on the steering wheel. "I guess that's right." He shot her a look. "You're pretty smart, you know that?"

"Carm's the one who gets straight As."

"There's more to being smart than getting perfect grades."

"Like what?"

"Like perseverance. Sticking with something and not giving up on it. That's totally what you do. And getting along with people, caring about others. That's something you're really good at, too."

Rosie wiggled in her seat. "I am?"

"You sure are." He studied her as he drove. "You really like to move, don't you?"

She wiggled her body even more. "Oh, yeah, baby."

"Maybe that's your thing."

She stopped moving. "What thing?"

"The thing you and I were talking about. Something for you

to do while Carm's at the rock gym. Something that's just your thing and no one else's."

She rocked in her seat. "This is a thing?"

"It is when you do it to a beat."

She rocked harder, straining against her seatbelt. "Bop, bop, a loo bop, a bop bam boo!" she sang out.

"That's it." Chuck grooved in his seat along with her. "I was thinking of dancing. You wouldn't have to climb up high on a wall and across ceilings or anything like that. Dancing is about staying on the ground and moving to the music."

Rosie swayed from side to side and tapped her foot on the floorboard. "I like that idea."

"Plus, you'd get to do it with other kids, which would be fun for you because you're such a people person. You like people, which makes them like you back. It's a good trait to have, a smart trait, one I'm trying to learn from you."

"You're trying to learn from *me*? Wow." Rosie settled back in her seat. "But somebody killed Barney. I don't like them. I *hate* them."

"The police will get them. I'm sure of it."

"Or we will."

"That's why we're on our way to the park—to see if there's anything we can learn that might help the police do their work."

He turned south off the highway and drove past the Mesa Verde Visitor and Research Center, which rose from a broad sagebrush flat beside the highway. High above the center, the crest of Mesa Verde was rimmed with the dark green piñons and silvery green junipers that gave the plateau and park their shared Spanish name.

The Visitor and Research Center was constructed of sandstone blocks and exposed beams to resemble a traditional Ancestral Puebloan housing structure. A wall of windows on the building's east side provided a commanding view of the La Plata Mountains north of Durango. Groves of aspen trees blanketed the upper slopes of the craggy peaks. Many of the trees were yellow with fall as the crisp, cold September nights ushered in the change of seasons.

Rosie pointed at the building as they passed. "We're going there on a field trip after we learn everything."

"I've been meaning to take you there myself," Chuck said. "You'll like it. There's a museum where they explain how Mesa Verde was the first national park ever established to protect the works of mankind instead of nature. Plus, there are windows to watch the curators do their work in the research side of the building. That lets visitors know Mesa Verde was created specifically to help preserve the indigenous history of North America, which is to say, it's all about what I do for a living—archaeology."

"And it's what we're learning *alllll* about in school."

Chuck nodded. "You got that right."

He showed his national park pass to the ranger in the entrance booth and began the winding climb up the park road to the top of the plateau, swinging the big pickup around the road's tight turns as they ascended. Cars and recreational vehicles streamed by in the opposite direction, descending from the plateau toward the park's sole entry-exit point as the end of the day approached.

Rosie wet a tendril of her curly hair between her lips and pulled it straight with her fingers. When she let go, the tendril tightened back up like a spring beside her ear.

The scene unfolded out the windshield as they climbed: the gray clay face of the plateau rising to the green border of the mesa top, the Mancos Valley spread below, a patchwork of alfalfa fields and grass meadows broken by rocky ridges. In the middle of the valley sat the small town of Mancos, its handful of streets set close beside the Mancos River.

The park road reached the crest of Mesa Verde four miles from the entrance station. As he always did at this point, Chuck slowed to take in the stunning view. The green-carpeted plateau slanted southward away from them, a tilted tabletop of piñon and juniper trees thirty miles across from east to west and twenty miles from north to south. The mesa fell away to the brown, high-desert scrublands of the Ute Mountain Ute reservation on the Colorado-New Mexico border. Canyons cut deep into the mesa top every couple of miles. The canyons ran from north to south, their vertical walls of buff-colored Cliff House Sandstone aglow in the afternoon sunlight. Puffy, white cumulous clouds sailed across the blue sky overhead.

"Why are we slowing down?" Rosie asked.

Chuck pointed through the windshield. "Look."

"At what?"

"Just look. What do you see?"

She shrugged. "Nothing."

"That's right. There's nothing here—no houses, no shopping malls, no skyscrapers—which means there's everything here."

"Like what?"

"Like everything that made me want to be an archaeologist."

He waved his hand at the canyons, worn over the eons into the sandstone surface of the mesa. The gorges began near the top of the slanted plateau as narrow fissures a few feet across. Eroded by runoff from thunderstorms and melting snow, they widened and deepened as they wound their way south, walled by cliffs that sliced straight down into the sloping mesa. Out of sight in roofed alcoves at the bases of the cliffs, long-abandoned Ancestral Puebloan villages faced out to the flat canyon bottoms.

"I first came here, to Mesa Verde, on a school trip when I was a kid, just like the one you've got coming up," Chuck explained to Rosie. "When the school bus came up over the top of the mesa to where we are now, I remember being blown away by the view—the piñons and junipers covering the top of the mesa in dark green, the light brown desert to the south, and, best of all, the shadowed canyons hiding their secrets."

"Secrets?"

"You've been learning about how the canyons here were home to thousands of people a long time ago, right? Just think what it was like back then—smoke rising from cooking fires deep in the canyons, farmers tending their crops, teams of workers building earthen dams and digging irrigation ditches to capture the little water that fell from the skies. There would have been potters firing clay urns in red-hot coals, flint knappers chipping away at chunks of obsidian, jewelry makers stringing necklaces with turquoise beads they'd traded for all the way from the Sonoran Desert."

"Ms. Jarvis says this place was a totally happening scene," Rosie concurred.

"Your teacher, right?"

"Yep. She says it was like a big city, except spread out in all the canyons."

"Until just like that—" Chuck snapped his fingers "—it wasn't. No more smoke from cooking fires. No more farming or building houses or making jewelry. The Ancestral Puebloans abandoned everything they'd built here, everything they'd created. Imagine how heartbreaking that must have been for them. How devastating."

Rosie stuck out her jaw. "It would have been really sad."

"I agree. That's what hit me the first time I came here as a kid. Mesa Verde seemed like it would have been such a cool place to live. When I learned that the people had left everything behind, and that they had just taken off, I couldn't believe it. Why would they leave such a beautiful place? It made no sense to me. I had to find out. As an archaeologist, that's the kind of question I've been trying to answer ever since."

"Ms. Jarvis says they left because it stopped raining."

"That's part of it, for sure. Probably the biggest part. The drought stressed the Ancestral Puebloans and other peoples living in the area, which led to fighting between them."

"Wars, you mean?"

"Not big wars. But smaller fights, yes. The archaeological record is fairly clear on that—the towers built by Ancestral Puebloans at high points along the canyon rims to keep a lookout for raiders, plus the defensive positioning of their villages, deep in the canyons, protected by cliff walls on three sides and stone roofs above. In a way, the Ancestral Puebloans probably became victims of their own success. They got really good at homebuilding and farming, which would have made them targets because of how successful they were. They were sedentary. That is, they lived in one place, here on the mesa. That means nomads—people who moved from place to place all the time—could attack them and try to take everything they'd worked so hard for."

Rosie turned to Chuck in her seat as they followed the main park road down the sloped mesa top.

"At the beginning of the drought," Chuck continued, "the Ancestral Puebloans would have been able to fight off the marauders. But the drought went on for years. The Ancestral Puebloans' crops probably would have failed, which would have made them poorer and hungrier and less able to defend themselves. At the same time, the nomadic people would have been more desperate, too. In years of normal rain, they hunted wild game and gathered nuts and berries for food. But the drought reduced the amount of game. The same for nuts and berries. So the nomads most likely would have turned to raiding the Ancestral Puebloans and their corn-filled granaries. In response, the Ancestral Puebloans would have had to devote more people to protecting their food stores, leaving fewer of them to tend their crops and maintain the dams and irrigation ditches that were critical to their survival as the drought dragged on. Each year things would have gotten worse—less food, less water, more attacks. The Ancestral Puebloans would have been under siege and starving, unable to care for their farms, their children, themselves."

"So they left," Rosie said, her eyes downcast. "That's the sad part."

"Based on the best information we've been able to put together, they had no choice. Mostly, they joined other sedentary societies living to the south along the banks of the Rio Grande, which had water flowing in it year-round, even in dry years. They joined other societies just emerging in the Southwest like the Ute and Hopi people, too. The Ancestral Puebloans' civilization here on Mesa Verde may have dispersed, but they brought their skills to the societies they joined, and helped those societies succeed in the generations that followed." He gazed at the broad expanse of the plateau stretching away to the south, cut by canyons. "In the meantime, their villages were abandoned and falling into ruin in the bottoms of the drainages here on the mesa."

"Until you came along to dig them up."

"I got here pretty late in the game. Lots of other archaeologists were fascinated by Mesa Verde way before I was. There's so much to be learned here—how to cope with extreme weather changes, and how to get along, or not get along, with one another in stressful times. To me, that's why archaeology is so important, because there's so much to be learned from what others went through long before we arrived on the scene."

"I just think it would be cool to dig up all the pottery and treasures and stuff."

"That, too. But it has to be done with total awareness of whose the stuff was—the Ancestral Puebloans'—and for their modern-day descendants."

"The Native Americans," Rosie said. "The indignant people. That's what Ms. Jarvis calls them."

"The *indigenous* people," Chuck corrected her with a nod. "Sounds like Ms. Jarvis really knows her stuff. She's definitely up to date with her terminology."

"She says the word 'Indian' is old-fashioned."

"She's right. In the same way, the Ancestral Puebloans used to be called the Anasazis, but not anymore."

"Why not?"

"To the Navajo people, *Anasazi* means 'ancient enemy.' But Navajos see the Ancestral Puebloans as their ancestors, not their enemies. Plenty of Native Americans don't like the term 'Ancestral Puebloan' either, though, because *puebloan* is a Spanish word, and Spaniards showed up here in the Southwest and ruled Native Americans by force five hundred years ago."

"That all sounds pretty confusing."

"That's because it *is* confusing. Which is part of what I love about archaeology—all the different peoples involved, and all the awareness you have to have of everybody's different points of view and why they feel the way they do."

"Barney loved archaeology, too, just like you, didn't he?"

Chuck clenched his teeth as he guided the truck down the road. "That's why we're here."

The main park road descended through the piñon-juniper forest from the crest of Mesa Verde to a long finger of the plateau known as Chapin Mesa. Deep canyons on either side of the thin finger of land contained the park's principal concentration of Ancestral Puebloan villages, including Spruce Tree House, Cliff Palace, and Balcony House. Half a mile before the start of Chapin Mesa, a secondary road branched off the main road. Chuck turned onto it as instructed by Samuel. Instantly, the traffic died away. The deserted road headed west past the heads of Navajo, Wickiup, and Long Canyons on the way to Wetherill Mesa, a slice of tableland between deep gorges on the park's remote western boundary.

The road was narrow and curvy, the driving slow and arduous. Chuck cursed to himself as he gunned the truck on the few straightaways and braked through the countless turns. He never should have left Janelle and Carmelita on their own back in town to drive all the way out here. Why in God's name had he agreed to head for the far reaches of Mesa Verde only three hours after Barney's murder in Durango?

5

The secondary road turned south after ten miles onto Wetherill Mesa, aiming for a handful of small Ancestral Puebloan villages known as Badger House, Long House, and Kodak House. Rather than follow the road to the villages at the southern tip of Wetherill Mesa, however, Chuck turned west yet again, still following Samuel's instructions, leaving the pavement for a dirt road headed toward the park's western border.

Dust billowed into the air behind the truck as he drove a mile through the forest to a turnaround spot and graveled parking area at the end of the graded dirt track. Samuel's black Ford pickup sat in the parking area between a pair of late-model vehicles—a silver mini SUV and a lime-green subcompact. The two vehicles were unfamiliar to Chuck, their shiny newness indicating they most likely were rental cars.

Chuck nosed his truck to a stop beside the subcompact and climbed out. A well-maintained hiking trail led south from the parking area. He helped Rosie down from the passenger seat and headed away from the trail with her into the untracked piñon-juniper forest to the west.

"Where are we going?" Rosie asked as she hiked behind Chuck through the patchwork of shade and sun created by the outstretched branches overhead.

"To a canyon."

"But there's only a bunch of trees."

"Just you wait. We're walking on Mesa Verde, which is a big, flat chunk of sandstone with just enough soil on it for trees to grow. Sandstone is one of the softest kinds of rock there is. It crumbles and washes away wherever water runs across it." He glanced back at her as they walked. "You can probably guess what that leaves behind."

"Canyons!" she cried.

"*Exactamente.*"

They emerged from the forest after ten minutes onto a sunlit bench of beige sandstone. The stone shelf ended abruptly twenty feet from the edge of the forest, falling straight down into a hundred-foot-deep canyon. The opposite wall of the canyon, a vertical cliff of matching tan stone, faced them a few hundred feet away. Here and there, boulders worn from the mesa top rested on the edges of the facing cliffs, poised to tumble to the floor of the canyon as the process of erosion gradually enlarged the gorge over geologic time.

"It's deep!" Rosie exclaimed, striding toward the edge of the cliff.

"Not so close," Chuck said, hurrying after her and grabbing her hand. "There's lots of loose stuff, big boulders and little pebbles, ready to fall into the canyon at the slightest touch. It could take you with it if you're not careful."

He peered down into the walled canyon. Ponderosa pine trees grew from the sandy bottom of the gorge, their needled tops nearly even with the canyon rim. Bunchgrass and thickets of scrub oak sprouted among the ponderosas in the canyon bottom. A narrow defile, ten feet deep and walled with sandy soil, cut down the middle of the canyon floor, channeling water that flowed into the gorge when rains came to the plateau.

Maintaining his grip on Rosie's hand, Chuck walked with her along the sandstone shelf to the head of a narrow cleft in the flat stone rim of the gorge as Samuel had directed. The cleft sliced steeply downward, a rock-walled slot descending all the way to the canyon floor.

Rosie smiled and clapped her hands as she looked down the chimney-like passage. "This'll be fun."

She entered the slot first, pressing her hands to the facing rock walls as she descended. Chuck followed close behind, ready to steady her if she stumbled. But she scrambled over chockstones and slipped past mountain mahogany bushes growing in the cleft without difficulty, reaching the bottom of the slot in less than five minutes.

Chuck followed Rosie out of the cleft and onto the flat floor of the gorge. The *chink* of a shovel striking soil echoed up the canyon to where they stood.

"Hear that?" he asked Rosie. "Maybe we'll get to do some archaeology after all."

"Bazunga." She looked up at Chuck and explained, "That means 'great.'"

The digging grew louder as they hiked down the canyon along the base of the cliff. High above their heads, the ponderosas thrummed as the afternoon breeze coursed through the trees' long needles.

Rounding a bend in the canyon, they came upon a dirt-floored, stone-roofed alcove eroded into the base of the canyon wall. The shadowed recess faced southwest from the bottom of the cliff, the overhanging roof shielding the dirt floor beneath it from rain and snow. Two women stood facing Chuck and Rosie on the far side of a depression dug into the floor of the cavern-like space. Samuel Horvat wielded a shovel in the neck-deep depression, the back of his head visible above the alcove floor.

At the appearance of Chuck and Rosie, the older of the two women crossed her arms over her narrow chest, observing their approach with piercing, electric-blue eyes. She was short and slight, weighing no more than a hundred pounds, and looked to be about Chuck's age, in her mid-forties. She wore dusty white sneakers, khaki slacks, and a cotton jacket over a bright white, button-up shirt.

The second woman was in her late twenties. She wore faded jeans and a crimson T-shirt with the blocky, easily recognizable *H* of Harvard University emblazoned on its chest.

An assortment of dig implements rested in the dirt beside the women—plastic hand scoops and metal trowels, a hatchet, a hammer and chisel, and stackable buckets made of heavy plastic. On a flat piece of sandstone, out of the dirt, sat a camera bag and zippered computer satchel.

Samuel tossed a shovelful of soil onto a pile of dirt at the edge of the cavity. A small cloud of dust rose into the air as the dry soil landed on the pile.

"Hey, there," Chuck called as he approached the depression with Rosie.

Samuel turned to them. Sweat gleamed on his forehead beneath the brim of the stained felt fedora he'd worn for as long as Chuck had known him. Samuel was well into his fifties, his face deeply lined from decades of work outdoors beneath the harsh, Four Corners sun. Thick, gray hair covered his ears and tumbled from his hat down the back of his neck to his shirt collar.

Chuck stopped at the edge of the depression and looked down at Samuel. The longtime Southwest Archaeology Enterprises archaeologist wore heavy leather boots, brown denim work jeans, and a heavy cotton shirt with the letters *SAE* embroidered in red on its left breast, the middle *A* shaped like an arrowhead.

Samuel stabbed the blade of his shovel into the dirt at the bottom of the cavity and rested his gloved hands on top of the shovel's handle. "Thanks for coming," he said to Chuck.

Rosie stopped at Chuck's side.

"And who might you be?" Samuel asked her.

"I'm Rosie."

Chuck put his arm around her shoulders, drawing her to him. "She wanted to come along. She's studying archaeology in school right now."

"Good for you, young lady," Samuel told her. He leaned the shovel on the side wall of the depression and said to Chuck, "I was just doing a little cleaning up. The walls were caving a bit."

He pulled a bandanna from the back pocket of his jeans, pushed his fedora to his hairline, and swabbed his forehead with the blue cloth. He tucked the bandanna back in his pocket, repositioned his hat, and looked up at Chuck, his lips flattening into a hard line. "It's true?"

"I'm afraid so."

"I didn't want to believe it, but the texts kept coming. That's why I called you."

Chuck turned his attention to the two women on the far side of the depression. "I don't believe we've met."

"Kyla Owens," the young woman introduced herself. "You're Chuck Bender, as in Bender Archaeological, right? I've heard a lot about you."

Kyla's brown hair was long and shaggy, falling past her shoulders from beneath the flat brim of a trucker's cap she wore low over her eyes. She was of medium height, stocky and thick limbed.

Samuel caught Chuck's eye from the bottom of the cavity. "This is Kyla's first time out West. She's a bit of a legend considering her age—Princeton undergrad, Yale PhD, now finishing up a post-doc fellowship at Harvard."

Kyla's face flushed. "I'm honored to be part of the team."

"She's been out here for a couple of weeks, doing some research for her fellowship advisor. She's been working in the Collection," Samuel said, using the nickname for the Mesa Verde National Park archives, complete with row upon row of climate-controlled artifact storage cabinets, in the research wing of the Visitor and Research Center.

The older woman leaned forward from where she stood at the edge of the depression next to Kyla. "I am Ilona Koskinen," she said with a thick Scandinavian accent. Her platinum-blond hair was parted down the middle. Bangs covered her forehead like a white picket fence, ending at her bleached-blond eyebrows. "I have come here from the National Museum of Finland in Helsinki."

Samuel asked Chuck, "What exactly happened in Durango?"

"What have you heard so far?"

"Not much. No one seems to know anything."

"I don't know all that much myself." Chuck related what he knew to Samuel, Ilona, and Kyla, keeping his account brief, and concluded to Samuel, "Then you called." He looked over his shoulder toward Durango. "To be honest, I'm kicking myself right now for having driven all the way out here."

"This won't take long," Samuel assured him. "Come on down here with me. Like I said on the phone, you have to see this with your own eyes."

The SAE archaeologist stepped aside, revealing a dark, oval-shaped opening the size of a manhole cover at the bottom of the depression. Pie-sized chunks of thatched sticks and mud leaned against the side of the cavity.

"Someone already opened this up at some point in the past," Samuel said. He pointed at the pieces of thatching. "Those had been set back in place over the opening. Kyla says they came right out when she pulled on them."

Chuck slid into the depression and stood over the dark opening with Samuel.

Rosie jumped up and down at the cavity's edge. "I want to see, too! Can I, please? Can I?"

The soil gave way beneath her feet and she tumbled down the side of the depression. Chuck caught her and placed her upright beside him.

SCOTT GRAHAM

"Oops," she said. She combed dirt from her hair with her fingers.

"Sorry about that," Chuck said to Samuel.

"Um, yeah, sorry," Rosie said, her eyes on the opening at the bottom of the cavity.

Samuel waved off her apology with a flick of his hand. "No harm, no foul." He held her gaze. "Have you ever seen a dead body before?"

"I've seen a dead goldfish."

He glanced at Chuck. "Okay with you?"

Chuck placed his hands on Rosie's shoulders. "She's a pretty tough cookie."

Samuel crouched next to the opening and crooked his finger for Chuck and Rosie to do the same. They squatted beside him and he aimed a powerful flashlight into the opening.

"Holy *shit*," Rosie exclaimed.

6

"I mean," Rosie revised, "holy shoot."

Chuck looked into the opening along with her. He sucked a sharp breath.

Samuel's flashlight illuminated a human corpse visible from the shoulders down. The corpse lay on its back on the dusty floor of a crypt-like space at the bottom of the depression. Cracked leather suspenders extended from the waistline of thick cotton pants that covered the lower half of the body. Beneath the suspenders, a coarse shirt covered the top half of the body. A thin layer of dust coated the corpse. The head of the body was cut off from view by the ragged edge of the opening.

Chuck attempted to make sense of the scene before him. The suspenders and clothing clearly dated the corpse to the late 1800s, but the body lay in a vault that, just as clearly, dated from the time of the Ancestral Puebloans who'd populated Mesa Verde hundreds of years prior to the nineteenth century.

Samuel angled the flashlight, aiming its beam at the corpse's head. "This is where it gets creepy."

Chuck squatted lower, peering into the opening. Rosie crouched closer to the bottom of the depression beside him.

"Geez," she said, putting a hand to her mouth.

Chuck stared at the corpse's head, lit by the beam of Samuel's flashlight. The skull was cleaved down the middle, nearly in two. Remnants of closely shorn brown hair clung to the split cranium of what appeared to be a male. His skin was still attached to his skull, his ears shriveled on either side of his head.

His teeth showed between lips that were dried and cracked and drawn back along the jawbone.

Bile rose hot and burning in the back of Chuck's throat. For the second time today, he was looking at the body of a murder victim.

"What is this?" he demanded of Samuel. "Who? How is this even possible?"

Samuel aimed his flashlight at the Finnish woman, Ilona, standing above them at the edge of the depression. "You'll have to ask her."

Ilona raised a hand, shielding the light from her eyes.

Chuck looked up at her. "You're here because of Gustaf Nordenskiöld, aren't you?"

She lowered her hand. Her Nordic-blue eyes glittered in the beam of light. "That is a fast understanding you have just made."

Chuck rose from his crouch. "A man was killed today in Durango. A friend of mine." Rosie stood up beside him. He squeezed her arm. "*Our* friend."

"I am sorry about your friend," she said. "I have just arrived in your country. I am here as a scientist, to perform a study."

Samuel lowered his flashlight. With the beam of light removed, the afternoon sun silhouetted Ilona from behind, her face now a pale moon in deep shadow.

Samuel directed his flashlight back into the opening. "She's here on account of this."

"Another murder victim," said Chuck.

"Not the corpse. I'm talking about the hidden chamber. The crypt. It's why Ilona invited me here, and why Kyla is here, too."

"And me, apparently."

"No. I asked you to come on account of the body."

"You've got a lot of explaining to do."

Samuel directed the beam of his flashlight toward the dirt wall of the depression. "Shall we?"

He climbed out of the cavity and, reaching down, helped Rosie and Chuck clamber out after him.

Chuck stood with Rosie, facing Samuel, across the depression from the two women. "Tell me what's going on," he said to Samuel.

"I don't know why Barney was killed today." Samuel paused for a beat. "But I suspect his death might well have something to do with the corpse here in the chamber."

Chuck turned to Ilona on the far side of the cavity. "Which means Barney's death might be related somehow to the timing of your arrival here."

Ilona lifted her chin. "I have no knowledge of this dead man you are speaking of."

"And I don't have any knowledge of you. So how about we start with who you are and why you're here."

"Yeah," said Rosie, at Chuck's side. "Let's start with that."

Ilona looked out at the canyon from the mouth of the alcove. The ponderosa pine trees grew tall from the floor of the gorge, their branches lit by the slanting rays of the afternoon sun. Her eyes came back to Chuck and Rosie and she addressed them both.

"I am the head curator for the national museum of my country," she said. Her command of English was strong. "Six months ago, I received a phone call from here in America. The call was from a woman named Elizabeth Mantry. She told me that her family name—her last name, as you call it—was Cannon when she was a girl, before she married. She lives in the town called Mancos, in the valley outside the national park. She told me she had information about an ancestor of her family, someone who had gone away from his home in the Mancos Valley more than a hundred years ago and never returned. Elizabeth told me she had studied the genealogy of her relatives and found a branch on her family tree that came to a sudden end. The branch was for a young man, a teenager, named Joseph Cannon."

Ilona glanced down at the dark opening at the bottom of the depression.

"Joseph Cannon was Elizabeth's great-great-uncle, as I think you call it," she continued. "He was the brother of Carl, Elizabeth's great-grandfather. Elizabeth learned all this from Joseph's journals. Joseph and Carl lived on a farm beside the Mancos River, where they grew food to sell to the gold miners working in the high mountains. One day, Joseph, the oldest of the Cannon children, went away with a man who came to the farm looking for workers."

The museum curator from Finland lowered her head in acknowledgment to Chuck.

"As you correctly understood, the man who came to the farm was Gustaf Nordenskiöld. You could say that Gustaf is the reason I am a curator. The Nordenskiöld family has a history that goes back and forth between the different countries of Scandinavia. Many families have such a history. Like the Nordenskiölds, my family, the Koskinens, is one of them. When I was in university, I became interested in my family history, just like the woman, Elizabeth, from Mancos. I learned that my family reached many of the countries of Scandinavia—Norway, Latvia, Lithuania, and, of course, Sweden, the country at the crossroads of all the Scandinavian region. One of the interesting stories from my family's past is that my three-generations-ago grandfather went on a journey of exploration to the Arctic with Baron Adolf Eric Nordenskiöld."

"He was Gustaf's father, wasn't he?" Chuck asked.

"You are right about that," Ilona replied with a nod. "After I learned that my old relative went on the journey to the Arctic with the baron, I studied more about the Nordenskiöld family in Sweden, and in Finland as well. You see, Koskinen is the most common surname in my country. On every street, you will meet a person with the Koskinen name. It is said the Koskinens are the little people who keep the country of Finland running. We are the plumbers and bakers and factory workers. But the Nordenskiöld family? They are the barons and baronesses and famous people. To me, a young Koskinen woman in university, they were a rare and extraordinary species, so I studied all about them. I learned that Adolf, the father, is the reason Gustaf, the son, came here, to Mesa Verde, at such a young age. Gustaf was only twenty-two years old at that time, and he was very sick from tuberculosis, but still he came to this faraway place and worked and worked, to prove himself worthy of being his famous father's son."

"That's what you suppose."

"No. That is what I know, from reading and studying Gustaf's writings."

"You still haven't explained why you're here," Chuck said. "Or why I'm here, either."

"I learned much about Gustaf's journey to this place," Ilona said. "I learned that he became friends with the Wetherill ranching family in the Mancos Valley. He was impressed by the Wetherills' knowledge of the Ancestral Puebloans, and he teamed with the Wetherill sons, Richard and Al, who were young men just like him. Together, the three of them explored the abandoned villages of Mesa Verde in the year 1891. Gustaf determined that a scientific study of the Ancestral Puebloan civilization needed to be completed very quickly, before it became too late. Already, at that time, the ancient villages of Mesa Verde were being destroyed by thieves interested only in money."

"Looters," said Chuck. "Pothunters. Grave robbers."

"Yes, looters, as you call them. They were digging up all the artifacts they could find from the abandoned Ancestral Puebloan villages. They even used dynamite to blow up the midden piles beside the villages and steal whatever survived the explosions. Gustaf convinced the Wetherills to join him in gathering and preserving as many artifacts as they could before everything was stolen or destroyed."

"Except Gustaf himself was seen as a looter. He was arrested."

"The real looters did not like that a person from Europe was gathering artifacts from Mesa Verde and shipping them across the ocean, even though Gustaf was doing it for safekeeping. So the looters convinced the local law people in Durango to detain Gustaf. Fortunately, he was released after only a few hours, and he quickly shipped home to Sweden the artifacts he had collected up until that time with the help of his hired workers. I am proud to say that through his studies and explorations my fellow countryman, Gustaf Nordenskiöld, helped give birth to the field of archaeology, and to the importance of preserving and studying the history of ancient civilizations."

Chuck frowned. "Wait. Your countryman? I know Gustaf's Mesa Verde collection ultimately ended up in Finland, but from what I remember, Gustaf was Swedish, not Finnish."

"It is true that his family lived in Sweden at the end of the 1800s. But the Nordenskiölds actually were an old and royal family from Finland. Adolf, the baron, was living in exile in Sweden because of his works against the bad government that had taken over Finland at that time. That is why, after freedoms were restored to the Finnish people, Gustaf's Ancestral Puebloan collection came to be in the National Museum of Finland—all except for some very important artifacts he sought but did not find, artifacts I learned about from Elizabeth, the woman from Mancos."

"Which is why you've come here, to America."

"No. It is why I have come here—" she swung her hand in an arc, taking in the alcove and the canyon beyond "—to Finland."

Turning to Samuel, Chuck jerked a thumb across the depression at Ilona. "What the . . . ?"

"Let her explain," Samuel urged.

Chuck directed a wary look at the museum curator, but she said to Samuel, "I do not think he will be convinced by me. You should be the one who tells him."

Samuel faced Chuck. "I honestly can't believe you, of all people, don't know where we're standing right now."

Chuck peered from beneath the roof of the alcove at the opposite wall of the canyon, visible through the trees a couple hundred yards away. "We're in a canyon, beneath a cliff, at the far western edge of Wetherill Mesa."

"We're not in just any canyon. We're in *Gunnel Canyon*," Samuel said, emphasizing the name. He gazed out from the alcove along with Chuck. "You can look at as many maps of the national park as you want, but you won't find this place on any of them. Gunnel Canyon is barely a hundred feet deep and runs for less than a mile before it dumps into the westernmost arm of Long Canyon." He turned back to Chuck. "You saw the trail from the parking area headed to the North Fork of Long Canyon, didn't you? You couldn't have missed it."

"Sure. But you said to head west, away from the trail, to the slot in the canyon rim and on down here."

"That's right. You no doubt noticed the route you took had no cairns, not a single marker of any kind. That's all on purpose. Gunnel Canyon isn't in the national park. As far as officialdom is concerned, it doesn't exist at all."

"You mean, it's outside the park boundary. It's on Ute Mountain Ute reservation land instead."

"No. I mean, it's not in the park, and it's not part of the reservation, either."

Chuck twisted his head, surveying the shadowed recess with its sandstone roof and dusty floor and century-old corpse in the hidden crypt at his feet. "You're telling me we really are standing in Finland right now?" he scoffed.

"That's exactly what I'm telling you." Samuel toed a groove in the dirt floor of the alcove. "The fact is, all of Mesa Verde is ancestral Ute land. These days, the mesa officially is divided between the national park and the Ute Mountain Ute reservation. Maps show the western boundary of the park coming right up against the reservation boundary. This little canyon, if it was mapped at all, would be smack-dab on the line between the park and the rez. But we're actually standing on a little sliver of no-man's-land, just enough to take in Gunnel Canyon and this alcove. We're not in the national park, and we're not on Ute reservation land, either."

Ilona broke in from across the depression. "You can now understand what it is that I am telling you," she said to Chuck. "We are in Finland—you, me, all the five of us. Gustaf declared this place for his family's historical country. Because his family was royalty in Finland, that is the country he had the authority to declare for."

Chuck grunted. "He just up and declared this canyon, in the middle of the United States—in the middle of absolutely nowhere back then—to be part of Finland?"

"He knew something was here that would change what everyone thought about ancient civilizations," Ilona said. "He knew it would be the archaeological discovery of a lifetime."

Samuel steepled his brow as he looked at Chuck. "Of all our lifetimes."

7

Chuck pointed through the oval opening in the buried chamber at the dead body. "What does the corpse have to do with this once-in-a-million-lifetimes find you're talking about?" he demanded of Samuel.

The SAE archaeologist looked at Ilona, who explained, "Joseph Cannon was a young man, little more than a boy, when he went missing while working for Gustaf. He never returned to the family farm. After Elizabeth called me, I sent an email to Michaela McDermott at Southwest Archaeology Enterprises. We made up a contract together, and she assigned Samuel to work with me. Samuel joined me here to search for the artifacts Joseph Cannon was looking for in 1891."

"Joseph wrote about it in his journal," Samuel added. "The one Elizabeth found."

Chuck addressed Ilona. "What made this Elizabeth woman decide to call you, all the way over in Finland?"

Ilona answered slowly, her reluctance obvious. "She knew about the effort to return the Nordenskiöld remains back here to America."

"Aha." Chuck explained to Rosie, "For decades, there was a battle between Ilona's museum and people here in the US to convince the museum to repatriate the remains."

Rosie scrunched her nose. "What's 'repatriate' mean?"

"To return something to its place of origin. You heard Ilona describe how Gustaf Nordenskiöld gathered artifacts from Mesa Verde and shipped them to Europe. But she didn't mention something else he gathered from here and shipped across the ocean, too—human remains."

Ilona lowered her head, her eyes on her dusty sneakers.

"Gustaf did more than ship Ancestral Puebloan pottery and jewelry and clothing out of the country," Chuck explained to Rosie. "His excavation team dug up skeletons and skulls of Ancestral Puebloans. He shipped those out of the country, too. Altogether, he shipped the remains of eighteen Ancestral Puebloans to Europe."

"Ooooo," Rosie said, her eyes growing large. "Like ghosts."

"More like Esther from Falls Creek than ghosts. The bodies of real people who lived and died and were buried by their loved ones here at Mesa Verde—until Gustaf dug them up and shipped them away. After which, they were kept locked up by Ilona's museum."

Rosie looked at the Finnish curator. "Why would you want to keep dead people in your museum?"

Ilona raised her head. "To study them. For science."

Chuck shook his head, his jaw stiff. "The museum had the remains for more than a century," he told Rosie. "There's no way anyone there was still studying them. The real reason the museum didn't want to return them had to do with money. The museum was worried that if it gave back the skulls and bones of the Ancestral Puebloans, it might have to give back everything else Gustaf took from Mesa Verde, too—the pottery, the clothing, the jewelry, all of it. The National Museum of Finland is well known for Gustaf's Ancestral Puebloan collection and didn't want to risk having to give it up. The good news is that Ilona's museum finally returned the remains, just a little while ago, and so far the museum has been able to hang on to the rest of its Nordenskiöld collection without any problems." Chuck glanced across the depression at Ilona, then continued speaking to Rosie. "In fact, I'm getting the sense that Ilona is here to dig up even more artifacts from Mesa Verde—from right here in this alcove—and ship them back to Finland, too—" he shot a sidelong look at Samuel "—with this guy's help."

Samuel stepped backward. "I'm just doing my job. Michaela is the one who negotiated the contract."

Chuck turned to Kyla, the post-doc fellow from Harvard. "What about you?"

"Samuel asked me if I wanted to help." She looked at Samuel.

"I'd heard Kyla was out here working at the park," he said. "I suspected Ilona and I wouldn't be able to do all the digging on our own."

"So," Chuck said, "with Kyla's help, you and Ilona were looking for the big discovery you mentioned, but you found the corpse instead." He glanced into the depression. The suspenders on the dead body were visible through the opening as two shadowy lines extending up the corpse's torso. "And you asked me to come out here because you have reason to believe Joseph Cannon's murder a hundred years ago and Barney's murder earlier today are somehow related. Have I got all of that right?"

"When the texts of what happened in Durango started coming in," said Samuel, "I couldn't *not* call you."

"You could have described to me what you found over the phone."

"I didn't think you'd believe me. We're archaeologists. We have to see these things for ourselves."

"You could have sent me pictures."

"No." Samuel shook his head. "It's not worth the risk."

"Your dig's some sort of a big secret?"

"Not necessarily a secret. Just quiet is all. The park service wants no part of it. Neither do the Utes. When the park superintendent and tribal president heard Gunnel Canyon was involved, they got together and declared the dig off limits to archaeological staff from the park and tribe both. See no evil, hear no evil, that's what they decided."

Chuck peered at the portion of the corpse visible through the opening and said grimly, "Regardless, evil came here a hundred years ago. And it came to Durango—to Barney, to my home—just a few hours ago."

Ilona drew her skinny frame up to full height, slightly taller than Kyla beside her. "There is no evil in the idea of the study I am here to perform."

"What's the intent of your study? What's this big discovery you're so hot about?"

She hooked a tendril of her platinum hair behind her ear with a thin finger. "You are right that I am coming here for Gustaf Nordenskiöld and for what he thought he would find here."

"But he didn't find it, did he? Because if he had, it would be in your collection back home in your museum. So I'll ask you again: What was Gustaf looking for? What brings you here now, more than a hundred years after he left?"

Ilona looked into the depression, then back at Chuck. "It is what Joseph Cannon was seeking on Gustaf's behalf."

Samuel picked up her explanation. "We're working under the assumption that the corpse is, or was, Joseph Cannon, and that his killer took what he was attempting to find."

"Which was *what*?" Chuck demanded.

Samuel looked across the depression at Ilona. She remained silent.

"Canopic jars," Samuel said.

Chuck gaped at Samuel. "Canopic jars? As in, *Egyptian* canopic jars?"

On the far side of the cavity, Kyla whistled. "I knew I was here for a good reason, I just knew it."

"Not Egyptian," Samuel said to Chuck. "Ancestral Puebloan. But yes, canopic jars all the same."

Rosie raised her hand and asked, "What are canop... canop...?"

"Canopic jars," Chuck finished for her. "They're ceremonial urns used for the storage of human viscera after death."

"Viscera?"

"The inside parts of the human body."

Samuel bent toward Rosie. "Thousands of years ago, the people of ancient Egypt stored the viscera of dead people in special vessels called canopic jars," he told her. "The jars were placed in tombs with the mummified remains of the deceased. That way, the organs could be returned to their bodies in their next lives."

"Hmm." Rosie pressed a forefinger to her chin. "That makes sense."

"But that was Egypt, on the other side of the planet, with their pyramids and underground tombs and elaborate burial rituals," Samuel continued. "As far as anyone knows, no other prehistoric peoples anywhere else on earth ever used canopic jars as part of their interment ceremonies—including the Ancestral Puebloans of Mesa Verde, whose society didn't even come into existence until thousands of years after the culture of the ancient Egyptians came to its end."

Rosie's eyes widened. "So if it turned out the Ancestral Puebloans *did* do that..."

"... it would be a huge discovery," Samuel said. "Massive. It could even open up the possibility of some sort of intercommunication between two ancient peoples separated in time by several millennia, and by the Atlantic Ocean as well."

Chuck inclined his head to Rosie. "It would be what Samuel said a minute ago—the archaeological discovery of all our lifetimes put together."

Ilona offered a pronounced nod. "I have studied Gustaf's journals and published works for many years. Even though he was only a young man when he came here to Mesa Verde, he was a very good scientist. He understood the bigness of what he was studying here. And then he heard some stories about the vessels, which made an even bigger excitement inside him."

"The canopic jars, you mean," Chuck said.

"That is correct. Everything fell into place in my mind after Elizabeth called me. That is when I contacted Michaela at Southwest Archaeology Enterprises."

"Why Michaela?"

"Her company is the biggest, no? And the website says they are always charging the littlest money."

"Michaela passed Ilona on to me," Samuel said. "After the park and tribal officials refused to let any of their staff get involved, Ilona and I decided we would keep the circle of knowledge small. We only reached out to Kyla, no one else. I figured she'd be up for it, and I was right."

Chuck turned to the young archaeologist from the East Coast. "You honestly agreed to participate without knowing what you were looking for?"

Kyla shrugged. "My advisor knows Samuel. Ilona checked out all right online. Samuel said it would be quick, just a day or two. I was stoked to get in on a legitimate dig while I was here at the park. I figured I had everything to gain and nothing to lose. And, holy moly, was I ever right." Her eyes gleamed. "Ancestral Puebloan canopic jars—who'd have ever imagined?"

Samuel clapped his gloved hands at Kyla. "You've got some seriously great shoveling abilities, you know that?"

Kyla's eyes glowed and her face flushed.

Turning away from her, Chuck scanned the alcove. The dirt floor of the recess was bare beneath the sandstone ceiling. No length of rebar protruded from the ground to mark a central datum point at the middle of the dig site from which all site measurements would emanate. Nor did a stringed survey grid stretch across the ground in measured squares. Instead, the excavation appeared to consist solely of the depression dug into the floor of the recess that led directly to the hidden chamber and the corpse within it.

Samuel followed Chuck's searching gaze around the alcove. "I know, I know. No datum point, no survey grid. None of the usual prep work."

"I assume you knew where to dig because the soil already had been disturbed where Joseph's body was entombed."

"We could see the disturbance plain as day," Samuel said with a nod. "Even after more than a century."

Chuck curled his mouth as he examined the rest of the alcove floor, which appeared smooth and undisturbed. "I don't see any other signs of past digging. How could this alcove possibly be here all these years, unsurveyed and undug except for the one place where you found the corpse?"

Ilona raised a finger, drawing Chuck's attention from across the depression. "Very easily, in a matter of fact. Gunnel Canyon is dry of water most of the months of the year, so the Ancestral Puebloans did not build any permanent housing structures here. With no housing structures, this canyon had no interest to early archaeologists and looters, and after the national park was made, Gunnel Canyon stayed off of the radar, as you say it."

"Until you showed up yesterday."

"Until *we* showed up," Ilona said with a look at Samuel and Kyla.

"I'm not here for canopic jars," Chuck said. "Or for Joseph Cannon. Or for whatever other secrets this site might hold. I'm only here on account of Barney's murder." He locked eyes with

Samuel. "You called me because of the timing between your discovery of the corpse—clearly the victim of murder—and Barney's killing at my house, is that right?"

"I think it's highly unlikely that what happened in Durango is merely coincidental with the timing of our discovery here," Samuel affirmed.

"Let's consider that timing, then." Chuck turned to Ilona. "When did you arrive in Colorado?"

"Three days ago. I am staying in Durango, at the Strater Hotel, where Gustaf stayed."

"That's where he was detained under house arrest, wasn't he?"

"He was required by the town officials to remain in his suite for a few hours, yes, until he was freed to go."

"It's worth noting that he was detained for doing exactly what you're doing here in this canyon today, a hundred years later—unauthorized Ancestral Puebloan digging."

"Whoa, there," Samuel said, raising his hands to Chuck. "Gustaf wasn't detained for looting. He was accused of trespassing on what were considered tribal lands before the establishment of the national park."

"That was the official charge. But we all know why he really was held."

"You and I also know he wasn't a looter. He was one of the world's first true archaeologists, performing scientifically sound studies in an attempt to stay a step ahead of the real looters." Samuel glanced at Ilona and Kyla before looking back at Chuck. "As for us, you called our dig 'unauthorized.' But nothing could be further from the truth. The park service has checked off on what we're doing here. The tribe has checked off on it. They just decided they didn't want to be involved, that's all."

"You didn't place a datum point. You haven't even put in a survey grid."

"We didn't have to."

"This isn't a normal archaeological dig, not by any definition. All you did was show up and start digging."

"And it paid off, didn't it?"

"For you, maybe." Chuck pointed at the corpse lying in the chamber. "But not for this guy. Someone took an ax to him, from the looks of it. Somebody murdered him, just like somebody murdered Barney behind my house earlier today."

"That's why I called you," Samuel said. "That's what I, we, want to know. Does anything you saw in town—with Barney, with your house—seem to connect with what you're seeing here?"

At last, Chuck understood why Samuel had invited him out to Mesa Verde from Durango. His cheeks grew hot as blood rushed to his face. "I can't believe you," he spat at the SAE archaeologist. "Barney's dead—he's *dead*—and all you care about is how his death might affect your dig. *That's* why you conned me into driving all the way out here, isn't it? Not so I could learn what I could for Barney's sake, but so you could learn what you could from me."

Samuel's eyes slid away. At the same instant, Chuck's phone buzzed in his pocket. He pulled it out to see an incoming text on the screen.

It was from Janelle: *Call me. Now.*

8

Chuck looked up from his phone. "I have to make a call."

"You'll need to climb out of the canyon to get it to go through," Samuel said. "Only texts make it down here to the canyon bottom, and even then, they only make it every so often."

"Are we done here?" Chuck asked, his voice sharp.

"You have to understand, Chuck," Samuel pleaded. "I wanted you to see what we found with your own eyes. Now that you've seen it, we'll suspend the dig. There'll be plenty of time to deal with the corpse later. It's been more than a century, after all. We agree with you: the first order of business is Barney."

"Barney? You don't care the least bit about Barney." Chuck glared at Samuel. His voice vibrated with anger. "This is only about the canopic jars to you. You didn't get me out here to show me the corpse. You lured me here to find out if anything I told you about Barney's murder might help you with your search for buried treasure." Chuck turned to Kyla, across the depression from him. "I'd be careful if I were you, Harvard. Sounds like you've built yourself a pretty good reputation in a short amount of time." He aimed one finger at Samuel and another at Ilona. "You wouldn't want to put all you've worked for at risk by trusting these two."

He spun away. Taking Rosie's hand, he led her out of the alcove and back toward the slot in the canyon wall.

"You're mad," Rosie said as she and Chuck retraced their steps up the canyon.

"I was," Chuck said. He took a steadying breath. "I'm not anymore."

"What are you, then?"

"I'm disappointed." He exhaled. "And, okay, I guess I'm still a little angry. I thought we would learn something by coming all the way out here that would help us with Barney. Instead, I got used."

They came to the cleft and scrambled up it to the canyon rim. Chuck dialed Janelle as soon as they reached the sandstone shelf at the top of the cliff.

Janelle answered by saying, "You have to get back here."

"What's going on?"

"Your old girlfriend just arrested Audrey."

Chuck squeezed his phone in his hand. "Sandra?"

"She's got Audrey stuck in the back of her police car. She's asking for you."

"Who? Audrey or Sandra?"

"Sandra. She wants to know if you want to press charges."

"Charges? For what?"

"For interfering with an active investigation on your property. It's my property, too, but she won't even acknowledge it. She'll only listen to you."

Chuck pressed the phone to his ear as he strode away from the edge of the canyon into the forest, heading back to the parking area at the end of the dirt road with Rosie a step behind. The piney scent of the trees filled the air. A chipmunk darted across the forest floor ahead of him. It stopped and rose on its hind legs, its nose twitching and its long tail waving like a flag, before disappearing behind the thick trunk of a gnarled, old piñon.

"Tell me what happened," Chuck said to Janelle.

"Carm and I went with Audrey, like we planned. First thing, we drove around the neighborhood until we spotted Barney's car. It was parked three blocks away. I'm sure Audrey has told the police where it is by now."

Chuck squeezed his temples between the thumb and forefinger of his free hand as he walked. "He obviously was hiding the fact that he was headed to our house."

"Agreed. Why else would he park so far away? Audrey and I looked in the car windows, but we didn't see anything that seemed out of the ordinary."

"What'd she say when you pointed out he clearly was on some sort of secret mission to our place, after he'd told her he was just going out for coffee?"

"I couldn't bring myself to mention it. She's heartbroken, Chuck."

"What'd you do after that?"

"We parked and headed for our house. There were lots of people lined up at the police tape at the end of the block. Twenty or so. They all started hugging Audrey. There hasn't been any official announcement yet, but everybody knows."

Chuck wound his way through the trees with Rosie. "That's Durango for you."

"Everyone crowded around her. I guess that's what attracted Sandra's attention. She came over and said she had a couple more questions for her. She lifted the police tape and escorted her toward the house. They'd only gone a few steps when Audrey started screaming and crying and trying to hit Sandra. More like flailing, really. I wouldn't really call it an assault."

"That's not how the cops will see it."

"No doubt," Janelle said in agreement. "Sandra put Audrey in handcuffs and made her get in the back of one of the police cars. Officer Anand, the officer posted out front, is keeping an eye on her while Sandra has gone back inside the house. She came over and filled me in. She seems reasonable enough."

"Unlike Sandra?"

"Sandra's never been reasonable, and you know it, not since the day I showed up in town—and in your life."

"Now is not the time," Chuck cautioned.

But Janelle stuck to the subject. "She's never gotten over you. It's right there in her eyes, every time we run into her around town. You see it, too; don't tell me you don't."

"She's married, Janelle. To another woman. They have kids, for Christ's sake."

"Have you seen those kids? Have you really looked at them?" Janelle's voice shook. "She must have picked a donor who looked just like you."

Chuck moaned. "Barney's dead, Audrey's under arrest, and we're talking about who someone's sperm-donor kids look like?"

"Who *Sandra's* kids look like. She's in our house right now, this minute, snooping around. Who knows what she'll find in there to try to incriminate you, just to get back at us. Or, me."

"Please. *Calmate.* Hang in there for me, for us. You have to."

A long second of silence passed before Janelle muttered, "Okay. All right," followed by a burst of air jetted through her lips. "I just need you to get back here as fast as you can."

Fifty yards ahead, through the piñon and juniper trees, the pickup glinted in the orange, late-afternoon sunlight. The scent of dust sifted through the forest.

"We're almost to the truck. We'll be back in an hour and a half, tops."

"How's Rosie doing? Is she good?"

"Rosie's always good." Chuck pivoted and walked backward, holding out the phone to her. "*¿Verdad?*"

"*¡Verdad!*" Rosie shouted into the phone.

He turned forward and put the phone back to his ear. "Ninety minutes, *cariña*," he promised.

* * *

Chuck turned off the secondary road and drove up the main road heading out of the park, approaching the edge of the plateau and the start of the four-mile descent to the highway. Rosie sat opposite him in the front passenger seat.

"What does 'repatriate' mean again?" she asked.

"It means returning human remains and funerary objects to their places of origin—that is, to where they were found, like Ilona's museum finally did with the remains and funerary objects that were taken from Mesa Verde back in 1891."

Chuck accelerated out of a curve and sped along a straight-away. With the onset of evening, the main park road was deserted in both directions.

"What are funerary objects?"

"Special items Ancestral Puebloans and other prehistoric peoples buried with their loved ones, like jewelry and pottery and fancy clothing."

"And like the canopy jars they buried with the dead people, too."

"*Canopic* jars," Chuck said. "And yes, I guess you could say that. In Egypt, anyway."

"And maybe here. That's why the lady came, right?"

"Yep."

"And because of the dead man. His name was Joseph."

"It sounds like that's who he was."

"What happened to him?"

"You saw his skull."

"It was almost cut in half. Was that from the autopsy?"

"No. It looks pretty clear that somebody killed him."

"Just like Barney."

Chuck nodded. "Whoever killed Joseph—assuming it is Joseph—left his body there, hidden away, all these years." He glanced at Rosie. "It didn't bother you, seeing the corpse?"

"The dead man? Nah. I thought it was cool. It was like a real archaeology thing. But those people were mad that they found him, weren't they?"

"They thought they were going to find a treasure—the canopic jars—but they found the corpse instead."

"They wanted to find the jars with vis . . . vis . . ."

"Viscera."

"Yeah. With viscera in them." She screwed up her lips. "That doesn't sound like a treasure to me."

"It's an archaeological thing, like you just said. An astonishing archaeological thing."

"Would that be a big enough deal that people would kill each other to get them?"

"Like Barney, you mean? Or the body in the chamber? Yes, in fact, they very well might. If the jars really do exist, they would change a lot of what we know about Ancestral Puebloan culture. The fact of the jars' existence would raise Ancestral Puebloans to a whole new level in terms of how spiritually advanced they were. That would be a huge deal—new information that would change how we see and understand Ancestral Puebloan culture."

"Wow." Rosie sat up straight in her seat. "When I grow up, I want to be an archaeologist and study the Ancestral Puebloans."

"Like me?"

"Just like you." She folded her hands in her lap. "And like the guy with the funny name."

"Gustaf Nordenskiöld?"

She giggled. "That's the name the lady kept saying."

"Nordenskiöld, Nordenskiöld, Nordenskiöld," Chuck repeated rapidly, eliciting more giggles from Rosie.

"I don't know for sure if I want to be like him, though," she said after she stopped laughing, "because he took those dead bodies."

"He shipped the skulls and bones of Ancestral Puebloans

back to Europe because he wanted to study what the people were like a long time ago, along with the clothing they wore and the items they used in their day-to-day lives. Taking the bodies was considered acceptable back then. Most archaeologists collected skulls and bones along with artifacts they found. The US government even collected the skulls of Native American men, women, and children massacred by the army. Eventually, though, Native Americans publicly objected to the removal of their ancestors' remains—as well they should have. They pushed for the passage of the Native American Graves Protection and Repatriation Act, which required the return of bodies and funerary objects to where they were found."

"If there's a law, why did that funny-talking lady keep on keeping all those old skeletons in her museum for so long?"

"Because the law only applies here in the US. It doesn't work in other countries."

"She's greedy, then." Rosie crossed her arms over her chest. "And mean."

"There's more to it than that. Lots of museums here in America have human remains and funerary objects from other countries that they don't want to give back, either. If the United States pushes real hard for the return of the Ancestral Puebloan remains from places like the museum in Finland, then museums in the US might have to give back their stuff to other countries, too."

"That makes them greedy and mean, too, just like the funny-talking lady."

"I'd say that sums up the situation pretty darn well—except that Ilona's museum, at least, finally gave back the remains and funerary objects taken by Nordenskiöld, so sometimes the right thing does, in fact, happen."

* * *

They reached the edge of the mesa. The park road tipped downhill, descending into the Mancos Valley. Far below, outside the park boundary, the highway cut across the broad valley floor from east to west. To the north, the La Plata Mountains sawtoothed the horizon. Hesperus Mountain, the highest peak in the range at more than thirteen thousand feet, punched the sky in the middle of the range. The peak was one of the Navajo Tribe's four sacred mountains, marking the northeastern corner of the tribe's traditional homelands.

Chuck guided the truck into the first switchback, his foot light on the brake pedal, driving as fast as he dared. The pickup leaned hard to one side, the tires squealing as they clung to the pavement.

Rosie leaned toward Chuck through the turn and sat up straight as they came out of the curve. "What can we do to make all the museums return all the dead people they've got?" she asked.

"I like how you think, you know that?" Chuck said. He relaxed his hold on the steering wheel as the road straightened. "Since NAGPRA—the repatriation act—doesn't work in other countries, it takes a big push by the public to convince foreign museums to give remains back."

"Is that what happened with the Mesa Verde dead people?"

"That's exactly what happened. Lots of folks in America argued for the return of the remains for a long time. In answer, for a long time, Ilona's museum made the excuse that Mesa Verde didn't have a good place to store the remains until they were reinterred. But that all changed a few years ago." He pointed through the window at the Mesa Verde Visitor and Research Center at the foot of the mesa below. "The new Visitor and Research Center has a state-of-the-art, climate-controlled facility for storing artifacts and human remains."

"So there finally was a place for the bodies to come back to?"

"Yep. Park archaeologists could store the remains and funerary objects in the center while they figured out the best place to rebury them. Then, when they decided, they could go ahead and do the reinterment."

"I bet the Nordenskiöld man was happy about that. He was a real archaeologist. He just didn't know any better about taking the bodies back then."

"Now that you mention it, I bet he was."

Chuck steered the truck into the next switchback. Rosie leaned away from him this time, allowing centrifugal force to press her upper body against the passenger door as the pickup swung around the outside lane of the curve, a few feet from the precipitous drop-off into the valley.

Chuck tapped the brakes as the truck rounded the switchback.

Blam. A gunshot-like blast sounded from beneath the truck as the front, passenger-side tire exploded.

The pickup canted hard to the right, lurching toward the side of the road and the abyss beyond.

Chuck slammed his foot on the brake pedal. He fought to keep the truck on the pavement, the steering wheel bucking in his hands. Chunks of tread from the blown tire thudded the truck's undercarriage as the pickup skidded straight toward the edge of the road.

PART TWO

"The Surgeon General is anxious that our collection of Indian crania, already quite large, should be made as complete as possible."

—Madison Mills, Surgeon, US Army,
January 13, 1868

9

Chuck battled the steering wheel, his foot plastered to the brake, as the last of the blown tire tore away from the metal rim. The rim gouged into the asphalt and the truck lurched, its frame wrenching.

Rosie shot her hands out in front of her. "Daddy!" she screamed.

The truck slid off the road, its front end plunging over the unguarded drop-off.

The truck's undercarriage and running boards slammed against the edge of the asphalt. The friction of the metal on the pavement halted the truck's skid a third of the way along its body, leaving the front end hanging over the void.

Chuck gripped the wheel, his hands shaking, and stared out the windshield at the valley floor hundreds of feet below.

"Daddy, Daddy, Daddy!" Rosie wailed. She unclipped her seatbelt, scrambled across the front seat, and pressed herself to him.

He released the steering wheel and hugged Rosie to his chest. With his arm tight around her, he opened his door to the mountainside falling away beneath the perched truck and positioned his feet on the running board, his back to the abyss. He drew Rosie after him and edged with her along the running board to the point where the truck frame met the side of the road. He stepped onto the pavement and backed away from the truck with his arms around Rosie's stomach, staring at the front end of the pickup hanging suspended in space.

When they were well away from the vehicle, he bent over her. "It's okay, *m'hija*," he said softly in her ear, calling on the Spanish endearment for "my daughter" Janelle used to soothe the girls. "It's all right. We're safe now. We're safe."

Rosie buried her face in his chest. "I . . . I was so scared," she said between gulping sobs. "I . . . I thought we were going to die."

"But we didn't." He stroked her hair. "We didn't."

She looked up at him with teary eyes, her sobs subsiding. "Not like that guy in the hole."

He managed a shaky half-smile. "Nobody came after us with an ax, did they?"

Which led him to consider: rather than an ax, what might someone have come after them with instead?

He took Rosie's hand and retraced with her the path the skidding truck had followed off the edge of the road. The acrid smell of shredded rubber filled the air. Hunks of sidewall and chunks of mangled tread littered the passage of the skidding truck.

The blown tire was only weeks old, its tread virtually unworn. It should not have failed on the curve—unless someone had induced it to do so.

Chuck picked up the pieces of tire scattered on the road, examining them one by one. He studied several smaller pieces first, finding nothing, then checked a large hunk of tread, roughly six inches square. When he twisted the large piece in his hands, a ripped seam appeared. The seam ran from the center of the piece of rubber to one side. He twisted harder, widening the seam. The rip ended in the middle of the piece of tire, where a small, circular hole punched all the way through the tread.

He looked up from the hunk of rubber. Something shimmered on the pavement in the last of the day's sunlight. He picked up the object. It was a steel carpentry nail, shiny and new, about three inches long, with a large, flat head. He inserted the nail through the hole in the hunk of tread. The circumference of the nail perfectly matched the diameter of the circular puncture.

Rosie pointed at the nail. "Was that in our tire?"

"I think so."

Chuck gazed out across the valley while he slid the nail back and forth in the hole. Tires punctured by lost or discarded carpentry nails were common enough in urban and populated rural areas, but not in a little-developed national park like Mesa Verde. Yet the gleaming, new nail in his hand somehow had come to be here in the park, and in the truck tire. In general, a nail through the tread of a tire led to a slow leak that emptied the tire of air over time. But the massive bulk of the heavy crew cab combined with the hard, downward turn off the mesa appeared to have led to the explosive failure of the nail-punctured front tire, nearly sending Rosie and him to their deaths.

He recalled the scent of dust floating in the air when he'd returned with Rosie from Gunnel Canyon to the end of the dirt road. Had another vehicle lifted the dust into the air as it departed ahead of them—after that vehicle's driver had positioned the carpentry nail under the front tire of Chuck's pickup with the point of the nail facing into the tread?

Chuck tightened his fingers around the hunk of tire tread. Joseph Cannon was dead, the victim of a murder perpetrated more than a century ago. Barney was dead, too, murdered earlier today. Now, Chuck and Rosie had nearly died. He shuddered. If the nail in the tire was no accident, meaning he and Rosie weren't safe way out here in the national park, then what sort of danger might Janelle and Carmelita be facing right now in Durango, where Barney had been killed?

A compact sedan appeared around the curve, descending from the top of the mesa, and came to an abrupt halt behind

Chuck's truck. The sedan's occupants, a middle-aged woman and a man in the passenger seat beside her, stared wide-eyed at the suspended pickup.

Chuck let them know he and Rosie were uninjured and waved them on their way. Returning to the truck, he grasped the rear bumper and lifted, grunting. The truck didn't budge.

"Good," he said to Rosie.

"It's not about to fall off the edge?"

"It likes the road better than the mountainside."

She wrapped her arms around herself. "So do I."

Chuck removed the spare wheel from beneath the bed of the pickup and laid it on the road beside the truck. He stood over the spare, staring at the tireless front end of the truck hanging in space.

"I can't change the wheel with the truck out in the air like that," he told Rosie.

"Well, duh," she said with an exaggerated roll of her eyes.

Warning her to stay back, he sidestepped his way along the running board and returned to the driver's seat. Cinching his seatbelt, he started the truck, put it in reverse, and goosed the engine. The rear tires bit into the pavement, but the truck didn't move. He depressed the accelerator further. The tires bucked and spun, raising a cloud of blue-gray smoke. Still, the truck did not budge.

He let up on the accelerator when flashing lights appeared in his rearview mirror.

A white park-service pickup truck, heading down from the mesa like the couple's sedan before it, eased to a stop behind the stranded crew cab. A uniformed ranger hopped out of the park-service vehicle, leaving the rooftop emergency lights flashing.

Chuck climbed out of the crew cab and met the ranger. The man was in his mid-thirties, tall and burly, his face burnished by the sun. He put his hands on his hips and stood in the middle of the road with the wide-legged stance of someone who knew what he was about.

"Man, oh, man," he said, shaking his head as he ogled Chuck's truck. He ran his fingers through his short, black hair. Leaning down to Rosie, he said, "That must've been pretty scary."

She nodded vigorously, her entire body rocking with her head. "Really, really, *really* scary."

"Are you all right?"

"Yep."

"That's the spirit." Straightening, the ranger asked Chuck, "Are you doing some work here in the park?"

Chuck followed the ranger's gaze to the Bender Archaeo-logical logo stenciled on the front door of the pickup. "I was showing my daughter what I do for a living. Rosie says she wants to be an archaeologist someday, like me."

"Or a park ranger," Rosie added quickly.

The ranger grinned at her. "Be careful what you wish for, y'hear?" He turned to Chuck. "Have you called a wrecker?"

"Not yet. Who knows how long it'll take for them to get here. I've got a tow strap in my toolbox, though. Shouldn't take more than a few minutes to see if we can do it ourselves." He cocked an eyebrow at the ranger. "You game?"

The ranger's grin widened. "You bet."

Chuck ran the nylon tow strap from the rear of his truck to the front of the ranger's pickup. With a series of smooth tugs, the ranger eased the Bender Archaeological truck back onto the road. Chuck insisted he could change the wheel on his own, prompting the ranger to shake Rosie's hand and inform her that he looked forward to the day she joined him in the ranger ranks—"It's way more fun than what your dad does for a living," he assured her—before returning to his truck and driving on down the road.

Half an hour later, Chuck and Rosie were on their way, too, the spare spinning smoothly on the front passenger side of the truck. The punctured piece of tire tread rested on the front seat between them, the nail protruding from the hole in its center.

They descended to the highway and turned toward Durango. Dusk blossomed pink and orange in the western sky behind them, reflected in the rear-facing mirrors.

Rosie plucked the steel nail from its hole in the tread and fingered its point. "It's sharp." She looked at Chuck. "Did somebody do it on purpose?"

10

Chuck shot a sidelong glance at Rosie. She'd proven herself a youngster of steel today, in the face of Barney's death, the sight of Joseph Cannon's corpse, and the nearly fatal plunge off the park road.

She could handle the truth.

"Yes," he told her as they ascended the west side of Mancos Divide, "I think maybe someone was trying to scare us."

Back in Durango, he parked on a quiet side street in the Grid district and walked with Rosie toward the house.

The last of the evening light filtered through the canopy of trees sheltering the neighborhood. Ahead, secured between folding barricades, crime-scene tape closed off the street leading to the house and the alley in back. Durango Police Department SUVs crowded the pavement in front of the house.

By now, a mobile command unit had joined the vehicles. The badge-shaped Durango Police Department logo emblazoned the side of the office-on-wheels, and a canvas front awning extended from its roof.

Spotlights rose on aluminum poles from each corner of the command unit. The lights shone on the house, illuminating the brick facade like a movie set. Pasta Alfredo, the cat Rosie had picked up as a stray a year ago in Arches National Park, crouched in the upstairs window of Carmelita's room, while Officer Anand sat in a folding chair in the front yard, facing the police vehicles in the street.

More than a dozen onlookers gathered in a group at the police barricades half a block from the house.

"Chuck," said a woman in the group. She approached him with her hand extended.

Chuck took the woman's hand as they met, far enough from the barricades to be out of earshot of the others. "Michaela."

Rosie continued to the police tape, joining those observing the crime scene.

In contrast to the casual, fleece-and-jeans attire of most Durangoans, Southwest Archaeology Enterprises owner Michaela McDermott wore dark pumps, a pressed navy skirt, and a matching blazer over an off-white linen blouse. The blouse was unbuttoned to reveal a bulky, silver-and-turquoise pendant at her throat. Michaela was in her mid-fifties. Her hair, dark blond streaked with golden highlights, flared past her ears. Her lips were lacquered with fire-engine-red lipstick, and her cheeks were stretched Botox-tight.

Michaela drew Chuck to her with a firm grip. Her gray eyes, visibly bloodshot, searched his. "I'm so sorry for what's happened, Chuck. I know Barney was a dear friend of yours."

The smell of alcohol on her breath washed over Chuck. He freed his hand from her grasp and leaned away from her. "And yours, I'm sure."

"He was so much more than just an employee of Southwest Archaeology." She wrung her hands. "All my employees are far more than just clock-punchers to me—your brother-in-law included."

Chuck narrowed his eyes at Michaela. "Clarence?"

"Such a hard worker," she responded. "In just the few weeks he's been with us, he's become a dear friend to me, just like Barney, and just like all my people. Clarence and I worked together just this morning, in fact. A Saturday, no less. He's been so willing to sacrifice for the SAE team, filling in wherever he's needed, working weekends, and such . . . such a . . . *friend*."

Chuck blinked. Weren't they supposed to be talking about Barney? "Have the police spoken with you yet?"

Michaela laid a hand flat on her chest. "Me? Why, of course. I told them everything I could think of. Everything." A deep *V* burrowed between her thin eyebrows and she shook her head, the highlights in her hair flashing beneath the streetlights. "But what little I have to offer, dear Chuck." She sighed. "What little I have."

Chuck grabbed his pant legs at his sides. *Dear Chuck*? What did she mean by that? Though he and Michaela had run their respective archaeological-contract firms in Durango for more than two decades, they were little more than nodding acquaintances around town. Chuck regularly worked in the field with Michaela's employees, when his contracts overlapped with those awarded to her firm, but he'd never worked directly with Michaela because she never worked in the field herself.

Instead, Chuck knew from his archaeologist friends at Southwest Archaeology Enterprises that the owner and chief executive officer of the firm spent her days in the expansive SAE offices, which took up the top floor of an ornate brick building overlooking Main Avenue in downtown Durango.

Michaela lived in a sprawling mansion in a gated community high on a mountainside above town. She and her husband, an attorney, regularly hosted fundraisers for local nonprofit organizations at their luxurious residence. The fundraisers were the sort of soirees at which Chuck would not have been comfortable—had he ever been invited, that is.

Michaela wrapped her fingers around the turquoise pendant at her neck. Her powder-blue eyelids fluttered. "When I met with Ilona Koskinen this morning, little did I know the awfulness this day held in store."

Chuck swallowed. First, Michaela had made a point of mentioning Clarence. Now, Ilona. "Sounds as if you know where I was this afternoon."

"Gunnel Canyon offers a fascinating slice of Mesa Verde history, does it not?"

Chuck worked to keep his face neutral. Michaela was veering ever further from Barney's murder. Or was she? "I imagine you met with Ilona here in Durango this morning, not out at the canyon," he said, playing along.

"Yes. At my office. The Gunnel Canyon dig is Samuel's responsibility. As I always say, I trust my project managers implicitly as well as explicitly. My contracts are their contracts, and I tell them as much. They've earned the right to manage their assignments as they see fit." She kept her gaze fixed on Chuck. "Despite the significant size difference between Bender Archaeological and SAE—and your lack of any project managers besides yourself, Chuck—I'm sure you can understand my need to relinquish control, to not allow myself to become a micromanager-slash-CEO."

"Oh, I'm sure I can understand," Chuck replied flatly. He studied her as closely as she appeared to be studying him. "What makes you bring up your meeting with Ilona?"

"I want to make certain you know we're on the same side, you and I."

"Who's talking about sides? My friend, Barney—your friend, too, as you just said—is dead, murdered. There are no sides here, Michaela. There's just the need to find whoever killed him."

"Of course, of course." She released the pendant. Her hand hovered at her throat. "My only goal, the sole objective of SAE, is to provide the police the correct particulars to solve this despicable crime—without overloading them with extraneous information that would merely serve to slow their efforts. That is what I have done." Her eyes tightened almost imperceptibly. "I strongly encourage you to do the same."

Chuck pressed his lips together.

"You should know," she continued, "that I mentioned Clarence's name to the investigators. I felt I had no choice."

"I see," Chuck said, his jaw clenched.

Michaela reached out to him, her fingers dangling in the chilly evening air. "Your brother-in-law has made himself so invaluable to me in just the last few weeks since he joined us." She paused for a second. "Precisely as he did for Barney."

"For Barney?"

"As a crutch to him. A support."

Chuck released his pant legs and twisted his hands into fists. "What are you talking about, Michaela?"

"In the short time since I hired Clarence, he and Barney had grown remarkably close. I simply made sure to point out that fact to the police."

"Clarence had nothing whatsoever to do with Barney's murder, and you know it. You were working with him just today. You know him well enough by now to know he's not a killer."

"Oh, I'm sure you're correct," Michaela said breathily. "Your brother-in-law is such a dear." She stroked the polished turquoise stone at the center of the pendant with her fingertips. "Regardless, Clarence's intimacy with Barney may have availed him of information that could prove helpful to the investigation. I therefore felt it important for the police to know and understand your brother-in-law's close association with Barney." She removed a pair of oversized sunglasses from an inner pocket of her blazer and pressed them over her eyes with both hands. She glanced over her shoulder at the crime scene, then leaned forward and said in Chuck's ear, her alcohol-laden breath warm on his skin, "Your turn, Chuck."

She marched down the street away from the house, the leather soles of her pumps clicking on the pavement.

Chuck turned to the house, his back to Michaela, willing the sense of menace she exuded to depart along with her.

Barney. That's who he was here for. And Audrey.

He texted Janelle to let her know he and Rosie had arrived. Taking Rosie's hand, he ducked with her beneath the yellow crime-scene tape and they walked up the street toward the house together.

Janelle and Carmelita appeared around the side of the mobile command unit. Rosie ran ahead, meeting them in front of the house.

"We had a wreck, *Mamá!*" she announced the instant she reached her mother.

Janelle looked at Chuck, who trailed a few steps behind, then back at Rosie. "You *what?*"

"Daddy didn't tell you?"

Janelle fixed her eyes on Chuck as he reached them. "Daddy?"

Chuck had spoken briefly with Janelle by phone on the way back to Durango from Mesa Verde, learning that Sandra was still holding Audrey pending his arrival. He hadn't mentioned the blowout and the truck's plunge off the park road.

"We had a flat," he admitted, kneading the back of Rosie's neck with his fingers. "We're fine."

His neck rub didn't serve to settle Rosie down.

"We went over the edge," she announced to her mother and Carmelita. "Somebody tried to scare us. Daddy said so. We were hanging way out in the sky like a bird. A ranger pulled us back on the road, and then Daddy changed the tire." She shrugged. "And here we are."

"Daddy?" Janelle repeated. She said to Chuck, her voice quivering, "Somebody tried to *scare* you?"

Before he could answer, Rosie nodded emphatically. "With a nail."

"We don't know what happened," said Chuck. He tightened his fingers on the back of Rosie's neck. "Not for sure."

"Ouch!" Rosie wriggled free of his grasp and pivoted to look up at him. "But you said—"

"I know what I told you," he cut in. "But we don't really know, and we probably never will."

Rosie's eyes went to a folding table set up beneath the awning in front of the command unit. Canned soda and bottled water lined the table, along with energy bars and muffins wrapped in cellophane.

Rosie put her hand to her stomach. "I'm starving."

"I was hungry, too," Carmelita told her. "They said we can have what we want. They gave us chairs on the other side, out of sight of all the people."

Janelle asked Carmelita, "Will you take your sister over there with you?"

The girls headed for the command unit.

Janelle turned to Chuck. "'Daddy'?"

"That's the good news. The only good news, really."

In the five years since Chuck had come into the girls' lives, Carmelita and Rosie exclusively had called him "Chuck"—until today. He was comfortable with the girls' addressing him by his first name, but Rosie calling him "Daddy" represented a positive change nonetheless.

"The blowout was pretty intense," he said. "She yelled it out when we came to a stop, and hasn't stopped using it since."

"Chalk one up for flat tires, I guess," said Janelle.

"Did you talk with Michaela McDermott any this afternoon?"

"A couple of times."

"What'd she have to say to you about Clarence?"

Janelle frowned. "She didn't say anything at all to me about him."

"You must have been too intimidating to her."

Janelle's lips drew inward. "What are you talking about?"

He aimed a thumb over his shoulder. "I ran into her just now, back there at the police tape. It was almost like she was waiting for me. She knew I'd been out at Mesa Verde. Did you tell her I was on my way here?"

"Now that you mention it, I guess I did. She asked. I didn't see any reason not to. Why?"

"She made a point of mentioning Clarence right away, like she considered him a prime suspect. She pretty much told me she'd said as much to the police."

Janelle's eyes flared. "That . . . that woman," she snarled. She looked past Chuck to the onlookers lined at the police tape at the end of the block.

"She's not there anymore. She took off."

Janelle's fingers curled into claws and her hands shook. "I'll kill her, I swear to God."

"She must have waited until I got here, just so she could tell me that."

"Why would she do that? What do you think she's up to?"

"She had alcohol on her breath. Some of the stuff she said made it seem like she was drunk. Other stuff, though, not so much." He shook his head, frowning. "I bet Clarence has told her how tough you are. She knew what you'd do to her if she said anything about him to you, so she hit me with her accusations instead. She clearly wanted to put us on notice for some reason."

He wagged his chin from side to side, baffled. Michaela also had mentioned her meeting this morning with Ilona. Like her blatant mention of Clarence, had that been on purpose? Or had it just slipped out? "I don't get it," he said.

Janelle's cheeks reddened. "You helped Clarence get on with Southwest Archaeology Enterprises. You pulled strings so he could go to work for Michaela."

"She's pretty much the only game in town at this point. I've been winning enough contracts to get by, but just barely. I'm not getting nearly enough work to keep Clarence busy, too. It was either help him get on with SAE, or he was going to spend the rest of his life as a bartender. Besides, from what he's said, the work he's been doing has been solid. Michaela has put him on all sorts of projects. I know he's not making a lot of money, but he's been getting lots of good experience." Chuck shrugged. "Maybe we're overreacting. Maybe she just thought she was being nice by filling us in. From what I know of her, she's never had much in the way of social skills. She's respected more for her business sense—for her ability to bid lower than anybody else and scoop up most of the Four Corners-area contracts that come along, especially over the last few months."

"She's barely paying Clarence minimum wage. Audrey mentioned how little money Barney was making at SAE, too, even after all these years."

Chuck trembled at the mention of Audrey's name. "Where is she? How's she doing?"

Janelle pointed at one of the bulky police SUVs slotted in front of the house. "She's still in there. They won't let her out, and they won't let me talk to her, either. I have no idea why."

11

Chuck approached Officer Anand, who rose from her folding chair in the front yard and spoke into a microphone clipped to her shirt collar. Sandra exited the house seconds later. She passed the young officer on the front walkway and stopped on the sidewalk facing Chuck.

"About time you got here," she said.

"Why are you holding Audrey?" Chuck demanded. "Her husband was murdered today. What are you, crazy?"

Sandra's eyes flicked to the line of parked SUVs. "She assaulted me."

"You must have done something to provoke her."

"Wrong."

"Wrong?"

"I'll let her explain."

Sandra crossed to the driver's side of the SUV Janelle had pointed out. Waving Chuck to the passenger side, she unlocked the doors with a remote and they climbed inside. Audrey sat in the back seat, her hands behind her, separated from the front of the vehicle by a thick sheet of heavily scratched plexiglass. Sandra spun a tiny, dash-mounted camera to face into the vehicle and depressed a button on top of the camera. A red light came on next to the camera's lens. Turning to face the back of the car, she slid open a panel in the middle of the safety glass between the seats.

"My wrists are killing me," Audrey said through the opening.

"Everyone in the back seat has to be cuffed," Sandra said. "Sorry."

Audrey's eyes glinted with tears. "I shouldn't be back here. You have no right." Her voice softened, the loose skin beneath her chin wobbling. "My husband is dead, and you've got me caged up like I'm some sort of animal."

"You're under voluntary detention, as you and I discussed. That's much better than being placed under formal arrest, which was your only other choice."

Audrey blinked away her tears. "Let's just get this over with. Jason will be here soon, besides which, I have to go to the bathroom."

Chuck turned sideways in the front seat, his back to the passenger door. "Did Audrey interfere with your investigation somehow?" he asked Sandra.

"She attacked me."

Audrey glared at Sandra. "You had no right to make the accusations you were making to me."

"They were questions—one question—that, rather than answer, you chose to assault me for asking."

"All I did was defend myself from your baseless—"

Sandra rapped her knuckles on the plexiglass, cutting Audrey off. "How about if we try this again?"

Audrey sat forward, still eyeing Sandra through the glass. "Fine."

"Where were you today between the hours of noon and two p.m.?"

Audrey turned to Chuck. "See? They think I did it. They think I killed my Barney."

"*That's* why you attacked Sandra?" he asked. "She's just doing her job."

"She has no right."

"You need to understand, Audrey, all of us are devastated right along with you. But Barney's killer is getting farther away with every minute that goes by." Sandra nodded as he continued. "They have to ask about you first. It's the rules, just like the handcuffs in the back seat."

Audrey grunted. Her gaze shifted from Chuck to Sandra. "I was at home, trying out a new pastry dough recipe for . . . for . . . Barney. No one stopped by. I wasn't on the phone." Her voice rose. "And no, I did not kill my husband."

Sandra cleared her throat. "Thank you for that."

"How about you?" Audrey demanded, eyeing Sandra through the scratched safety glass.

"Me?"

"If you're asking about me, I'm allowed to ask about you, too, aren't I? Where were you from noon to two today?"

Sandra extended her jaw. "My job is to—"

"Your job is to catch my husband's killer," Audrey broke in. "You've kept me cooped up in here forever. I've had plenty of time to do some thinking. One of the things I've thought about is why you'd lock me up in here—me, the wife of the murder victim. And I've figured out the answer. Everybody knows you and Chuck were quite the hot item together a few years ago. My husband was found dead earlier today behind Chuck's house—that is, behind the house of your ex-boyfriend."

Chuck held his breath. Sandra's face was a mask, still and frozen.

"Rumor has it you never got over Chuck," Audrey said. "Even your wife knows it, or so they say."

"This has nothing whatsoever to do with your husband's—" Sandra began.

"Oh, yes, it does," Audrey countered. "It has plenty to do with it. Somebody broke into the house of your former boyfriend today, which led directly to my husband's death."

When Sandra said nothing, Audrey repeated, "So tell me, officer, where were you at midday today when my husband was murdered?"

Sandra placed her hand on the butt of her service pistol, holstered at her waist. "I was in bed, coming off a string of nights," she said. "I was just about to get up when the call came through. I'm on the homicide response squad for the department. Durango's too small to maintain a full-time team. I dressed and came straight here, and I've been here ever since."

"Who were you in bed with? Your wife? I suppose you can get her to vouch for you."

"That's enough. I won't—"

"Who?" Audrey demanded.

The question hung in the air.

"No one," Sandra admitted. "Cheryl was at work. The kids were at daycare."

Audrey sat back. "So. You haven't got an alibi for my husband's murder, and you're handling the investigation."

After a moment of silence, Audrey's chin began to tremble, followed by the rest of her body. She dissolved into tears, her head bowed and her hair draping her face.

Sandra addressed Audrey's lowered head through the opening in the plexiglass. "I answered your questions. Now, I'd appreciate it if you would answer mine. I appreciate the names you provided me when I came to your house earlier today. Now that more time has passed, I simply need to know if you've had any more thoughts about why Barney was at Chuck's house today, and if you've thought of anyone you know of who might have meant him harm."

Audrey stopped crying. She hiccupped and raised her head, looking at Sandra through her fallen hair. "I don't know why Barney came here." She tossed her head, flipping her hair out of her face. The makeup around her eyes was splotched and runny. "It's Chuck who should know. It's his house."

"You have no idea?" Sandra insisted. "None whatsoever?"

"Barney said he was going out for his 'cuppa.' That's what he calls it." She swallowed. "Called it. Every day when he's home, he goes out in the afternoon for a cup of coffee. I'm sure he took advantage of being out of the house to swing by here, for whatever reason." A tremor entered her voice. "It had to be bad timing, a case of wrong place, wrong time."

"Is there anyone you can think of, anyone at all, who might have wanted to hurt your husband?"

Audrey shook her head. "Everybody loved Barney. No one was ever mad at him for anything, ever."

"We're working on the assumption that he was in Chuck's study for some reason, looking for something. Any thought as to what that might have been?" Sandra made no mention of the postcard.

"Someone else must've broken into the house. I bet he was trying to stop it. I bet that's what got him killed. That's my Barney. That's my husband, Jason's father."

"Could it have had anything to do with the dig he was working on?"

Audrey sniffled. "The hours have been steady for him, finally. He was working on the dig in Cortez, for that new subdivision they're putting in."

"I understand he was working with Chuck's brother-in-law. What do you know about him?"

Chuck flinched.

Audrey didn't look at him. "Just that Barney liked him," she answered Sandra. "He said Clarence was someone who really wanted to learn. They went out for drinks a couple times after work. That's about it."

Chuck caught Audrey's eye through the plexiglass. "What about Barney's other coworkers? What about Samuel Horvat?"

"What about him?"

"What about others from Southwest Archaeology Enterprises besides Clarence? Somebody broke into my study—which is something Clarence, as my brother-in-law, wouldn't have had to do. They went through my files. They were after something having to do with archaeology, that much seems clear."

He didn't mention the postcard either, following Sandra's lead.

"What makes you bring up Samuel, in particular?"

"I was just throwing out a name along with Clarence's," Chuck fibbed, seeing no reason at this point to mention the dig in Gunnel Canyon.

Audrey looked at Sandra. "Clarence was new. Everybody else at SAE has been there for years. That would seem to count for something."

Sandra dipped her chin. "Maybe so."

Audrey squirmed in her seat. "I really need to use the bathroom."

"Anything else?" Sandra asked her.

Audrey shook her head, then nodded. "Just that—" her eyes flicked to Chuck in seeming apology before returning to Sandra "—I think you should talk to Clarence."

Sandra summoned Officer Anand, who helped Audrey out of the back seat and removed her handcuffs before accompanying her to the command unit.

When Sandra was alone with Chuck in the police car, she pressed the button on the top of the dashboard camera, holding it down until the red light on the front of the camera went out.

"Samuel Horvat?" she asked, turning to him.

"I was with him this afternoon," Chuck said. "He called and told me he had something he wanted to show me out at Mesa Verde, on account of Barney's murder."

Sandra straightened, her back to the driver's door. "I need to hear this."

Chuck described his trip to Gunnel Canyon. He told her

about the presence of Ilona Koskinen and Kyla Owens with Samuel at the dig, and the discovery of the century-old corpse in the unearthed chamber that had prompted Samuel to call Chuck in Durango.

He didn't mention the true objective of the excavation—the canopic jars—or the blowout caused by the nail in his tire. He wasn't ready to go that far with Sandra. Not yet, at any rate.

"He called you from the park?" Sandra asked when he finished.

"Yes." Chuck hesitated. "At least, I assume so."

"What about Janelle?"

He stiffened. "What about her?"

"Are she and her brother close?"

"What are you suggesting, Sandra?"

"I'm just asking every question I can possibly think to ask."

"That's all?"

"Unexplained murders are rare in Durango, Chuck. Easy solves, sure. A drug deal gone bad, a drunk taking a knife to someone in a bar, a husband-wife murder-suicide—those happen everywhere, including here." She nodded toward the front of the house and the alley beyond. "But this? An out-and-out murder in the middle of the day, right in the center of town, with no immediately clear motive or perpetrator? This sort of thing happens in Durango, like, never."

"So . . . ?"

"So, every homicide course I've ever taken says the best chance to solve an open-ended case is for everybody on the investigation team to consider all possibilities, and based on those possibilities, follow up with all persons of interest right away, asking as many questions as possible as quickly as possible. The goal here is a fast solve, before the public gets frightened, because a frightened public is an angry public."

"You're already worrying about public backlash?"

"The chief checked in with me an hour ago. He's already gotten calls from the mayor, the city manager, the president of the college. You know the Durango bubble—all the problems of the world are out there somewhere, far away, while everything's always just peachy here in our little mountain town . . . until it isn't. And when it isn't, people get scared, and then they get mad, just to cover up how scared they are. Barney's shooting is a big deal inside the Durango bubble, which means I'll be asking anybody and everybody I can all the questions I can possibly think to ask, no matter how many toes I end up stepping on— yours included."

"Wait. Shooting? Did you just say Barney was shot?"

"What'd you think happened?"

"I saw a lot of blood. I assumed he was stabbed."

"No. He was shot several times. Small-caliber. Probably .22. We'll know for sure when the ballistics come back. Which reminds me, you told me once that you would only ever own long guns—rifles and shotguns for hunting. You said pistols were only good for killing people, and you wanted nothing to do with them." She held his gaze. "Is that still true?"

"Yes, it is," Chuck said without hesitation. "My guns are locked in my gun safe in the garage. My *long* guns. No .22s. No pistols, ever. I'll be happy to show you or whoever wants to look whenever you want."

"That'll be necessary soon enough," she said with a nod. She sighed. "The shots are what led to all the bleeding. People heard some popping noises, but nobody saw anything until a neighbor found him lying in the alley. By then, the perp was gone and Barney was dead."

"What made you bring up Clarence's name with Audrey?"

"He's the newest hire. He worked with Barney pretty steadily the last few weeks, from what Michaela McDermott told me. Plus, like Audrey said, they even went out socially."

"But you know Clarence."

"I *barely* know him. I met him the one time, when we ran into each other in town and you introduced him to me." Her voice softened. "At this point, Chuck, my job is to keep an open mind. I know Audrey isn't thinking straight. But often enough, what people in her situation have to say proves helpful, no matter how stressed they are when they say it. Or, maybe, *because* of how stressed they are. That's one of the reasons I was willing to hold her for so long. Sometimes what people say when they're under pressure leads to something useful, and that leads to something else even more useful after that." She paused. "Your brother-in-law included."

12

Chuck collapsed on the couch in Clarence's living room. Janelle sank into the sofa's sagging cushions next to him. Clarence set a bag of take-out burritos on the coffee table and dropped into the easy chair. The girls sat on the carpet, leaning back on their hands, their legs stretched in front of them.

Chuck, Janelle, and the girls had departed the scene of the murder fifteen minutes ago. Sandra had offered no indication when they'd be allowed back inside their house, refusing to let them so much as grab a change of clothing from their bedrooms, and telling them merely to "sit tight and let us do our work."

They'd called ahead to Clarence, who had picked up the burritos while they walked to his apartment.

Janelle still wore her paramedic uniform, her name stenciled above her shirt pocket. Chuck and the girls remained in their climbing-gym outfits, Chuck in his fleece top and sweats, the girls in hoodies and loose bottoms over their climbing tights.

Chuck recounted his and Rosie's visit to Mesa Verde, including the discovery of the corpse in the alcove and the possible existence of Ancestral Puebloan canopic jars. He summarized his discussion with Audrey and Sandra in the police car, ending with the shared focus the two were placing on Clarence as a suspect, along with Michaela's accusatory focus on Clarence as well.

Chuck rubbed his face with his hands. He'd been powerless three years ago when Clarence had been summarily suspected of murder by the police in a predominantly white town in northern Colorado merely because of his brown skin. Unlike that instance, racial profiling did not appear to be the case with Barney's murder. But Michaela's fixation on Clarence, seconded by Sandra and Audrey, was maddening nonetheless.

"I just don't get it," Chuck muttered, lowering his hands.

"I do," said Janelle beside him. "It comes down to what you said Sandra said: Clarence is the new guy with Southwest Archaeology Enterprises. Plus, he was getting tight with Barney, and he was a few blocks away, alone, with no witnesses to account for his whereabouts, at the time of Barney's murder."

"But it's all circumstantial. Complete conjecture."

Clarence tightened his fingers around the arms of his chair, the blood draining from his face. "*Jesu Cristo, hermana,*" he said to Janelle. "You've almost got me believing I did it myself."

"That's the problem," she said.

"So what's the solution?"

"One thing's for sure: we're not about to sit tight and do nothing."

Clarence's shoulders slumped as he visibly relaxed. "That's my sis."

He scooted to the front of the easy chair, pulled the foil-wrapped burritos from the bag, and lined them on the coffee table. Selecting the largest, he peeled the foil from one end and took a monstrous bite. The aroma of beans and jalapeño peppers filled the room as he slumped back in his seat.

"Mmm," he said, chewing. "I so needed this."

The girls took burritos as well.

Janelle stared out the front window. Like Chuck, she appeared to have no appetite. Turning to Clarence, her face stiff, she said, "Barney's dead, you're under suspicion for his murder, and you're stuffing your face like nothing's happened."

Clarence swallowed. "I didn't do anything, *hermana*. I got faith them cops'll find the killer. I told 'em everything I know—

which, okay, isn't much—when they came and interviewed me this afternoon. They didn't arrest me after they got done with their questions."

"Not yet."

"Between the three of us," Chuck said, "we're probably in as good a position as anyone to get a handle on this."

Rosie stopped chewing. "What about me?"

"And me?" Carmelita seconded.

"The *five* of us are in the best position to figure it out," Chuck said.

Rosie held her partially eaten burrito aloft like a torch. "I vote for the foreign lady. She talks weird."

"She was forty miles from our house, at the dig site, when Barney was killed," said Chuck.

"She could be the mastermind," Carmelita reasoned. "She might be directing everything from behind the scenes."

"That's one possibility, I guess."

"And Samuel," said Rosie. "He helped me out of the hole. He was nice, and you know what they say about nice guys: they always finish last."

Carmelita punched Rosie's shoulder. "What's that supposed to mean?"

"It means he's in last place, so he's the killer. Get it?"

Carmelita rolled her eyes at Rosie and turned to Chuck. "Of everyone," she said to him, "I vote for Uncle Clarence's boss. She was hanging around the house all afternoon. She's the first one who accused Uncle Clarence, isn't she?"

"I think so."

"Well, we know Uncle Clarence didn't do it."

Clarence lifted an eyebrow. "We're *pretty sure* I didn't."

"Close enough," Carmelita said, aiming a fleeting smile at him. "Michaela could be the killer, and she's accusing you to shift the blame."

Clarence raised his shoulders to his ears, his thick studs glinting in each lobe. "Seems as good an idea as any." He took another bite of his burrito.

Janelle looked around the room. "We should start with the 'why' questions. Why was Barney at our house? Why was he holding the postcard of Esther when he died? Why might someone else have wanted the postcard enough to kill Barney? Or, why might someone have wanted to break into our house along with Barney? Or instead of Barney?"

"That's a lot of questions," said Rosie.

"Without answers," said Carmelita.

"Plus," Chuck noted, "there's another 'why' question I can't figure out. Why would Sandra hold Audrey in the police car for as long as she did, waiting until I got there to question her?"

"Because," Clarence said, "Sandra is Sandra and you're you."

"What's that supposed to mean?"

"She was holding Audrey to get to you," Clarence explained. He turned to the girls. "Chuck was a hot tamale around these parts before your *mamá* came along and took him off the market. The one who thought he was the hottest was Sandra."

"The cop?" Carmelita asked.

"*Sí.* I bet she wanted to spend a little more time with Chuck, so she held onto Audrey to make sure she got to."

"No, no, no," Chuck said.

"*Sí*, sí, *sí*," Clarence maintained.

"There's another way to look at it," Janelle said. "I agree Sandra was holding onto Audrey to make sure she got to talk to Chuck." An ominous tone entered her voice as she continued. "But maybe for a different reason than you're thinking."

"What's that?" Clarence asked.

"Maybe she also sees Chuck as a suspect, along with you."

Clarence stopped chewing.

Chuck said to Janelle, "I was with the girls at the gym, with people all around me. My alibi is rock solid."

Rosie waved her burrito, her eyes growing large with understanding. "I get it," she said to her mother. "You think Sandra might be thinking of Chuck as a mastermind, controlling Uncle Clarence, like Carmelita was saying about the foreign lady."

Clarence waggled a finger at the girls. "Don't nobody control me, *sobrinas*."

Janelle said, "Your nieces know that. But does Sandra?"

Chuck clasped his hands, his elbows on his knees. Sandra certainly would know he wasn't capable of murder, or of orchestrating a murder, either. He shivered. But just how certain was he of her certainty? For that matter, how certain was he that Sandra wasn't capable of murder, or of orchestrating a murder, herself?

He faced Janelle. "Sandra didn't say anything to me about my being a suspect along with Clarence."

"She wouldn't have wanted to show her hand. She just wanted to watch you, listen to you, see you in action. She held Audrey so she could do that without you having any idea."

"But why would I direct Clarence to break into my study? Why would I have him kill Barney behind my own house? Talk about leading the police right to my doorstep."

Janelle shrugged. "Stranger things have happened."

"You really think Sandra sees me and Clarence as suspects?"

Janelle held Chuck's gaze. "I'm just saying it's possible, which means we might as well decide what we're going to do next based on that possibility."

Chuck slipped out of bed before sunrise.

He and Janelle had spent the night in Clarence's bedroom at Clarence's insistence. Chuck had slept little, spending much of the night replaying the events of the previous day in his head, while Janelle had tossed and turned restlessly beside him.

Having received Janelle's whispered approval of his intended destination, he tugged on his clothes in the dark and crept out of the bedroom, easing the door closed behind him. Clarence snored on the couch in the living room. The girls breathed softly, curled in blankets on the floor.

Chuck pulled on his sneakers, grabbed one of the leftover burritos from the coffee table, and left the apartment. He forced himself to eat the soggy, bean-filled tortilla as he headed downtown. Normally, he'd have enjoyed the pre-dawn walk through the quiet streets, accompanied by the chirps of awakening birds and the chatter of early-rising squirrels in the trees. Now, however, he trudged through the neighborhood with his head down, plagued by visions from yesterday—Barney's body beneath the bloody sheet in the alley, the century-old corpse with the cleaved skull in the unearthed crypt, and the blown tire and Rosie's terrified scream as the truck skidded toward the abyss.

Chuck texted Samuel requesting Ilona's room number when he neared the Strater Hotel. He waited, phone in hand, in the Victorian-era hotel's lobby. Parlor settees upholstered in crushed velvet graced the high-ceilinged entry hall, its walls covered in mahogany paneling and glittery foil wallpaper. The smell of fresh coffee filled the air, making his stomach rumble.

Before he could track down the source of the smell and pour himself a cup, his phone lit up: *222*. He texted a thumbs-up to Samuel, climbed the thickly carpeted stairs to the second floor, and rapped on the varnished, solid-wood door to room 222.

A plaque next to the door identified the room as the Louis L'Amour Suite. A framed paragraph below the plaque read:

"Louis L'Amour is the world's bestselling Western author. He lived most of his life in Los Angeles, but spent every August for many years in Durango to get a feel for the Old West settings of his novels. He always stayed at the Strater Hotel, and always in this room, directly above the Strater's Diamond Belle Saloon. He claimed the sound of the Diamond Belle's honky-tonk piano reverberating through the floorboards helped him focus on his work."

The door opened. Ilona stood in the entry. She wore ballet slippers and a thin, ankle-length robe tied at her waist. Her white-blond hair was loose, framing her wan, makeup-free face.

Despite Chuck's unannounced arrival, she stepped back and said, "Please, you may enter."

"Sorry to barge in on you like this," he said as he strode past her through the doorway. He turned to face her in the center of the spacious room, which was furnished with a vintage, carved writing desk, a tall, multi-drawer dresser, and an oversized, four-poster bed, all fashioned from dark mahogany.

She closed the door and leaned her back against it, her hands behind her. "I believe I understand why you are here. You are trying to connect the dots, as you call it."

"That's right. I believe you're the linchpin somehow."

"I do not know the word 'linchpin,' but I do not think it means 'killer,' am I right?"

"I don't think you killed Barney. But I do think it's possible, likely even, that your arrival here set something in motion that led to his murder."

As with his surprise appearance at Ilona's door, Chuck imagined his blunt assessment would catch the Finnish museum curator off guard. But she merely nodded and said, "I told the police officers the same idea when they came here to my room last night, after I returned from Mesa Verde with Samuel."

She waved Chuck to a love seat beneath the corner windows overlooking Main Avenue. Like the settees in the lobby, the small sofa was upholstered in red velvet. "Please, sit," she said.

He lowered himself to the couch.

She crossed the room and perched on the edge of her unmade bed, her hands on the mattress on either side of her. "I am sorry that your friend has died. I hope that my travel here is not a part of it. I will tell you everything I can think to tell you, everything I have told the police." Lifting her hands from the bed, she gripped her thighs through her robe with slender fingers. "In truth, Samuel and I are thinking perhaps you are the linchpinning person, not me. That is the reason Samuel called you yesterday in the car, after he learned about the death of your friend."

"In the car? I thought you were at the dig site yesterday when Samuel heard about Barney."

"We were on the way to Gunnel Canyon from Durango at the time that Michaela called Samuel about your friend."

Chuck frowned. "Michaela called Samuel?" Yesterday in the alcove, Samuel had made no mention of the phone call from the owner of Southwest Archaeology Enterprises.

"There were many texts, also," Ilona said. "We decided we must turn around and go back to Durango. But then, right after Michaela called on the phone, Kyla called on the phone, also. She told us of her find, and we went on to the canyon very quickly."

Chuck drew a breath. "Are you saying Kyla breached the chamber and found the body on her own, without you there?"

Ilona nodded. "It happened very fast. We started the digging only the day before. Kyla wanted to dig more yesterday, before we arrived. She was very excited. Samuel gave her the permission."

Chuck recalled his early years as an archaeologist, when the anticipation of what he might discover on any given day was so powerful he could barely contain himself. No doubt Kyla was equally excited about her first opportunity to dig in the West—

particularly at a little-known site in the heart of Ancestral Puebloan territory.

He studied Ilona. By describing the timing of the phone call from Michaela as having reached her and Samuel while they were on the way to Gunnel Canyon from Durango, the museum curator had as much as admitted that she and Samuel might, in fact, still have been in town at the time of the break-in and Barney's murder. Her admission seemed open and unaffected. Was her openness calculated? That is, was she offering information up front that she knew Chuck would learn soon enough on his own? Or was she simply being honest and forthright with him?

The answer could lie in what connections, if any, Ilona might have had to Barney. Did she know anything, for instance, about the postcard Barney had clutched in his hand at the time of his death?

Chuck sat forward on the love seat. "Do you know who Esther is?"

A veil fell over Ilona's eyes. For the first time since Chuck's unannounced arrival at her hotel room, it appeared he'd gotten to her.

"Yes, of course," she answered after a pause. "The mummy."

"One of the most perfectly preserved sets of mummified human remains ever discovered in North America. But I'm sure you know all about that."

"I know Esther was discovered far away from the excavation in Gunnel Canyon, not even at Mesa Verde."

"It sounds as if you know where Esther's remains were discovered instead."

Ilona pointed out the corner window, up Main Avenue. "In a valley very near here. To the north."

"Most people think Mesa Verde was the only place Ancestral Puebloans ever lived."

"But I am not most people. I may be a long distance from my home, but this area is a part of my deep studies over many years. I know that the early Ancestral Puebloans populated the Animas River Valley around Durango centuries before their civilization reached its peak at Mesa Verde."

Chuck nodded. "Old-time Durangoans talk about how, when developers graded the streets for the Crestview neighborhood on the west side of town in the 1950s, townspeople picked up hundreds, if not thousands, of pottery shards and projectile points unearthed by the bulldozers."

"It is the same with the old Sámi artifacts in the north of my country."

"Which brings me to my primary question." Chuck looked Ilona in the eye. "Are you staying here at the Strater in Durango, a long way from Mesa Verde and Gunnel Canyon, only because Gustaf Nordenskiöld stayed here a hundred years ago, as you said yesterday? Or are you here for some other reason—something that specifically has to do with Durango—and, perhaps, Esther?"

Ilona's fingertips dug deeper into her thighs. She didn't answer.

"You and I both know how much Esther looked like the mummies of ancient Egypt. I always assumed it was nothing more than a coincidence. But that's because I'd never heard any talk of the possible existence of Ancestral Puebloan canopic jars."

Ilona released her legs and curled her hands in her lap. "I do not know anything of what you are saying."

"Sure, you do." Chuck sat back in the sofa. "You just said you know Esther was found near Durango rather than at Mesa Verde. You admitted yesterday you're here in America in search of Ancestral Puebloan canopic jars. You must at least have considered the possibility of a connection between Esther and the canopic jars you're searching for. Why deny it? Esther was the very first thing that came to my mind yesterday when Samuel admitted to your search for the jars."

Ilona opened her hands in her lap with visible effort, her fingers shaking as they straightened. "I was saying just now only that I do not know of a connection between the mummy, Esther, and any *Egyptian* canopic jars," she said.

"You're saying, then, that you *do* know of a connection between Esther and canopic jars in general, just not ones from Egypt?"

"No," Ilona said firmly, her neck muscles tight. "The canopic jars are a rumor, nothing more."

"A strong enough rumor, however, that you found it worth coming all the way here from Finland to investigate."

"The excavation started out as planned. We found the disturbed ground in the alcove and began to dig. But," she admitted, "the discovery yesterday of the body was a surprise."

"Not as much of a surprise as Barney's murder yesterday behind my house."

She looked at the floor. "No, not as much as that."

"I find it difficult to understand why, when Michaela told Samuel about the murder, the very first thing he did was call me."

"He didn't call you until we learned about the body, after Kyla opened the hole and found it. He thought you would want to learn about it."

Ilona's response reminded Chuck of the reason he'd stormed out of the alcove yesterday. Why had Samuel—and Ilona, too, for that matter—been so intent on convincing him to come to Gunnel Canyon immediately after hearing of Barney's murder? He bit down hard on his lower lip. He was missing something. What was it?

"Because you left the canyon so quickly yesterday," Ilona said, "Samuel would like very much to meet with you again today. He wants to talk more about the discovery of the body and what you think it might mean about your friend, Barney."

"Samuel needs to ask me that, not you. And he'll have to tell me what he thinks first."

"That is what he will do, then," Ilona said simply. She stood up from the edge of the bed. "We are all wanting the same thing. We will meet together and talk about all our ideas. We wanted to meet with you last night, but it was too late when we finally returned to Durango after changing over the tire on Samuel's car."

Chuck's jaw dropped. "You had a flat on the way back from Gunnel Canyon yesterday?"

"A flat, yes, that is what you call it. A metal nail went into the tire of Samuel's car and let out all of the air."

13

Chuck stood with his back to the counter in Clarence's tiny kitchen, spooning cold cereal into his mouth. Between spoonfuls, he reported on his visit with Ilona to Janelle and Clarence, both eating cereal as well, Janelle standing with her back to the sink and her bowl in her hand, Clarence seated at the small dinette table set against the wall, his bowl on the table in front of him. The girls remained cocooned in their blankets on the living room floor.

"She acted like she was expecting me," Chuck said.

"At six in the morning?" Clarence scoffed. "You've gotta be kidding me."

"She *acted* that way." He paused. "Although I did ask for her room number from Samuel. He probably called her to make sure it was okay to give it to me, in which case, she'd have known I was coming."

"What'd you get out of her?"

"She was fairly forthcoming, as far as I could tell. Everything she said aligned pretty well with what we already know. Still, I got the sense she was hiding something. I just don't know what it is yet."

Janelle set her spoon in her bowl. "Did you learn anything new from her?"

"One potentially big piece of information. I had assumed Ilona, Samuel, and Kyla were at the dig site in Gunnel Canyon all day yesterday. But Ilona said she and Samuel were driving to the site when they heard about Barney's death."

"How far from Durango were they?"

"She didn't say."

"But . . ." Janelle urged.

"But yes, it has occurred to me that they could, in fact, have been in Durango when Barney was killed."

"So, Samuel might have been in Durango, or this Ilona woman, or both of them together."

"I can't even begin to imagine—" Chuck began.

But Janelle continued, gazing at him across the top of her cereal bowl. "The same with the Harvard student."

"Kyla?"

"She supposedly was at the dig site, right? But you've now been told that she was there alone, with no witnesses to place her there."

Clarence swallowed a mouthful of cereal. "Never trust them East Coast types," he declared.

"What else did you find out?" Janelle asked Chuck.

He stopped with his spoon halfway to his mouth. Slowly, he set the spoon back in his bowl. "They had a flat on the way back from the dig site last night. They found a nail in their tire."

Janelle and Clarence exchanged glances.

"Yeah," Chuck said in response to their silence. "I know how that sounds."

"The nail in your tire was no accident," Janelle said. "Some unknown someone sabotaged the cars at the canyon, yours and theirs both."

"Most likely," Chuck said.

"'Most likely'? What do you mean? There's no question someone sabotaged the cars."

"Agreed. I'm just saying that we might actually know who did it. One of the three of them—Samuel, Ilona, or Kyla—could have put a nail in their own tire just to throw us off of them. It could have been all three of them in on it together, or just two of them."

"But why would any of them, or anyone else, put a nail in your tire? What's to be gained from that?"

"That's the part I can't figure out."

Clarence took another spoonful of cereal. "So what do we do now, *jefe*?" he asked Chuck, his mouth full.

"You don't do anything. Not for the time being, at least. They've already got you in their crosshairs. The last thing we want is for you to do something that would put yourself even more at risk."

"I take it you have something of that sort in mind for yourself?"

"I do." Chuck looked at Janelle. "If I can talk you into it."

Chuck sat in the front passenger seat of Janelle's mini SUV while she drove north on Main Avenue. The girls slumped, half asleep, in the vehicle's cramped rear seat. They'd left the big, burly—and highly conspicuous—Bender Archaeological pickup truck behind at Clarence's apartment complex.

Half an hour ago, Chuck had outlined his plan in Clarence's kitchen.

Janelle had agreed to it immediately. "I don't want to wait around until Sandra decides to come after us, too," she said. "I think seeing if we can learn anything on our own is a good idea."

Chuck exchanged a flurry of texts, finalizing his meeting with Samuel and Ilona for later in the day.

Clarence exhaled as they left his apartment. "Just promise me you'll be careful," he said. "This ain't no game we're playing."

Now, as they drove up Main, Chuck leaned forward and peered through the windshield at the sun-washed blue sky overhead. Another clear fall day was on the way for southwestern Colorado.

They turned off Main Avenue at the north end of Durango and wound out of the city limits alongside Junction Creek, a tributary of the Animas River flowing south out of the mountains. The road climbed past homes on subdivided parcels along the creek bottom.

They stayed on Junction Creek Road at the turnoff to the county road leading up Falls Creek, adjacent to Junction Creek. The pavement turned to gravel where private property ended and National Forest land began. They passed out of cell phone service range as the road grew more remote and slanted sharply upward, ascending a broad shoulder of mountain separating the Junction Creek and Falls Creek drainages. As they climbed, the lower-elevation ponderosa pines and thickets of scrub oak gave way to higher-elevation fir and aspen.

Atop the ridge, the rugged San Juan Mountains appeared in the distance. The sprawling Weminuche Wilderness area, the largest protected wilderness in Colorado at half-a-million acres, encompassed the remote mountain range, which needled the eastern horizon with spire after spire of gray granite.

Chuck aimed a finger at the turnoff to an old logging track leading away from Junction Creek Road. "That's us."

Janelle parked at the rusted, single-bar gate that blocked the long-unused track. Chuck climbed out of the SUV and swung a water-and-snack-filled daypack onto his back.

Rosie, now wide awake, leapt from the back seat and clambered onto the rear bumper. Clinging to the roof rack, she stood on her tiptoes and gazed into the distance. A gust of wind coursed over the mountain, tossing her curly hair. She put her hand to her forehead, shading her eyes from the morning sun. "This is sooooo beautiful," she declared.

Janelle smiled. "You look like the captain of a ship."

"Land ho!" she cried. She jumped down from the bumper and said excitedly to Carmelita, who stood yawning beside her, "This view is totally bonus, isn't it, Carm?" Without waiting for an answer, she said to Chuck, "I can't believe we've never come up here before."

"Junction Creek Road is only open a few weeks in the summer and fall after the snow melts." He took in the expansive view. "You're right, though. It's beautiful." He settled the pack on his shoulders. "Ready, set?"

Carmelita pointed past the gate at the abandoned logging road. The track was overgrown with brush and tall grass. "That way?"

"*Sí.* To the end of the old road and down, down, down from there."

"Sweet," said Rosie.

"But," Carmelita reminded her, "that means up, up, up on the way back."

"Ohhh," said Rosie.

Chuck tapped the bottom of his daypack. "Clarence stocked us up. We'll be fine."

"Besides," said Janelle, "we're doing this for Barney. We're trying to help the police, remember?"

"That's right," Rosie said. "I almost forgot."

"You *did* forget," Carmelita admonished her.

"Well, Carm, probably so did you."

Chuck tensed, ready for a squabble. But the mention of Barney's name must have had a sobering effect on Carmelita, because she shrugged and said simply, "You're right. I did, too."

The abandoned track dwindled away after a few hundred yards, where the ridge fell precipitously to the flat floor of the Falls Creek Valley a thousand feet below. Beyond the undeveloped meadows of the creek's bottomlands, separated by a low ridge of serrated sandstone, the equally flat floor of the Animas River Valley spread north of Durango. The land along the river was squared by county roads and chockablock with subdivisions.

Chuck paused with Janelle and the girls at the end of the track, studying the forested slope that plunged away from their feet. Far below, a flash of white showed through the trees. The white was the top—and, from their position high above, the only visible portion—of the majestic sandstone escarpment that framed the east side of Falls Creek Valley like a white curtain.

"See there?" Chuck asked the girls, pointing down through the trees at the shelf of rock shimmering in the sun. "That's where we're headed."

Rosie moaned. "That's a looong ways."

But Carmelita said, "Cool. Looks like it's gonna take some serious scrambling to get down there."

Rosie looked from her sister to the steep slope, her face brightening. "Yeah," she declared. "Way cool!"

"Besides," Chuck said, "remember what we're headed down there for."

"Barney," Rosie said soberly.

"And what else?"

"Archaeology!" she cried.

She set off down the mountainside with Carmelita beside her.

14

"Hold up!" Chuck called ahead to the girls when they neared the top of the escarpment.

Carm and Rosie waited in the deep shadow of a stand of firs, squatting beneath the boughs of the trees. Chuck stopped with Janelle behind the girls.

"Check this out." Carmelita held up a small object clenched between her finger and thumb.

Chuck leaned over her shoulder. The object, the size of a quarter, was made of black, glass-like stone—obsidian. Its flaked edges gleamed, the cupped facets along its sides reflecting the rays of sun streaming through the branches of the firs.

"It's an arrowhead," Carmelita said.

"A projectile point," Rosie corrected, pride in her voice. "That's what Ms. Jarvis says to call them." She gazed at the small, sharpened bit of glassy stone. "Maybe it was used on an arrow, or maybe on a teeny, tiny spear. That's what Ms. Jarvis says."

"It was sitting right on top of the dirt," Carmelita said.

"That's the sort of thing that shows we're never the first ones to be anywhere," said Chuck, "not even way up on a mountainside like this. It's what I love about my work: the connectedness of the past to the present."

"That sounds pretty trippy," Carmelita said.

He smiled down at her. "It does, doesn't it?"

Rosie reached for the projectile point. "I want to be trippy, too," she said. "Give it to me, Carm. Gimme, gimme!"

Carmelita closed her fingers over the point and jerked her hand away from Rosie. "You forgot to say please."

"I didn't forget. I just decided I wouldn't."

"I guess you don't want to see it very much, then."

"Pleeeeease," Rosie whined, her eyes on Carmelita's closed fist. "Please, please, please."

"Oh, all right."

Carmelita handed the point to Rosie, who turned it over in her palm and fingered its edges. "It's a perfect triangle."

"They knew what they were doing," Chuck said. "You know what to do with it when you're finished looking at it, right?"

"Pocket it," Carmelita said quickly. Then, she grinned.

"Carm!" Rosie scolded. She looked up at Chuck. "Ms. Jarvis says we have to leave it where we found it."

"Ms. Jarvis is right. When you put it back, other people can find it and appreciate it, too."

"But archaeologists take stuff like this all the time, don't they?" Rosie asked.

"Whatever they take, they study and catalog and display to the public as much as possible. They do it—*we* do it—on behalf of everyone, so it's considered okay."

The projectile point glittered in Rosie's palm. She dropped it to the ground. It slid a few inches down the hill and came to rest against a small, gray stone flecked with green lichen. Together, the projectile point and lichen-covered rock formed a pleasing miniature tableau.

"Nice," Carmelita said.

She stood up. Rosie rose beside her. Chuck looked past them, scanning the mountainside below. Fifty yards down the slope, the rock outcrop extended horizontally from the forested ridge, a bench of white stone leading thirty feet to a sheer, hundred-foot cliff. The slope resumed at the bottom of the cliff, descending gradually for a quarter mile to the broad Falls Creek Valley floor. Falls Creek Road bisected the near side of the valley from south to north where the gentle slope ended and the flat bottom of the valley began. Thick stands of scrub oak and a handful of soaring ponderosas grew on the gentle slope between the base of the escarpment and the road. On the far side of the road, an open meadow of grass, tawny brown this late in the year, extended eastward to the rocky ridge separating the Falls Creek drainage from the Animas River Valley beyond.

The Falls Creek meadowland north of Durango had been slated for development in the 1960s, prompting locals to mount one of the earliest land-preservation efforts ever undertaken in the United States. The effort was successful, and the land was transferred to National Forest ownership. The meadow was now a popular hiking, dog-walking, and mountain-biking venue a ten-minute drive from town.

Peering through the trees, Chuck noted more than a dozen vehicles parked in pullouts along the road, and just as many hikers and bikers on the network of trails that cut through the meadow beyond. While the meadow east of the road was open to all comers, signs along the roadside warned visitors that venturing to the towering sandstone escarpment bordering the west side of the valley was prohibited.

"Let's stay in the trees," Chuck said to the girls, speaking softly despite the distance of several hundred yards to the hikers and bikers on the trails.

"Why are we being sneaky?" Rosie whispered back.

"No need to call attention to ourselves."

Carmelita caught Chuck's eye and pointed south along the escarpment, her brow furrowed in question. At his answering nod, she stepped over the projectile point and led the way through the trees, digging her sneakers into the steep slope for traction, parallel with the upper bench of white stone. After a quarter of a mile, the stone escarpment disappeared into the forested slope. Where the escarpment ended, Carmelita descended the hillside next to the rock outcrop.

She waited at the base of the escarpment, shielded from the county road and meadow beyond by a dense thicket of scrub oak. Chuck, Janelle, and Rosie joined her behind the screen of trees. To the north, the escarpment loomed a hundred feet above their heads. The white sandstone cliff formed a sweeping cirque half a mile across, bounding the west side of the valley. At the far end of the escarpment, a roofed alcove faced south, dark as a cave, from the base of the cliff.

A car drove down Falls Creek Road toward town, out of sight beyond the oak thicket. When the sound of the car engine faded, Chuck pointed across the cirque at the distant alcove. "See that?" he whispered.

"It looks like where we were yesterday, at Mesa Verde," Rosie whispered back. "Does it have a dead body in it, too?"

"It used to. A whole bunch of dead bodies, in fact. Remember how I told you the abandoned villages under the cliffs at Mesa Verde were being looted and destroyed back in the 1800s?"

Rosie nodded. "That's why they made the national park, to protect them."

"That's also why, before it was a national park, Gustaf Nordenskiöld sent artifacts from Mesa Verde back to Europe, to keep them from being sold on the black market and disappearing forever into the private collections of rich people. He dug up dead bodies, too. The very same thing happened here at Falls Creek."

Rosie, Carmelita, and Janelle gazed past Chuck at the shadowed recess as he continued.

"After Mesa Verde became a national park, looters turned to other Ancestral Puebloan sites that hadn't been protected yet. They trashed lots of places in the process. For decades, it was an all-out race between archaeologists and unscrupulous looters to see who could get their hands on artifacts first."

Rosie frowned, her nose crinkling. "What does 'unscrupulous' mean?"

"Jerks," Carmelita offered. "People who don't care about history, who only care about themselves."

"*Exactamente*," Chuck said. "Early on, archaeologists purchased artifacts from looters to keep them from falling into the hands of private collectors. But that only encouraged the looters all the more. Eventually, archaeologists stopped buying stolen artifacts. But the looters are still at it today, destroying sites all over the world."

"What about here?" Carmelita asked, aiming her chin at the alcove beneath the escarpment. "Was it looted or dug by archaeologists?"

"Both, I guess you could say, but not until decades after Mesa Verde became a national park. That was because the alcove here appeared to be empty. It wasn't until the 1930s that someone realized it might, in fact, be worth exploring, because by then archaeologists had figured out that the earliest predecessors of the Ancestral Puebloans had been nomadic. They're known today as the Basketmakers, because they made lightweight baskets out of grasses and reeds to transport their goods from place to place."

"But," said Rosie, "Ms. Jarvis says Ancestral Puebloans made all sorts of fancy pottery—plates and bowls and all kinds of cool stuff."

"She's right. But that wasn't until they started living in the same places all the time. Pottery is heavy and fragile and hard to lug around."

"Which is why," Carmelita said, "they used baskets when they were nomadic."

"The Basketmakers," said Rosie.

"You got it. Both of you." Chuck pointed across the cirque at the shadowed alcove. "The Basketmakers spent time right there, under the cliff." He stepped aside so Janelle, Carmelita, and Rosie had a clear line of sight to the recess with its bare dirt floor. "See how there are no obvious housing structures under the overhang like the ones at Mesa Verde? That's why nobody paid the alcove here any attention for so many years—until a woman from Durango figured out its importance. Her interest led to the big discovery we talked about on the way to Audrey's house yesterday."

"The mummyyyy," Carmelita said, drawing out the word.

15

Rosie stuck her arms out in front of her and walked in place, her head lolling to one side. "Gaaaah," she gurgled. "I'm dead. I'm a mummy!"

"Hush," Janelle warned, glancing toward the road.

Rosie dropped her arms, her lips turning downward in a pout.

Janelle arched an eyebrow at Chuck. "No surprise it was a woman who figured it out."

"No surprise, too, that a guy took all the credit for it."

"Do tell," Janelle said, her voice thick with sarcasm.

"The woman's name was Helen Daniels. She had a job putting unemployed men from Durango to work during the Depression. She happened to be an amateur archaeologist as well, and she was frustrated by all the looting of ancient Basket-maker sites going on back then. She put the men in her group to work excavating known Basketmaker sites in and around Durango. She wanted to create an archaeological record of the sites before they were ransacked by looters. In the process, her team unearthed a number of early Ancestral Puebloan skulls."

"Mummies!" Rosie exclaimed.

"At that point, just crania," Chuck explained, "not whole, mummified bodies. Helen wrote a letter to a professional ar-chaeologist about the skulls, but he refused to come look at them. He didn't like the fact that Helen was excavating Ances-tral Puebloan sites as an amateur with a team of untrained dig-gers. But Helen was on a mission. She knew it was up to her and the members of her team to learn what they could before looters stole everything. Under her leadership, her team excavated sites all around Durango—near the college campus, next to Trimble Hot Springs, at Folsom Park in the middle of town."

"And here," Carmelita said.

Chuck nodded. "She heard there were ancient pictographs in the alcove, so she brought her team out here from town to check them out. Sure enough, there were paintings of humans and animals and even a flute player on the alcove roof. But the bad news was that there was evidence of recent digging by looters in the floor of the alcove as well."

"Uh-oh," said Rosie.

"Uh-oh is right. Helen and her team made sketches on paper of the pictographs for the historical record. A few weeks later, she returned on her own and took a good look around. By then, she'd developed a pretty keen archaeologist's eye. She noticed that a space between two fallen slabs of sandstone at the far end of the recess was stuffed with debris, and it didn't look to her like the debris had gotten there through any sort of natural process. She brought another amateur archaeologist, a guy named Zeke Flora, to the alcove and pointed out the debris in the space between the rocks. 'That's the place to dig,' she told him."

"She was smart," declared Rosie.

"Very," Chuck agreed. "Zeke knew it, too. He took Helen at her word, and they began to dig. Sure enough, the space between the slabs of rock turned out to be a burial site packed with Basketmaker bodies and funerary objects. In all, they found nineteen bodies interred between the rock slabs. One of them, an elderly woman, still had gray hair attached to her skull. The body of a young girl had been buried with a string of red and black beads wound around her legs, and a necklace of olivella shells—transported all the way from the Pacific Ocean, a thousand miles away—draped around her neck. As soon as

Zeke saw the bodies, he claimed them as his own. Helen wrote in a letter to her family how angry she was at Zeke for taking possession of the find. In the end, though, his claim didn't turn out so well for him."

"Good," said Carmelita.

"When it came to archaeology, Zeke was barely a step above being a money-grubbing looter. That's what led to his downfall—Esther, in particular. She was the most well-preserved of the bodies Zeke and Helen found in the alcove."

"Finally, the mummy," Rosie whispered.

Chuck nodded. "All the bodies were mummified—that is, preserved through the process of desiccation—thanks to the fact that they were buried here in the Southwest with its dry air, and out of the weather underneath the overhanging roof of the alcove. The body of a young woman was the finest of them all. She'd been interred for more than a thousand years, but she looked as if she'd died only a short time ago. Her skin was still in place over her body. She had a full head of black hair. Her eyebrows and eyelashes were intact, along with her fingernails and toenails. Her tongue was still in her mouth, and her eyeballs were still in their sockets."

"Yuck," said Rosie.

"When Helen and Zeke found her, she was lying on her back on a cedar-bark mat beneath a rabbit-fur blanket, with her arms crossed over her chest. They decided to give her a name— Esther—which is something else we would never do these days. Zeke transported her and the other bodies to his house in Durango. He cleaned them in the worst possible way, using water and scrub brushes. Then, he told three professional archaeologists what he and Helen had found. Only one of the three, Earl Morris, came to look at the human remains. Back then, Earl was the foremost archaeologist in the Four Corners region. When he saw Esther and the other bodies, he knew he had to do everything he could to protect them. That meant getting them out of Zeke's hands, because Zeke was threatening to sell them on the black market."

Rosie narrowed her eyes. "He was an asshole."

"*Rosie*," Janelle reprimanded.

"But he *was*."

Chuck hurried on. "Zeke knew he'd make lots of money selling the mummified bodies to private collectors, which meant Earl had a problem. He couldn't legally buy the bodies from Zeke because they'd been found up on the mountainside in the National Forest, rather than on private land in the bottom of the valley. Instead, Earl came up with the idea of 'borrowing'—" Chuck made air quotes with his fingers "—the bodies from Zeke for the same amount of money Zeke could have sold them for on the black market. After Earl took possession of the bodies, Esther became a big star. She was displayed in Washington, DC, to big crowds of people. After that, she was put in a glass case in the front room of the Mesa Verde National Park Museum. Thousands of tourists came to see her—until, finally, people began to realize how bad it was to show off a dead body in public like that."

"Well, duh," said Carmelita.

"Actually, there were people who continued to argue that displaying Esther was educational and that the museum should keep showing her in her glass case. But the other side finally won out." Chuck tipped his head at Carmelita. "Your side. She was stored away, out of public view. That was in 1971. Twenty years later, the Native American Graves Protection and Repatriation Act was passed. NAGPRA required all indigenous remains and funerary items that had been dug up and removed anywhere across the United States to be returned to their places of origin." Chuck looked over his shoulder at the alcove. "So back Esther went."

Rosie gaped at him. "She's here?"

"Somewhere close by, anyway. That's why we're here."

"Wowzers."

Carmelita looked from the alcove to Chuck. "What about Zeke, the guy who sold her? You said things didn't go too well for him."

"After he sold Esther and the other bodies to Earl Morris, Zeke spent the rest of his life trying to get them back. First, he said he'd only loaned them to Earl and demanded their return. Then, he sued Earl to get them back, but the courts said no. Finally, he wrote letters and magazine articles calling Earl and other professional archaeologists a bunch of crooks. He even sued Mesa Verde National Park, saying the park owed him a share of the money it made by displaying Esther as a tourist attraction."

"But he didn't even discover Esther," said Carmelita. "The lady, Helen, figured out where to look."

"In Zeke's mind, Esther and the other bodies were his, and that was that."

"What happened to him?"

"He never got another penny, and he died a bitter old man."

"Did they return Esther and the others to the alcove?"

"I'm almost certain they didn't. The alcove is too well known. Looters would have dug them back up in no time."

Carmelita scanned the curved length of the cirque. "Where, then?"

"I'm not sure. The reburial was kept secret to fend off looters. But we can assume the bodies were reburied somewhere near where they were found. That's the whole idea of repatriation, after all."

Rosie looked at the ground beneath her feet. "They might be buried right here, underneath us."

"My guess is they were reinterred somewhere along the base

of the cliff, just not in the original alcove. That would be more in keeping with where they were interred in the first place."

Rosie gazed at the base of the escarpment. "Let's find them."

Carmelita shook her head. "That's exactly what you're *not* supposed to do."

Rosie bit her lip. "I guess you're right." She turned to Chuck. "But I want to see Esther *sooooo* bad. That's why we're here, isn't it?"

"We're here on account of Esther, yes."

"And the canopic jars."

"Right."

Carmelita frowned. "Wouldn't digging up canopic jars be just as bad as digging up bodies? They're funerary objects, aren't they?"

"We're not here to dig up anything," Chuck said. "This whole area, from Falls Creek Road to the escarpment, has been closed off to the public for decades. That's why things like the projectile point you found are still right out in the open around here."

"But aren't we the public?"

"There are no signs up above, on Junction Creek Road, telling us to stay away, which gives us plausible deniability."

Rosie ducked her head. "But we're still hiding in the bushes," she whispered.

Chuck lowered his voice to match hers. "And that's why we're going to make our visit here a quick one. We'll break into pairs so we can go twice as fast. *Mamá* and Carm will work from the north end of the cirque back to the south. You and I will work from south to north. We'll meet in the middle."

"What are we looking for?" Carmelita asked.

"Any sign that people have been poking around here recently."

"Why?"

Chuck drew in the corners of his mouth. How much did the girls deserve to know?

He looked at Carmelita and Rosie. Yesterday, Barney had been murdered in the alley behind their home, meaning they had as much interest in solving Barney's killing as Chuck and Janelle—which, in turn, meant they deserved to know everything he and Janelle knew.

"Because of the postcard," he said.

16

"They made picture postcards of Esther and sold them by the thousands while she was displayed in the museum," Chuck explained to Carmelita and Rosie. "Just like the one I had in my files at home—the one Barney was holding when he was found yesterday."

"What does the postcard have to do with why we're here?" Carmelita asked.

Chuck's eyes went to the cloudless sky, his thoughts cascading backward through time.

"I was brought in as a consultant during the process of repatriating Esther and the other bodies," he explained. "That was years ago. At the time, Michaela McDermott had just started up Southwest Archaeology Enterprises. She put in a really low bid and won the contract to perform the repatriation. I got a call from Donald Cuthair pretty soon after that. Donald was the historical preservation officer in charge of the federal grant covering the cost of the repatriation. The rules of the grant required him to select the lowest bidder, which was Michaela and Southwest Archaeology. He called me when it became clear Michaela didn't have any idea what she was doing."

Chuck looked at his feet. The moldy scent of decomposition rose from the thick layer of brown leaves blanketing the ground beneath the oak thicket. He raised his head and continued.

"She was just getting started, so it came as no surprise that she was in over her head. Besides, NAGPRA had just been passed, so the whole process of repatriation was a brand new thing. Everybody had different ideas about how it should be done. Michaela wanted to make a big, public event out of the reburial, with local Ute Mountain Ute people drumming and dancing while television cameras rolled, before the actual reinterment was performed in private, in a secret place where looters wouldn't find the remains. Donald figured she just wanted the free publicity the public event would generate for her company. When I met with him, he gave me the postcard with the picture of Esther on it. Michaela had given it to him with the idea of having the picture blown up as a poster to display at the event she had in mind. He insisted I take the postcard off his hands. To him, it was haunted, cursed even. He didn't want anything to do with it, but he wasn't about to give it back to Michaela, either. I took it from him to make him feel better. But what was I to do with it? I couldn't just throw it away. Distasteful as it was, it was still part of the historical record. I ended up putting it in my files, along with my write-up of my consultation with Donald. I hadn't thought about it for years—until yesterday."

Chuck's gaze drifted along the escarpment as he concluded his story.

"I agreed with Donald that he shouldn't let Michaela push him into doing a big, public ceremony for the repatriation. Ultimately, he made sure the reinterment was kept entirely private. I never learned where Esther and the other bodies were reburied. There was no need for me to know. I just assume it was somewhere near here, where they were originally found."

"What about Barney?" Rosie asked. "Why did he have the postcard of Esther?"

"We don't know the answer to that. Not yet. That's one of the things we're trying to figure out."

Janelle looked at her wristwatch, then at Chuck. "We'd better get moving."

* * *

While Janelle and Carmelita wound their way through the dense stands of scrub oak, heading for the alcove at the far north end of the cirque, Chuck and Rosie walked the short distance to the base of the cliff at the cirque's south end.

"We really don't know where to look?" Rosie asked him.

He put his hand to the rock wall rising high above them. "I do have one place in mind. But, to be honest, I'd rather not find anything there or anywhere else along here. Esther and the others deserve to rest in peace."

"What about the canopic jars?"

"We don't even know if they exist."

They walked along the bottom of the cliff, screened from the road by oaks that grew tall at the foot of the wall, where they were nourished by rainwater and snowmelt running off the rock face and gathering at the escarpment's base.

For the most part, the cliff rose straight up from the foot of the escarpment. Here and there, however, runoff had worn small alcoves into the base of the rock.

Chuck climbed with Rosie into the miniature recesses as they came to them. The small, roofed alcoves were uniformly a few feet high from floor to ceiling and no more than twenty feet deep. All showed signs of bird and animal habitation—rodent pellets, bat guano, gatherings of twigs for nests—but none revealed signs of human presence, recent or ancient.

Chuck knew of only two recesses in the cirque large enough to have accommodated humans. One was the prominent south-facing alcove at the north end of the cirque that had served as temporary home to the Basketmakers, and as the original place of interment for Esther and the other bodies.

The second large alcove, in the southern half of the cirque, faced north, away from the winter sun, making it uninviting for human habitation. When Chuck had met with Donald Cuthair before the repatriation, Donald had mentioned the large, north-facing alcove as one of several locations under consideration for the reinterment. The alcove was hidden from the valley floor behind a thick stand of scrub oak, its existence known to only a few people.

Chuck shoved his way through a barrier of oak branches growing close against the cliff wall, then held the branches aside for Rosie. Beyond the tree branches, a bench of dirt climbed along the base of the escarpment. Chuck clambered up the slope, offering Rosie a hand at the steepest points. At the top of the dirt ramp, the north-facing alcove opened into the base of the cliff. Chuck stood in the mouth of the recess, riveted by the scene before him.

Rosie arrived at his side. "Holy bejeezcos," she said, staring.

More than a dozen pits had been dug knee-deep into the flat, dirt floor of the alcove. Nearly every square inch of the thirty-by-forty-foot base of the recess had been disturbed, the earth piled next to the holes. A stone slot at the back of the recess was chipped and scarred by blows from a hammer. The dusty floor was swept clean of footprints.

Chuck strode with Rosie past the pits to the rear slot, making fresh tracks in the dust as he crossed with her to the back of the alcove. The slot was a foot across and head-high at its opening, narrowing to nothing after only a few feet. Chisel marks marred the interior walls of the shallow cleft.

"It's a miniature cave," said Rosie, studying the narrow opening with Chuck. "It looks too small for bodies, though, or even jars."

Chuck turned from the cleft to face the pocked floor of the alcove. "What about all these holes? Do you think they found anything in them?"

Rosie surveyed the floor of the recess along with him. "Nope."

"Why not?"

"All the holes look the same. If they found something, I bet they would have dug deeper to get it out."

Chuck squeezed her shoulder. "They might have found something that was buried really shallow, but I tend to agree with you—it looks more likely that they didn't find anything."

"Are you glad we came?"

"I'm not happy to see this place all dug up, but it definitely adds a piece to the puzzle."

"What does it mean for Barney?"

"I have to believe that whoever killed Barney was—"

A car engine growled, then another, and yet another, approaching on Falls Creek Road from the direction of town.

17

Chuck scurried with Rosie past the holes to the front of the alcove. Through breaks in the oak brush that screened the mouth of the recess, he spotted several vehicles driving up the county road. A Durango Police Department SUV led the procession despite the fact that the car was miles outside its jurisdiction. A La Plata County Sheriff's Department cruiser followed the police SUV. Next came an olive-green US Forest Service pickup truck. Another pickup followed. It bore the Southwest Archaeology Enterprises logo on its door.

Chuck gripped Rosie's arm as the string of vehicles stopped at the side of the road, directly opposite where he and Rosie stood in the mouth of the north-facing alcove. Five people left the four vehicles and gathered at the edge of the road, facing the recess. Sandra was one of the five, having climbed from behind the wheel of the lead police SUV. She gestured at the brush-screened alcove and addressed the others, though she was too distant for Chuck to hear what she was saying. Having exited the other vehicles, a uniformed deputy sheriff and a man and woman in green forest-service attire stood with Sandra at the side of the road, along with Southwest Archaeology Enterprises owner Michaela McDermott.

"They're coming here, to where we are," Rosie whispered, her voice quavering. "They'll arrest us!"

Chuck bent and spoke softly in her ear. "We didn't pass any 'No Trespassing' signs the way we came. We haven't done anything wrong."

Rosie glanced behind them at the pocked floor of the alcove. "They'll think we did this."

"Not if we're not here."

"What about *Mamá* and Carm?"

Chuck looked north, across the cirque. "They're . . . they'll . . ."

Rosie pointed beyond the curved north end of the escarpment, where the white sandstone cliff ended at a swath of forested mountainside similar to the steep slope down which they'd descended at the south end of the cirque. "They'll climb up and around the other way. I know they will."

Chuck let go of her arm. "I bet you're right."

At the road, the members of the group returned to their vehicles, retrieved daypacks, and slung them over their shoulders.

"Let's get out of here," Chuck whispered to Rosie.

He snapped a leafy branch from a scrub oak at the mouth of the alcove and used it to sweep away their tracks across the floor of the recess. He descended the dirt bench with Rosie, heading back the way they'd come while continuing to brush away their tracks with the branch.

A glimpse through the scrub oaks revealed that the officials had left the road and were hiking toward the north-facing recess, winding single file through the thickets of scrub oak that blanketed the gentle slope below the cliff. Michaela walked at the front of the line, leading the others toward the alcove abandoned a few minutes ago by Chuck and Rosie.

"They're coming!" Chuck hissed to Rosie, his heart racing.

He discarded the branch and scampered with her along the base of the cliff away from the recess, counting on the oaks to shield them from the view of the oncoming officials. Where the escarpment met the steep slope they'd down-climbed an hour ago, Rosie charged up the slope ahead of Chuck, her stocky legs propelling her upward as steadily as a mountain goat. Chuck struggled to keep up, his breath coming in harsh gasps.

She turned north at the top of the escarpment and side-hilled through the fir forest above the cliff.

Chuck slowed behind her. They were safe now, shielded from the officials' sight by the flat shelf at the top of the escarpment. A moment later, he spotted Janelle and Carmelita approaching across the mountainside from the north end. Rosie waved furiously at her mother and sister and ran to meet them.

Janelle hugged Rosie and shot a fiery look at Chuck as he reached her and the girls. "You didn't tell me we'd be followed," she whispered, her voice tight.

"I figured it would be days before anyone would think to come here," he said, his voice low. "But it's a good thing. It really is."

He turned to the valley and squatted. The officials remained out of view, nearing the base of the cliff below. The sound of their voices as they called out to one another carried to the top of the escarpment, though their words were unintelligible.

Rosie left Janelle's arms and crouched next to Chuck. "They're going to the hole in the rock we were just in, like I said," she whispered, her voice shaking. "It's right below us."

Carmelita settled on her haunches, her arms around her legs, at Chuck's other side. "They haven't spotted us," she said quietly in his ear. "What do you think they're doing?"

"Either they know something we don't, or they're here for the same reason we are—they're trying to figure things out."

"Which do you think?"

"I have to believe they know something. They've got Michaela McDermott with them. She's the woman whose company won the bid to reinter the Falls Creek remains."

"That's who Uncle Clarence works for, right?" Carmelita asked.

Chuck nodded. "Barney worked for her, too. I'd give anything to hear what they're saying to each other."

Carmelita leaned forward, her eyes on the flat shelf of rock leading to the edge of the cliff. "They can't see us up here from down below. We can sneak out there and listen."

He gazed at the hikers and bikers making their way along the trails in the broad, open meadow on the far side of the road. "But we'd be in full view of everybody else."

"They'll think we're part of the group."

He glanced at Carmelita. She made good sense. "Roger that." He twisted to look up at Janelle behind him. "Did you spot anything in the main alcove?"

"We saw the pictographs you mentioned, and the slabs of rock. We didn't see anything that seemed unusual, though. The space between the slabs was empty. There wasn't any sign of recent digging. No sign anybody'd been there for a long time, in fact. What about you?"

"We saw more than enough for all of us." He pointed through the trees at the white shelf of stone and the north-facing alcove out of sight directly beneath. "Somebody's been digging down there, right where Michaela and Sandra and the others are heading."

Carmelita rose from her crouch and started down the slope toward the stone shelf at the top of the escarpment.

Janelle reached after Carmelita, her fingers closing on air. "Hold up, *m'hija*," she called softly.

Carmelita halted in the shadows beneath the last of the firs.

Janelle put her mouth to Chuck's ear. "Do you think it's a good idea?" she whispered.

"Like Carm said, they won't be able to see us from below. They won't know we're there." He looked her in the eye. "We're here for Barney, to try to help. And for Clarence."

Janelle grimaced.

"We'll be careful," Chuck promised her.

Rosie waved her hand. "I want to come, too."

"Sorry," Chuck told her. "This is a two-person job, like our trip to Mesa Verde yesterday."

Carmelita crooked her finger at Chuck and crept from the forest onto the stone shelf. Chuck trailed her through the last of the trees and out onto the flat pan of rock. Ten feet from the drop-off, Carmelita lowered herself to her hands and knees. She crawled forward to the edge of the cliff and lay prone on the rock, her chin resting on her hands. Chuck crawled to her side. They peered over the edge of the cliff together. Sandra, Michaela, and the others were not in sight. Instead, the sound of their wheezing breaths reached the top of the cliff as they climbed, out of sight, into the alcove below.

A male voice Chuck did not recognize griped, "You didn't tell us we were going on a frickin' expedition."

The sound of the man's voice rose up the face of the escarpment, his words easily discernible.

"They don't make sheriff's deputies like they used to," came Sandra's voice in retort, her words equally clear.

After more huffing and puffing from the members of the group, Chuck recognized Michaela's voice: "Here we are."

"Jesus," the deputy exclaimed. Chuck envisioned the man gawking at the pits in the floor of the alcove. "Somebody dug the hell out of this place."

"This is exactly what I was afraid of," Michaela said.

The heavy breathing from the group members subsided.

Sandra said, "They swept away their footprints."

"The brush marks appear awfully fresh," Michaela noted. "So does the digging."

The deputy said, "Check out the back wall." His voice grew louder, resonating upward as he approached the rear of the recess. "Somebody hacked away at the slot back here. I wonder what they were after?"

"And," said Sandra, "who they were."

Michaela said, "That much, at least, is coming into focus."

"Oh?" Sandra said.

"Don't play dumb with me, Officer Kingsley. You know perfectly well who I'm referring to."

A beat of silence passed. Chuck envisioned Sandra and Michaela facing each other across the alcove while the rest of the group looked on.

Michaela insisted, "Must I say his name out loud for you?"

Chuck turned his head, his ear over the edge of the cliff.

"I don't think—" Sandra began.

"Come now," Michaela broke in. "You're the one who told us you invited Chuck Bender to come out here with us this morning. But for some inexplicable reason you received no response from him. From what I'm seeing here, I think the reason you didn't hear from him is becoming increasingly, I might even say glaringly, obvious."

Chuck jerked his head back from the edge of the cliff.

"You honestly believe he was responsible for this?" Sandra said. "And for Barney Keller's murder, too?"

"It occurred in his backyard, didn't it?"

"He was at the rock gym, in public, when it happened."

"His brother-in-law wasn't. Clarence Ortega, my newest hire."

Carmelita grasped Chuck's wrist, her nails digging into his skin.

"You're making quite a leap with your reasoning," said Sandra.

"Maybe I am," Michaela said. "But that's what we're supposed to be doing, isn't it? That's why we came all the way out here."

"I didn't invite you out here with me to make accusations. I invited you for your expertise. Let's keep our focus on that, shall we? As the expert on scene, what do you think was found from all this digging?"

"Nothing," Michaela said. "Because there's nothing here to be found. It appears our little subterfuge all those years ago is still paying off. When I performed the repatriation with Donald Cuthair, he dropped hints that this alcove had been selected as the site of the reburial. That idea is still out there online if you look hard enough. The hints were Donald's idea, as was his suggestion to instead put the bodies right back where they were found."

"How could you have done that without their being stolen again right away?"

"I'd tell you, but then I'd have to kill you." Michaela laughed, a short, harsh honk. "Just kidding. I know everyone here today is on a need-to-know basis, so I'll tell you exactly what we did. We brought in hydraulic jacks and lifted the boulders in the alcove."

"The ones that formed the space where the remains first were found?"

"That's right. The bodies originally were interred above ground between the rocks. Donald suggested reinterring them beneath the boulders. A brilliant solution, I have to admit. We jackhammered out a spot in the rocky floor of the alcove beneath the rock slabs, making the reinterment location inaccessible to looters using shovels. We placed the bodies and funerary objects in the space we'd opened up, within a few feet of where they'd first been laid to rest. Once we set the boulders back in place, it looked just like before. We performed the reinterment in the middle of the night. The workers were required to sign nondisclosure agreements."

"How many workers were there?"

"Five, maybe six."

"That gives me half a dozen more persons of interest to track down," Sandra said. "You'll have to get me their names."

"If I can find them."

"Not if. You'll find them," Sandra said, her voice firm. "In the meantime, the question remains: Why would someone have come out here and done all this digging?"

"That's easy. Because of the postcard."

"But what was it about the postcard? What did Barney know that led to his death?"

"We'll get there. We *will* get there. It's been less than twenty-four hours. We already know, based on what we're seeing here, that we're on the right track."

"You mean, my investigation is on the right track."

"Of course," Michaela said icily. "*Your* investigation. But if this were *my* investigation, I know who I'd be interviewing next—and it wouldn't be my old reinterment workers. I'd be bringing Chuck Bender in for some serious questioning. Clarence Ortega, too."

18

Audrey leaned far back in the easy chair beside the couch in her living room, her feet extended on the chair's upraised footrest. Her eyes were closed and a damp washcloth rested on her forehead. Fresh flower arrangements on the coffee table and end tables perfumed the room.

Chuck stood in front of the television mounted on the living room wall. Janelle and Clarence sat on the couch facing him, while the girls sat cross-legged on the floor.

In the Falls Creek drainage, Chuck and Carmelita had retreated from the edge of the escarpment and recounted what they'd overheard to Janelle and Rosie.

In response, Janelle had reasoned to Chuck, "Sandra will nab you if we go back to Clarence's. She'll arrest Clarence soon enough, too. We need to warn him to get out of his apartment."

A string of earlier texts from Sandra had appeared on Chuck's phone when they'd returned to phone service in the Junction Creek valley. The texts asked him to contact her, no doubt so she could request that he accompany her and the others to Falls Creek. Janelle had texted Audrey and Clarence, asking Audrey's permission for them to return to her house on the west side of town, and alerting Clarence to meet them there as well.

At the house, Audrey reported that her son, Jason, had arrived in Durango from Denver and was at the grocery store picking up food for additional relatives slated to begin arriving later in the day.

In the living room, Chuck told Clarence of Michaela's contention that the two of them were responsible for Barney's murder.

Clarence stared up at him from the couch. "Michaela is blaming us to shift suspicion away from herself," he said. "That has to be it."

Audrey made a stifled squeak through her nose and opened her eyes. "You really think Michaela killed my Barney?"

"No," Chuck said with a sharp shake of his head. "I've known her for a long time. She's a manipulator, sure. A hard-nosed businessperson. But I can't wrap my mind around her being a murderer."

"I don't know about that," Clarence countered. "She threw me under the bus yesterday right off the bat. Now, she's throwing you under, too."

"True," Chuck said. "Which means, if I'm right, then what's she up to?"

Rosie rocked from side to side on the carpeted floor. "She wants the canopic jars and she'll do anything to get them. That's what archaeologists do, right? They go after treasures."

"I've been wondering about that myself," Chuck admitted.

"You said they're worth a fortune."

"But Samuel would have to be in on it with her. Ilona, too. And Kyla. That's a pretty big crowd."

"Well," Janelle noted, "you're meeting with Samuel and Ilona in two hours."

"I was thinking of canceling."

"That's the last thing you should do."

"What if they bring Michaela along? What if Sandra shows up and arrests me?"

Clarence drummed his fingers on his knees. "I trust Samuel. I learned a lot from him the couple times I was assigned to work with him. If anybody has any good ideas about what's going on, it's him."

Chuck looked from Clarence to Janelle. "You both think I should keep my meeting with them?"

They nodded together.

"Desperate times . . ." Clarence began.

". . . call for desperate measures," Janelle finished. She paused. "I can't believe I'm about to say this, but I'm beginning to think you should call Sandra back and meet with her, too. The more I think about it, the more convinced I am that she won't arrest you. In fact, I think you should try to meet with her before you meet with Samuel and Ilona."

Chuck stopped pacing and stared at her. "You can't be serious. After all the things you've said about her still being in—"

Janelle raised her hand, silencing him. Rising from the couch, she said to Audrey, "Would it be okay if Chuck and I talked out back?"

"Of course," Audrey said. She adjusted the cloth on her forehead and settled back in her seat.

Chuck pulled the back door shut after Janelle and faced her on the concrete patio that took up half the fenced area behind the house. Beyond the back fence, ridges swathed by piñons and junipers climbed away from the edge of town toward Perins Peak. The mountain's prominent east face of golden sandstone towered above the lower ridges like the prow of a ship.

A pair of mountain bikers whooped as they sped through the trees behind the house, traversing one of the several trails that led up and over and down and around the ridges at the foot of the peak. These days, the forested hillsides west of town were the province of bikers and hikers and trail runners. A thousand years ago, the same hills had been the hunting grounds of early Ancestral Puebloans.

"I can't believe you want me to talk to Sandra," Chuck said to Janelle. "I know full well what you think of her."

"You have no idea what I think of your old girlfriend. You only know what you think I think of her."

"Tell me, then."

Janelle cleared her throat. "Yes," she admitted, "I do believe Sandra is still in love with you. But that doesn't mean I distrust her. Just the opposite, in fact. I know I said last night that I think it's possible she considers you a suspect. I still think that's true. But if I'm right, that just means she's doing her job—even while she still cares for you." She looked Chuck in the eye. "You're not the easiest guy to like sometimes, stubborn as you are. But you're easy to love. I knew that as soon as I met you, which is why I had no trouble marrying you after knowing you for only a few weeks. And it's why I had no problem trusting you with Carm and Rosie, either. With you, what I see is what I get. You're an open book, Chuck, and I love that about you. More to the point, I love you for that. Which is why it doesn't surprise me that someone else might love you, too—might still be in love with you—for the same reasons. And it certainly doesn't bother me, because I'm the one who has you. The girls and I do, that is."

He opened his mouth to respond, but she shook her head at him and continued.

"Plenty of girlfriends of mine have had crushes they've never gotten over. I don't see that as being the case with Sandra, though. You've told me she took your breakup hard. But the point is, she took it; she moved on. She's got a good life for herself now, with a wife and kids and a seriously kick-ass job. Whatever she might feel toward you now doesn't matter. What I see in her eyes when she looks at you, or maybe just what I imagine I see, doesn't matter either. What matters is who she has proven herself to be at this point in her life. From what I know of her, she's a good mom and she's a good cop. Which means the best thing you can do for yourself, and for Clarence, is reach out to her. She's on your side. I believe that, and you have to, too."

"You're putting an awful lot of faith in her."

"Because I do have faith in her."

Chuck sucked air through his teeth. "I just don't understand why."

"I don't need you to understand," Janelle said. "I just need you to be willing to go with me on this."

She stood on tiptoe and kissed him. He pulled her close and, looking past her at the hills rising at the edge of town, took his first deep, full breath since Barney's murder.

Then he recalled Audrey's insistence, in the police car last night, that Sandra reveal her alibi for Barney's murder—and Sandra's grudging response that, in fact, she'd been alone at the time Barney had been killed.

He quivered and released Janelle.

At the same instant, someone yelled from inside the house, "I oughta kill you, too!"

19

Chuck and Janelle hurried through the back of the house to the arched entry leading to the living room. A young man had joined Audrey, Clarence, and the girls in the room. Two plastic grocery bags hung from each of his hands, the bags' leaden contents of cans and jars visible through the thin layers of plastic.

The young man glared at Audrey, seated in the easy chair across the coffee table from him. He hunched his shoulders and heaved the four grocery bags at her. The heavy bags arced through the air and crashed down on the glass top of the coffee table, short of where Audrey sat. The tabletop shattered into hundreds of tiny squares. A flower arrangement tumbled through the table's brass frame along with the groceries. The flowers sprawled on the floor beneath the table and water spilled from the vase, soaking the carpet.

The thin plastic grocery bags split open, spraying canned vegetables, boxes of dried pasta, and jars of sauce around the room. One of the cans bounced off the table's brass frame and struck Clarence's shin. He yowled and jumped up from the couch, holding his leg. The girls leapt to their feet and backed to the wall of the living room.

Audrey slammed down her footrest and rose from her chair, the washcloth falling from her forehead to the floor. The young man leaned toward Audrey, reaching for her throat with outstretched fingers.

Clarence released his leg and stepped between Audrey and the young man, who shoved Clarence hard in the chest. The young man was lanky and well over six feet tall. Clarence swung him up and over and down to the carpet on his back in a single, fluid move, falling on him with a resounding *thump*.

"Oof!" the young man cried as Clarence landed on top of him. "Get the hell off me!" he hollered, his voice muffled as he struggled under Clarence's hulking body, his arms and legs flailing.

"Jason!" Audrey commanded. "That's enough. You hear me? Calm down. That's *enough*."

Beneath Clarence, Audrey's son stopped squirming.

"Are we good?" Clarence asked him, rolling to the side.

"Yeah," Jason muttered. He sat up and massaged his shoulder as Clarence climbed to his feet.

Chuck hadn't seen Jason Keller since the only child of Audrey and Barney had left Durango to attend a private college back East several years ago. By all appearances, Jason had been happy, healthy, and well-adjusted when he'd gone away to school. Now, however, half a dozen years later, Jason appeared emaciated. His face, partially hidden behind a sparse beard, was waxen, his brown hair greasy and unkempt. A tattoo of a leafy vine ran up his thin neck from his shirt collar to the lobe of his ear. Two more tattoos wrapped around his arms below his shirtsleeves, a length of barbed wire around one skinny bicep, a ribbon of two-lane highway around the other. Additional tattoos dotted his forearms.

Clarence bent forward, rubbing his shin.

"Tell him you're sorry." Audrey stepped past the shattered table and stood imperiously over her son with her arms crossed.

Seated on the carpet, Jason shook his head and drew in his shoulders.

"I said—" Audrey began.

"I'm okay," Clarence interrupted her, straightening. "I don't think he meant to do that to your table."

"Of course he didn't," Audrey snapped, her eyes on her son. "He was aiming for *me*."

Clarence offered Jason a hand. "Come on, bud. Let's get you up."

Jason took Clarence's hand and climbed to his feet. Clarence again positioned himself between Jason and Audrey. Jason looked at the floor while Audrey scowled past Clarence at her son.

Clarence turned to Chuck and Janelle in the arched entry. "He kinda lost it there for a minute."

Audrey harrumphed. "He has no self-control, not anymore."

Jason lowered his head.

Clarence faced Audrey. "You gave it to him pretty good when he came in here."

"Not half as much as I should have." She turned to Chuck and Janelle. "I gave him a full grocery list, everything precisely spelled out. All he had to do was follow it. But where's all the fruit I put on the list? Where are the vegetables? The lettuce? Tomatoes? Bananas and apples? He showed up with cans and jars, nothing else."

"I did the best I could," Jason protested. He directed a defensive look at Audrey before focusing again on the floor. "We don't know who's coming," he said to the carpet. "Or how many. We don't know when they'll get here or how long they'll stay. I figured canned would be best."

"Well, you figured *wrong*," Audrey said. "You completely ignored my list, and when I pointed it out to you, you threatened to kill me and then you chucked your bags at me."

He raised his head once more. This time, he held his mother's gaze, his eyes flaring. "It never changes, does it? You're as nice as can be to everybody else in the world. But when it comes to me, I can never do anything right."

"It's my job to be demanding of you. Somebody has to tell you the truth about yourself. If not me, your own mother, then who do you expect is going to make you—"

"Your son just lost his father," Janelle said to Audrey, taking a step forward. "You just lost your husband." She glanced around the room. "We just lost a friend. There's nothing easy about this, not for any of us. We have to give each other the space we all need."

Audrey huffed. "If the police would just get a move on."

"They are," Jason said to his mother. "Sandra is doing everything she can."

"Sandra? Are you referring to Officer Kingsley?"

Jason nodded stiffly.

Chuck stepped from the arched entry to Janelle's side. "You've been speaking with her?"

"Why shouldn't I?" Jason said. "This is my father we're talking about."

Audrey addressed Chuck. "Jason worked with Officer Kingsley last year. He interned with her."

"It wasn't an internship," Jason interjected quickly. "I shadowed her for a shift. I did one of those ride-alongs with her."

"Barney set it up," Audrey explained to Chuck. "He said he wasn't going to mention it to you. He didn't want to upset you."

"Upset me?"

"He knew Officer Kingsley from when the two of you were together. But this was about our son. It had nothing to do with you. Jason was floating around Denver after college, not having any idea what he wanted."

"I was not—" Jason began.

But Audrey pressed on. "That ridiculous degree he got, in whatever self-designed major he made up, it cost us a fortune." She spoke as if Jason wasn't in the room. "And what good was it doing him? He had no job, no prospects. I was the one who said he should get serious. What was so wrong with being a cop? He was a Durango kid. He'd hunted, shot guns plenty of times. I knew that part wouldn't faze him. It was time he grew up and made something of himself."

"Barney felt the same?" Chuck asked.

"Of course he did. It was his money that had gone to waste for Jason's college years, right along with mine. A quarter of a million dollars, and for what?"

"I did what you asked," Jason said to his mother. "I came home. I went on the ride-along with her."

"But what good did it do? You went right back up to Denver, to your worthless roommates and their worthless ways, while we were down here trying to pay off all the loans we took out for you. You keep saying you're going to help out, but you've never come up with a cent—even though every time we see you, you've somehow managed to pay for another tattoo on that worthless body of yours."

"Enough," Janelle said. She glanced at the girls, their backs to the wall and their eyes round as dinner plates, before turning to Jason. "Is there anything you've found out from speaking with Officer Kingsley that might be helpful to us?"

"What do you mean, helpful to you?" Jason said. "It's my father who's dead."

"He was killed at our house."

"I don't care if he was killed on the moon."

Janelle appraised Jason, her look calculating. "Where were you yesterday?"

Jason grew still. "What do you mean?"

"Where were you at midday yesterday, when your father was killed?"

Chuck put a hand on Janelle's shoulder. "We don't need to—"

"Oh, yes, we do," Janelle said, her voice firm. "I want nothing more than to get Carm and Rosie away from this . . . this . . . mess. But not until we get the answers we need." Again, she addressed Jason. "So, where were you yesterday?"

Jason extended his arm. He aimed a finger at a tattoo above his wrist of a spider with its eight legs wrapped around an assault rifle. "I was playing *Enemy Invasion*."

"Where?"

"In Denver, before my mom called about . . . with the . . . news."

"You were online? Will it have been time-stamped?"

Jason's eyes darted around the room. He lowered his arm. "Well, actually, I wasn't officially playing. I was stalking. That is, I was there watching, studying up on others. It helps when you compete."

"You never officially signed in?"

Audrey broke in before Jason could respond. "Oh, no, you don't. I see where you're going with this, and I will not have it. This is *my* husband we're talking about. *My* son." She pointed at the front door. "Get out," she commanded. "All of you. Now." She faced Janelle and said venomously, "You have no right to accuse my son of anything. He just lost his father." Her voice broke. "I just lost my husband." She paused, steadying herself, her feet planted in the brown carpet next to the broken coffee table. "Out," she said to Janelle. "Before I call Sandra on you."

"I can't believe you, *hermana*," Clarence said to Janelle when the two of them reached the sidewalk with Chuck and the girls. "You just accused that guy in there of murdering his own dad."

"Everyone else is accusing you of murdering Barney," Janelle said. "We might as well add some names to the list. Besides, there's clearly enough friction between Jason and his mother to at least make it a possibility."

"He knows guns," Chuck noted. "Audrey said so."

"He's even got one tattooed on his arm," said Janelle.

"And," Carmelita chimed in, "he said he wasn't signed in to his video game yesterday. He totally could have been here instead of in Denver."

"Totally," Rosie agreed, her eyes on Carmelita. "He threatened to kill his mom, and then he threw stuff at her, too. He's a baaaad guy."

They retreated across town to Clarence's apartment.

Clarence paced two steps each way in his cramped living room. "Okay," he said, resuming their discussion, "I'm not saying Jason did it, but I'm not saying he didn't do it, either." He looked at Janelle. "The thing I'm getting fixated on is the whole thing with Sandra."

Janelle nodded. "Her name keeps coming up. She seems to be everywhere." She widened her eyes at Chuck.

"You honestly still think I should meet with her?" he asked.

"Absolutely," she said.

20

Chuck sent a text to Sandra's personal number. To his surprise, she responded right away, agreeing to meet alone with him.

She swung by the apartment and picked him up in her private car, a crossover SUV with a booster seat in back. Though she'd been in uniform at Falls Creek three hours ago, she now wore plain clothes—jeans and a zippered sweater.

"Thanks for meeting me like this," Chuck said to her as he slid into the passenger seat, "instead of hauling me in."

She shrugged as she pulled away from the curb. "The chief gives us plenty of leeway to do what we think best."

She suggested they take a walk on the college campus, on a mesa three hundred feet above downtown, explaining, "It'll be deserted up there on Sunday afternoon. No one will bother us."

She parked in one of the empty lots on the edge of campus and they headed on foot toward the clock tower rising in the middle of the central quad.

"You're really, seriously, not going to arrest me?" Chuck asked.

"Why would I do that?"

"Because Michaela wants you to."

"What makes you say that?"

"I'm not just saying it. I know it. I was up on the cliff above the alcove at Falls Creek this morning, listening to all of you."

She stopped in mid-stride, grabbed his arm, and spun him to her. "You were *where*?"

"I hiked down from Junction Creek Road." He didn't mention the presence of Janelle and the girls. "I guessed you'd head out there."

"You hiked?" She dropped her hand from his arm. "You guessed?"

"I suspected, put it that way."

Her eyes grew large. "The brush marks in the dirt . . . you were there before us, weren't you?"

"I saw what you saw," he confirmed. "The holes, the hammering in the back slot. I climbed around to the top of the cliff when you showed up. Your words came right up to me." He looked her in the eye. "You sounded like you agreed with Michaela when she named Clarence and me as Barney's killers."

"Letting people have their say is part of the process. I told you that last night."

"Even when they falsely accuse someone of murder?"

"Even then."

He grunted. Was Sandra telling the truth? Last night, she had turned off the camera in the police car when she'd been alone with him, assuring there would be no potentially incriminating record of their conversation. And she was meeting on her own with him now, out of uniform and in private, at seeming risk to her career.

He took a moment, sizing her up. He saw only the woman he'd known when they'd dated—open, honest, forthright. Nothing about her said "killer" to him.

"Okay, you win," he said. "The whole world can call me a murderer if they want to, and they can call Clarence a murderer, too, as long as we get our hands on the real one."

They set off again, crossing the quad and angling between dormitories and classroom buildings, headed toward the rim of the mesa on the far side of campus.

"Do you agree with Michaela," Sandra asked, "that nothing was taken from the alcove?"

"I do." Chuck found himself quoting Rosie: "The holes were all the same depth, and there were lots of them, which would point toward an extensive search but no specific discovery. Same goes for the hammering at the slot in back. Crude and, from what I saw, most likely unsuccessful as well."

"Michaela thinks they—or, you—were looking for the reinterred bodies. Do you agree? Or could the search have been for something else instead?"

He caught his toe on a crack in the sidewalk and took a stumbling step before he caught himself. It sounded as if Sandra knew about the rumored canopic jars. He wasn't about to mention them before she did, however. "Going after the reinterred bodies makes the most sense, particularly if you consider the postcard Barney was holding."

They passed the expanse of practice fields that bordered campus, nearing the mesa rim.

"I assume you overheard Michaela say that the reburial actually was done beneath the boulders in the north alcove. Do you believe her?"

"I don't believe anything she says, ever. I know she's wrong to suspect me and Clarence, of course—if she really does suspect us, that is."

"What are you suggesting?"

"Your meeting me unofficially like this tells me you don't believe her either—not that you possibly could, I imagine, given our past together. The obvious next question for both of us, then, is why she would falsely accuse me. The only answer I can come up with is that she's hiding something about herself, something she wants to cover up by accusing others."

"I don't see her as a murderer."

"I don't either. She did admit to me, though, that she was in town alone yesterday."

"I was in town alone yesterday, too. That doesn't make me Barney's murderer any more than it does her."

Chuck kept his eyes on the sidewalk in front of him. "I'd have thought she might have been at Mesa Verde."

A second of silence passed between them.

"You're referring to the canopic jars," Sandra said.

Chuck halted and waited until she turned to him. "How long have you known?"

"I was a street cop when you and I were together, but I'm a homicide detective now—part-time, anyway. It's my job these days to learn about things like the canopic jars and how they might figure into Barney's death. It's good, challenging work, and I love it." Her gaze shifted, her eyes taking on a melancholy look. "I admit it took me a long time to get past our relationship. To get past you. Cheryl came along at the right time. So did my promotion to homicide. It gave me something bigger than myself to focus on. I know you broke up with me because of how unhappy I was. To your credit, you were man enough to tell me so. The chief saw how unhappy I was, too. I'd been on streets for ten years at that point, doing the same old, same old. He gave me the choice of stepping up to homicide or stepping out, and he gave me a week to decide. That was the same week I met Cheryl. The fates were aligned. I went back to his office and told him, yeah, stepping up sounded good to me."

"I'm glad for you."

"I'm glad for you, too, Chuck. Really, I am. You weren't exactly filled with joy yourself when we were together. I'm happy for what Janelle has given you. Your girls, too."

Chuck smiled as he shook his head. "Kids. Talk about something bigger than ourselves to focus on. Maybe that's what we both needed, even more than our new partners."

"No. Everything starts with our partners. You and I were as wrong for each other as Cheryl and Janelle are right for each of us. You and me—the two of us, together—were doom and gloom. You figured it out before I did, which made it hard for me. But now, looking back, I know the decision you made for both of us was the right one. The worst thing we could have done is have kids together."

Chuck held Sandra's gaze. "*Bastante bien,*" he agreed, the Spanish a nod to his new life with Janelle.

They resumed walking toward the edge of the mesa.

"The canopic jars," Chuck urged.

"Like I told you last night, I've been questioning as many people as I can as quickly as I can, and listening hard to their answers, pretty much nonstop since yesterday." Sandra paused. "There's a woman in Mancos. I spoke with her last night. Michaela slipped up and mentioned her."

"You're sure it was a slip-up?"

"Fairly sure, anyway. Michaela didn't give me the woman's name. She just brought her up in passing. I tracked her down from there."

"Elizabeth Mantry," Chuck said.

Sandra looked sidelong at him as they walked. "That's right."

"What's her number? I want to talk to her, too."

"You know I can't give you that."

"I know you can't *officially* give me that."

"What's that supposed to mean?"

"I know you can't send her number from your phone to mine in any sort of traceable way. But if I just happen to catch sight of it on your screen..." He shrugged. "Besides, if you tracked down her number, I'll be able to do the same. It'll just take me longer."

"There's no need for you to talk to her. I already did that."

"You're a police officer. Who knows what she might be

willing to say to me, Barney's friend, compared to how careful she'd have been with you."

Sandra sighed. She stopped, thumbed her phone, and held it up to Chuck with a phone number facing him.

He tapped at his phone, entering the number. "Thanks."

She lowered her phone. "You'd have found it soon enough on your own, like you said. It's not like she's hiding or anything."

"What'd you learn from her?"

"The biggest thing she told me is that there's a dig going on over at Mesa Verde that might have some bearing on Barney's death."

"I was going to mention that."

"When?"

"Well, now, I guess. The dig is on the west side of the park, outside the park boundary. It's a fairly big deal, on account of what they're looking for."

"The jars, you mean."

"It was the Elizabeth woman, in Mancos, who clued you in about them, I take it, not Michaela?"

Sandra nodded. "Michaela hasn't been overly forthcoming with us, to be perfectly honest. She knows what's at stake for her. A murdered employee, his death clearly related to his work—that is, to her company. She's being very circumspect about what she says."

"Not when it comes to naming me and Clarence as suspects."

"No, not when it comes to that."

"She must have known you'd track down the woman in Mancos. How'd you get her name, anyway?"

"Samuel Horvat, the archaeologist with Southwest Archaeology Enterprises, gave it to me."

"You *have* been talking to everyone."

"So have you." Another sidelong look. "I heard you visited the Strater this morning, bright and early."

"I'm trying to talk to as many people as I can as quickly as I can, too, just like you."

"You're supposed to leave the investigating to us. You could get yourself hurt—or worse—going out and playing detective on your own."

"None of this is play to me. Barney was my friend. He was killed at my house, because of something having to do with my work. I've got my family to think about."

"Understood. But I needed to say it."

"You obviously know about the museum curator from Finland, Ilona Koskinen."

"I know about Kyla Owens, too."

"Did Samuel tell you he and Ilona weren't at the dig site yesterday at the time of Barney's murder? They supposedly were on the way there from Durango—which means they easily could have been in town at the time of Barney's death."

"No, he did not mention that fact." Sandra's eyes tightened. "That leaves Kyla alone at the dig site at the time of the murder, with no one to vouch for her, either."

"Seems your persons-of-interest list keeps getting longer—a lot longer than just Clarence and me, as Michaela would have it."

"She's on the list, too. For all that I don't see her as a murderer, she still has to be."

"What about the Mancos woman, Elizabeth?"

"I've only spoken with her by phone at this point, but her alibi for yesterday is rock solid."

"Regardless, I'm going to speak with her, too."

"I'm telling you not to, officially." Sandra took another step before continuing. "But if you learn anything, I'd appreciate hearing it from you."

"Speaking of learning something, there's someone else I think you should add to your list."

"Let me guess: Jason Keller, Barney's son."

"You're way ahead of me."

"He's been on the list from the start. Family first, family always, then move on from there."

"Is that why you held Audrey in your car for so long last night?"

A slight hitch entered Sandra's step. "No," she admitted.

"That had to do with another person of interest?"

"Yes."

"Me."

Sandra gazed straight ahead.

"That's what Janelle suspected," Chuck said.

"She's smart, your wife."

"Like you."

"For the record, I didn't suspect you. I don't. But the murder occurred at your house. I know you were at the gym, but that wouldn't necessarily clear you, not entirely."

"So, when Michaela started badmouthing me . . ."

". . . I figured, seeing as Audrey gave me the opportunity, I'd better cover all the bases and give you another look."

"Which you're still doing, meeting with me right now."

"That's my job."

"Just so we're clear," said Chuck, "my job—protecting my family—means I'm still checking you out, too."

They crossed the road bounding the west side of campus and stopped at the rim of the mesa. The view was commanding—the squared blocks of the Grid neighborhood at the foot of the plateau below, downtown Durango beyond, and the soaring face of Perins Peak framing the scene to the west.

A runner passed them on Rim Trail, the dirt path skirting the mesa's edge. The jogger continued on the trail past the head of Durango's SkySteps. Constructed of heavy timbers staked into the hillside, the stairway connected the college campus with town in five hundred winding steps, making a popular climb-and-descend workout for the town's many hardcore athletes, and a direct, if demanding, foot commute to and from campus.

The afternoon sun warmed Chuck's face. At the foot of the mesa, wind swept through the trees that hid much of the Grid, their uppermost branches pirouetting in the gusts. The roof of Chuck's house showed amid the waving branches, along with a police SUV still parked out front.

The hum of traffic on Main Avenue filled the valley, reaching the top of the mesa. Chuck flinched when another sound overwhelmed the sound of the traffic—the high-pitched screech of an emergency siren.

PART THREE

"Unless [human] remains are placed back in the ground, spirits can't continue the path to another spirit world."

—Ernest House Jr.,
Ute Mountain Ute repatriation expert

21

Chuck peered from the edge of the mesa at a police car racing south on Main Avenue, red and blue lights flashing on its roof. More emergency sirens joined that of the police car, those of an ambulance and fire truck that rolled out of the Durango Fire and Rescue Station, adjacent to downtown on the banks of the Animas River. A jolt of electricity shot down his spine as the three vehicles turned into the Grid, their screeches reverberating in the air above town.

A fourth siren added to the cacophony filling the valley, this one rising from the Durango Police Station. The lights of a police vehicle blinked as the car squealed away from the station, across the street from city hall, and entered the Grid.

Sandra pulled her phone from her back pocket. "Kingsley here," she barked into it, her eyes pinned to the speeding emergency vehicles below.

The vehicles threaded their way through the neighborhood, cornering right and left, nearing Chuck's house. Their lights flickered through the wind-whipped branches of the trees lining the street.

Sandra nodded as she listened to her call. "Got it," she said.

Chuck's phone vibrated in his pocket. He pulled it out to find an incoming text: *Help mechuck youhavetogot*

Sandra lowered her phone and said to him, her words clipped, "You're on your own. I can't have you with me."

"Of course."

She sprinted back the way they'd come, across the road and

past the practice fields and on toward her car on the other side of the campus.

Chuck stared at his phone. The garbled text was from his neighbor, Beatrice Roberts. He ran to the head of the SkySteps and started down the long set of stairs connecting the mesa with the Grid. He gripped his phone in his hand as he descended the stairway, hoping to feel the vibration of another incoming text from Beatrice.

Two more police cars sped into the neighborhood below. Visible through the swaying branches, the cars converged not on Chuck's house, but on Beatrice's house next door.

Chuck reached the foot of the stairway. He sprinted down the street. Turning left, he headed for Beatrice's house. Residents looked on from their front porches as he ran past. His quads burned and his heart pounded. Ahead, police SUVs were parked haphazardly in the street, the same as yesterday. Today, however, the police cars were parked not in front of Chuck's house, but in front of Beatrice's, their emergency lights flashing, and they were joined by the ambulance and fire truck. Firefighters in brimmed helmets and oilskin jackets waited outside the truck, while the ambulance and police vehicles were unattended.

Chuck crossed Beatrice's front yard and ran up the steps two at a time to her porch. The front door to the house stood ajar. He slowed, catching his breath, and stepped into the foyer.

The house was a brick Victorian like Chuck's, with compact rooms off a central passage. The hallway ran the length of the interior, past a small living room, study, and master bedroom to the combined kitchen and dining area at the back of the house.

Chuck hurried down the passage. The rooms on either side of the hall were packed with furnishings—an overstuffed sofa and easy chairs in the front room, an imposing wooden desk in the study, a sleigh bed and tall dresser in the bedroom.

First responders huddled in the kitchen at the end of the hallway, their backs to Chuck. He paused in the doorway.

A mishmash of plug-in appliances crowded the kitchen counters. The farmhouse sink on the far side of the room was half-full of dirty dishes. Virtually every square inch of wall space was covered with framed family photos.

Beatrice lay on her back on the linoleum floor in the middle of the room. Her eyes were closed, her arms limp at her sides. She wore her normal daily attire: a heavy sweater over a loose cotton housedress, with wool socks and leather clogs on her feet. The pasty skin of her lower legs, speckled with age spots, showed between the hem of her dress and the top of her socks.

Two paramedics crouched over Beatrice's still form, one on each side. Two additional paramedics and four police officers stood in a circle around them. One of the standing paramedics was Mark Chapman, Janelle's shift supervisor, and one of the police officers was the thirty-something officer with the thick mustache who yesterday had shown Chuck the postcard of Esther.

The mustachioed officer turned to Chuck in the kitchen entry. "You can't be in here."

Chuck held up his phone, still grasped in his sweaty hand. "She texted me. She asked me to come." He looked down at Beatrice. "Is she all right? What happened?"

On the floor, Beatrice moaned weakly. The police officer spun back to her.

Mark grasped Chuck's elbow and drew him into the hallway. Janelle's supervisor was middle-aged and paunchy. Silver hairs speckled his close-cropped, black beard. White slivers of T-shirt peeked between the stretched front buttons of his uniform shirt.

"We don't know what's going on with her yet," Mark told Chuck. "Did you say she texted you?"

"She asked for my help. Then it gets jumbled."

"Can I see?"

Chuck handed over his phone. Mark stared at its screen.

"Thanks," he said, returning the device. "That helps."

"How so?"

"The four of us from Durango Fire and Rescue were the first ones on scene. She was semi-conscious when we arrived, trying to talk."

"Trying?"

"She wasn't making much sense."

"Did you recognize anything she said?"

"Maybe." Mark paused. "I'm not sure."

Chuck waited.

"Okay," Mark said. "There was something I think I picked up." He glanced down the hallway, then back at Chuck. "She was agitated, as I said, and clearly confused. You could put it down to that—to her confusion."

"You could put *what* down to her confusion?"

Mark hesitated, then said quickly, "The word I thought I recognized. Words. Two of them." His eyes went to Chuck's phone. "With you here, and with what it looks like she was trying to text you, I'm thinking maybe I did recognize them correctly. They were weird, out of place—until you consider who was killed yesterday back in the alley, and what he did for a living, and her trying to text you just now."

"The words were . . . ?"

"Mesa Verde."

Chuck rocked back on his heels. "Are you sure?"

"No, I'm not sure at all. It's just a guess, but . . ." Mark's voice trailed off.

"Thanks," Chuck told him. "From Janelle, too."

"It's great having her on our team," Mark responded. "She's got what it takes."

"I couldn't agree more."

"She'll get on full-time soon enough. In fact, if I have anything to say about it—which I do, plenty—the next position that opens up will be hers."

Mark preceded Chuck back into the kitchen.

One of the kneeling paramedics pressed her fingers to Beatrice's neck, below the jawline, her eyes on her wristwatch.

The other paramedic put his gloved hand to Beatrice's shoulder and asked, "Beatrice? Mrs. Roberts? Can you hear me?"

The elderly woman's eyes remained closed. She made no further sound.

The paramedic probed Beatrice's gray hair with a gloved hand. His fingers came away from the back of Beatrice's head red with blood.

A hard knot formed in Chuck's stomach. Beatrice had been healthy and able-bodied for as long as he'd known her. She made her own meals and did her own housekeeping. If she'd fainted just now, it was the result of a new medical problem, or one she'd kept to herself. But the timing of her injury, a day after Barney's murder out back, suggested the possibility she'd been attacked instead—particularly in light of what she'd apparently said to Mark before losing consciousness.

Why, however, would someone have attacked a seemingly harmless old woman?

"Lucky she was able to call 911," the male paramedic said.

Mark stood over the two kneeling paramedics. "She's not regaining consciousness," he said to them. "This is a scoop-and-run. Let's go."

Mark spoke on his phone while the other three paramedics lifted Beatrice onto a gurney and wheeled her out to the waiting ambulance, trailed by the police officers.

Alone, Chuck stepped to the south-facing window in Beatrice's kitchen. From its raised position at the rear of the house, the window overlooked his backyard, which was enclosed on all sides by the head-high wooden fence that prevented Durango's voracious town deer from reaching the backyard flowers and garden.

Chuck took in the view of his yard through the kitchen window. The vantage point made Beatrice the only potential witness to yesterday's break-in. He kicked himself. Why hadn't he asked Sandra if she'd interviewed Beatrice yet? Moreover, why hadn't he contacted Beatrice himself? After all, her texts had been the first he'd received yesterday, alerting him to the turmoil at his house.

If Beatrice had shared with others something she'd witnessed yesterday, and if word of what she'd seen had leaked to Barney's murderer or murderers, then they'd have had no choice but to eliminate the witness to their crime.

But if Barney's killers had decided to silence Beatrice, they certainly would have silenced her permanently. Instead, Beatrice remained alive, injured but not dead. Why?

Chuck called Sandra.

"I hadn't gotten to it yet," she said when he asked if she'd interviewed Beatrice. "There wasn't time yesterday. The trip to Falls Creek was higher priority this morning. Then, when you called, meeting with you took precedence, too."

Chuck studied his quiet backyard from Beatrice's window. "It doesn't look like there's anyone from the department at my house anymore."

"Our team finished the initial site investigation this morning. An evidence-gathering team is on the way from Denver to perform a more thorough sweep. Given the high profile of the case, the chief thinks they're worth the expense. I tried to convince them to come today, but it's the weekend. They won't get here till tomorrow. We're rotating officers at your house until the evidence team shows up, but they're mostly staying out front in their vehicles."

"That means someone could have snuck into Beatrice's house from the back alley without being seen. She's not one to lock her doors."

"From what I'm hearing, they think it was an accident. A fainting episode, most likely."

"A suspiciously coincidental accident, if you ask me."

"I wouldn't disagree." The sound of rustling clothes came over the phone. "I'm heading to the hospital as soon as I get back in uniform. I'll see what I can learn from your neighbor when she comes around."

"*If* she comes around."

"I'm hoping."

"So am I."

"As for you, Chuck, I need you to stay put."

"I'm not about to run away," he assured her.

No farther, at any rate, than Mesa Verde.

22

Chuck dialed Elizabeth Mantry's number as he hurried the few blocks from Beatrice's house to Clarence's apartment.

A woman answered. He introduced himself as an archaeologist friend of Barney's. "I'm sure the Durango police already asked you this," he said, "but where were you at midday yesterday?"

"What is this?" she demanded. "Are you working for the cops or something?" Elizabeth's voice was rough and weathered, like a stiff brush scrubbing concrete.

Chuck took long strides, almost jogging. He didn't answer.

"Sorry to disappoint you," she said, filling in the silence, "but I worked the counter at Mancos Bakery all day yesterday. I saw everybody in town there, and they saw me. I gave her the names of people I remembered talking to."

"Her?"

"The officer I talked to yesterday."

"I understand you told her about the dig going on at Mesa Verde."

A note of pride entered Elizabeth's voice. "I'm the one who got the whole thing rolling."

"On account of the canopic jars?"

"You know a lot about what's going on, don't you?"

"I'm a friend of Barney's, a good friend. Or, I was."

"Samuel Horvat is the archaeologist doing the dig. Is he a friend of yours, too?"

"He and I have known each other a long time."

"He's the one who told you about them?"

"The jars? Yes."

"That's the big question, right there: Do they exist? It's why Ilona came over here. It's what she and Samuel are supposed to be finding out. But now, after your friend's death, they're saying the dig is going to be shut down, who knows for how long. The whole thing's turning into a total disaster."

Chuck blasted air through his nostrils. The far bigger disaster was what had happened to Barney. "I understand you contacted Ilona on account of your great-uncle's papers."

"Yes, siree. My great-*great*-uncle. After I ran across them, I did a lot of poking around online. From what I could tell, Ilona seemed the best person to talk to. Turned out I was right. She started making plans to come over here right after I first emailed her. She's been as excited as me about this whole thing from the get-go."

Chuck paused at the final intersection before Clarence's apartment complex, letting a car pass. Could that be it? Was Ilona so excited about the jars she was willing to commit murder to get her hands on them?

"Thanks for your time," he said to Elizabeth. "I have to go."

Back in Clarence's apartment, Chuck filled Janelle, Clarence, and the girls in on what had happened to Beatrice, and his follow-up phone conversation with Elizabeth Mantry. He proposed that he head for Mesa Verde on his own.

"Never," Janelle said. "Either you stay here with us, or the girls and I are coming with you, the same as this morning."

Chuck groaned even as he recognized that Janelle was right. The presumed attack on Beatrice proved danger continued to lurk in Durango in the wake of Barney's death, which meant it would be good for all of them to get away from town for a few hours while Sandra and her fellow officers continued their work.

As for Ilona, if she was in any way guilty, she'd be on the run after her attempt to silence Beatrice. She most assuredly would not be headed back to Gunnel Canyon.

"Fine," he said.

"I've had enough of sitting around here," Clarence said. "I'm coming, too."

Chuck nodded. Safety in numbers. "I don't want to take the truck, though. It's too recognizable. And we can't all squeeze into Janelle's car."

"I'll take my car, too," Clarence said.

Chuck, Janelle, and the girls piled into Janelle's SUV. They headed out of town with Clarence following in his old, dented sedan. They'd discussed whether Chuck should postpone his scheduled meeting with Samuel and Ilona, and decided it would be better for him to be a no-show and leave them wondering—especially Ilona—for the time being.

The girls wore earbuds in the back seat, their heads bobbing to their music.

Janelle glanced at Chuck as she drove. "You're certain the park is safe?"

"Safer than town, anyway."

"That's not overly reassuring."

"The cops are keeping an eye on our place, but that didn't keep Beatrice safe, right next door."

"You're assuming she was attacked. But we don't know that yet."

"We do if Mark is correct about what she said, and I have to believe he is. How could he have come up with 'Mesa Verde' on his own?"

"Pretty easily, if you ask me. From what you said, Beatrice was essentially unconscious when you saw her. Who knows how mentally aware she was before you got there."

"All we're doing is heading up on the mesa to check on the dig, the same as when we went to Falls Creek this morning."

"Where we found out that the alcove had just been dug illegally. *Criminally.*"

"And where we also found out that the authorities were right on top of it." Chuck aimed his thumb at the bright, sunny afternoon outside the car. "It's not as if we're heading into the heart of darkness. We're going to a national park, patrolled by rangers, along with hundreds of other tourists."

He didn't mention the nail in the truck tire that had nearly proved deadly at the end of yesterday's visit, but Janelle did it for him.

"Rosie made it sound like the blowout was a lot worse than you admitted to," she said.

"That's Rosie for you."

Janelle tightened her hands on the steering wheel. "I've got half a mind to turn around."

"If I'm right and Beatrice really was attacked, then Durango is not where we want to be right now."

She drew her lower lip between her teeth. "I'm glad we're together, then." Her eyes went to the rearview mirror. "Clarence, too."

"I'm just glad to get away from town—and from Michaela and her ridiculous accusations—for a few hours, anyway."

They left the highway and ascended the main park road to the top of the mesa along with the steady stream of traffic flowing into the park. Beyond the crest of the plateau, where the other park visitors continued south on the main road to Chapin Mesa, Janelle turned at Chuck's direction onto the twisting side road leading to Wetherill Mesa. She drove slowly on the deserted secondary road, negotiating its tight curves.

"I can't believe how quiet it gets when you leave the main road," she said. She glanced behind her at Clarence's sedan. "I'm glad we've got two cars."

"It's only a few miles farther."

"And then a dirt road?"

"It's short, less than a mile long."

"A side road off the main park road, then a dead-end dirt road after that. We may not be heading into the heart of darkness, but we're definitely heading for the middle of nowhere."

"We're doing this on Barney's behalf, to help with the investigation," Chuck reminded her, the argument growing weaker with each repetition.

"We're doing this for ourselves, too," Janelle said. "For you and Clarence."

They reached Wetherill Mesa. Chuck pointed her onto the dirt road. Clarence fell back, trailing the cloud of dust raised by the SUV.

Chuck peered ahead as they approached the end of the road. Sunlight shimmered off the roof of Samuel's black pickup truck, which was parked in the gravel opening beyond the turnaround. It looked as if Samuel, like Chuck, would be a no-show at the meeting in Ilona's room at the Strater scheduled for thirty minutes from now.

Janelle eased the SUV to a stop next to Samuel's pickup. Clarence parked beside them. They gathered outside the cars.

Chuck pointed at the black truck. "That's Samuel's. He promised to suspend the dig. He's supposed to be meeting me and Ilona in Durango right about now."

"I bet he's gathering tools and shutting things down," said Clarence. "He's probably just running late. He's not a murderer. I've worked with him enough over the last few weeks to know that much for sure."

"I don't trust anybody anymore."

"Maybe he'll have some answers for us."

"If we can figure out what to ask him."

Chuck led them away from the parking area, retracing the route he'd taken with Rosie yesterday through the piñon-juniper forest to Gunnel Canyon.

Though Carmelita continued to wear her earbuds, Rosie chattered away to her sister as they walked behind Chuck.

"We came this way yesterday," Rosie explained to Carmelita. "There's a cliff. And a crack in the rock. It's way cool. Just wait till you see the dead person. You're gonna freak, Carm. I swear to God, you'll just freak out."

"*Gosh*," Janelle corrected Rosie.

They hiked deeper into the forest.

Janelle said from behind Chuck and the girls, "This is way more remote than you made it sound."

"We're just doing some exploring, like this morning," he said, glancing back at her. "Besides, Rosie's right: the site is way cool. I swear to gosh."

They reached the canyon rim and walked along the cliff edge to the walled cleft extending to the floor of the canyon. Carmelita plucked out her earbuds and passed Chuck, taking the lead down the cleft. Clarence followed her into the cleft. He contorted himself, squeezing his belly through the narrowest portions of the slot in the cliff.

"Come *on*, Uncle Clarence," Rosie admonished, following him downward. "Carm's getting ahead of us."

"*Es difícil*," Clarence said between heavy breaths.

"No, it's not. *Es facil.*"

"*Para ti.*"

"*Sí, para mi.*"

She passed Clarence halfway down the slot, where the facing walls widened for a few feet.

"Wait up, Carm!" she called ahead, hurrying down the cleft.

Carmelita reached the foot of the slot and stood looking up from below until Rosie reached her, after which the girls headed down the canyon together.

"Wait for us!" Chuck called to them from where he was trapped behind Clarence.

They did not reappear at the bottom of the slot. He cursed beneath his breath and urged Clarence to hurry.

"I'm going as fast as I can." Clarence defended himself, placing each foot with care as he descended. "You didn't say *nada* about this crack in the rock."

"I didn't think I needed to."

"I gotta lose me some pounds," Clarence said between grunts.

"You always say that."

"I always mean it, too."

Clarence reached the bottom of the cleft and bent forward, his hands on his knees, gasping for air. Chuck and Janelle joined him on the canyon floor.

Chuck rested his hand on Clarence's back. "I hate to think what going back up is going to do to you." He looked for Carmelita and Rosie, but they'd already passed from sight around a bend in the canyon.

Clarence straightened. "I'll make it." He gulped. "I'm almost sure of it."

Janelle started down the canyon. "We have to catch up with—"

The combined screams of the girls filled the air, resounding off the canyon walls, from the direction of the alcove.

23

Chuck sprinted down the canyon with Janelle and Clarence. Ahead, the girls' screams died away. He wound through the ponderosa pines, his feet digging into the sandy floor of the canyon. He rounded a bulge at the base of the sandstone wall and skidded to a halt at the sight of Carmelita and Rosie standing stock-still at the edge of the alcove. Janelle and Clarence stopped beside him.

The girls faced away from Chuck. Beyond them, on the floor of the alcove, Samuel Horvat lay on his back in a pool of blood. His body was hacked and mutilated. One of his arms lay across his unmoving chest, the other was splayed outward.

Chuck hurried past the girls and collapsed to his knees at Samuel's side. Up close, the fact that Samuel was dead was horribly obvious. Samuel's torso was slashed and bloodied. Brain matter showed in breaks in his skull. Bits of his cranium were scattered in a puddle of dark blood beneath his head. A larger pool of blood spread from under his back.

On the ground next to Samuel lay the object that clearly had been used to kill him—the rubber-handled hatchet from among the dig implements that yesterday had been arrayed next to the depression. The hatchet's gray steel head and black handle were smeared with blood.

Chuck sank back on his haunches and looked over his shoulder to see Clarence step between the girls and draw them to him, his arms around their shoulders.

Janelle approached and knelt next to Chuck. She pressed her fingers to Samuel's neck below his jawline. "Nothing."

She pointed at the liquid pooled in the dirt beneath Samuel's body. It was dark red, almost black, its surface filmed. "He wouldn't have lived long with that much blood loss."

Chuck took Samuel's left hand in both of his. The skin of the hand was cold to the touch and ghostly white. Samuel's eyes, sunken in their sockets, gazed unseeing at the roof of the alcove twenty feet above. His right hand was deeply slashed between the thumb and forefinger, where he apparently had sought to defend himself from one of the blows of the hatchet. Another blow from the hatchet had ripped through his shirt and several of his ribs, exposing lung tissue beneath.

Chuck's breath caught in his throat. Samuel was dead, murdered in the same vicious manner as Joseph Cannon a hundred years ago. But Samuel's body had been left out in the open. As with Barney yesterday, Samuel's murderer had made no attempt to conceal the crime.

Logic said the killer already had left the canyon and driven away, leaving Samuel's pickup as the sole vehicle they'd encountered at the end of the dirt road. But if that was not the case, then there were all sorts of places for a killer to hide amid the ponderosas and thickets of scrub oak at the bottom of the canyon.

Chuck scanned the section of canyon floor visible from the alcove. Sunlight streamed through the tall ponderosas, speckling the ground. He spotted no signs of movement.

Janelle scrambled to her feet. "We have to get out of here. We have to leave. *Now.*"

Chuck nodded. "We have to get to the canyon rim and call this in."

He released Samuel's hand and turned to the girls and Clarence. Rosie's face was buried in her uncle's arms, but Carmelita looked past Chuck and Janelle, surveying the scene of the murder with cool eyes.

Chuck bit the inside of his cheek. Carmelita was doing what he should have done by now.

He turned back and studied the scene along with her—the entire scene, not just Samuel's dead body and the bloody hatchet.

The depression in the floor of the alcove remained as before, several feet deep, dirt mounded waist-high beside it.

He rose and stepped past Samuel's body to the edge of the cavity. The opening to the chamber at the bottom of the depression was the same size as yesterday, the sheered sticks and cracked mud lining its mouth as before. Through the opening, however, the position of Joseph Cannon's body in the crypt was different.

"Somebody moved the corpse," he said over his shoulder to the others.

Carmelita leaned forward, poised to approach the depression, but Chuck raised a hand to stop her. No need for her to see Samuel's maimed body any closer up.

"The corpse in the hole?" she asked, straightening.

Chuck peered through the opening at the body of Joseph Cannon. "He was on his back. Now he's on his side."

Joseph had been yanked sideways so roughly his body and clothing had come apart. The bones of his ribcage showed through rips in his shirt. His pants had fallen away from the lower half of his body, revealing his pelvis separated from his femur by several inches.

Icy fingers wrapped themselves around Chuck's stomach, making him shiver. Samuel's brutal murder and the rough treatment of Joseph Cannon's body were of a similar piece. He could think of only one answer that explained both actions. Someone must have believed the canopic jars were to be found in the secret chamber—jars so valuable they justified murder, along with ravaging a century-old corpse.

He checked the dirt floor of the alcove and sides of the depression for any telltale tracks of Samuel's killer or killers. But the floor and cavity were marked by the many feet of those who'd been here over the preceding two days, making it impossible to determine if any particular prints were associated specifically with Samuel's murder.

He slid to the bottom of the depression and directed the light of his phone through the opening and into the chamber. Joseph Cannon's bones glowed white in the light. Hard shadows cut from his contorted frame to the dusty floor of the vault.

Chuck steadied the beam. For most of the length of Joseph's body, the dust beneath the place where his corpse had lain for the past hundred years was marred by the recent movement. Beside where the young man's calves had lain, however, two undisturbed circles a few inches across were indented in the dusty soil. The circles were the size of the bases of Egyptian canopic jars—the likely size of Ancestral Puebloan canopic jars as well, if they existed.

Dropping to his knees, Chuck leaned his head into the opening and shone his light to illuminate the full interior of the chamber. As with the dirt beneath Joseph's corpse, the dusty soil immediately surrounding the young man's body was broken and disturbed. But beyond Joseph's head, at the far end of the vault, several more circles the same size as those beside his calves were indented in a patch of undisturbed soil. The circles formed a straight line across the floor of the chamber. The only other disturbances in the soil were from the wide-legged tracks of common darkling beetles, which had wandered past the circles, and the narrower tracks of rarer European meat beetles. Unlike the darkling beetle tracks, the tracks of the meat beetles passed directly over the circular indentations in the dusty floor of the chamber.

Chuck withdrew his head from the opening and sat back, trembling.

Samuel was dead. Any jars that had been in the chamber were now gone.

But Kyla had opened the vault yesterday, after which she'd been joined by Samuel and Ilona. That's when any jars hidden in the chamber would have been revealed and undoubtedly removed, which meant Samuel's brutal murder today was too late to have been part of any effort to steal the rumored—or now, based on the circles indented in the dusty floor of the secret vault, seemingly real—Ancestral Puebloan canopic jars.

All of which made no sense whatsoever.

"We have to go, Chuck," Janelle said to him from outside the depression.

He scrambled out of the cavity. "*Sí*," he agreed tersely.

Clarence swung Carmelita and Rosie away from the scene of Samuel's murder. "I'll take point," he said.

Lowering his arms from the girls' shoulders, he led the way back up the canyon along the base of the cliff.

"Why did we ever come here?" Rosie whimpered, a step behind Clarence.

Janelle put her arm around Rosie as they walked. "No one should have to see anything like that, *m'hija*."

"I feel bad for him."

"That's good to feel that way. That's how I feel at work when I see people who have been hurt or who have died. It's not easy to go through something like that, but then again, it shouldn't be."

Chuck said to Rosie from the end of the line, "I never should have brought you here today."

"No," said Carmelita, a step ahead of him. "It's good we came. We'll be able to tell the police what happened."

Rosie sniffled. "You think it'll help, Carm?"

"I'm sure it will."

Janelle fell back from the girls and Clarence and spoke softly to Chuck, so only he could hear. "Tell me more about Ilona, the woman from Finland."

Chuck slowed with Janelle. He kept his voice low as well. "She doesn't seem the ax-wielding type, if that's what you mean. Besides, she's tiny, barely a hundred pounds."

"What if she took him by surprise? I'm sure he trusted her. Judging by the depth of the injuries, it looks like the hatchet was really sharp. Killing him might have required less strength than you'd think."

"Regardless, it would have required complete insanity."

"How much do you really know about her?"

"Not a lot. But what I do know doesn't lend itself to her killing Samuel. She seemed perfectly sane when she was here in the canyon yesterday. Likewise when I met her in her room at the Strater this morning. Plus, she believes she has full legal rights to be excavating in the canyon. She told me Finland actually claims Gunnel Canyon as its own property. I can't imagine she's right, or that the United States ever would recognize such a claim. But from her point of view, whatever she discovers here is hers to do with as she pleases, no murder necessary." He shook his head. "We just need to get to the rim so we can call and let Sandra put the pieces together."

"Do you trust her?"

"Sandra?" Chuck ran a hand along the cliff wall, warm from the sun, as he walked. He hadn't yet had the chance to talk with Janelle about his meeting with his former girlfriend on the college campus. "You're the one who said *you* trusted her."

"I'm asking what you think. I was surprised by the fact that she came to get you in her personal car. As far as the timing goes, she could have driven straight from Beatrice's house to Clarence's apartment to pick you up."

"I can't for the life of me see her as Beatrice's attacker. I can't see her as Barney's killer either. And as far as Samuel is concerned, there wouldn't have been enough time for her to have come over here earlier today at any point."

"What about Michaela?"

"I can't think of any reason for her to be killing off her own employees."

"Unless Barney and Samuel got wind of something she didn't want them to know."

"Maybe she was planning to steal the canopic jars, and they found out."

"Money," Janelle said. "Greed."

"The strongest human emotion," Chuck agreed. "There's a fortune to be made selling the canopic jars on the black market."

"If the jars even exist."

"They very well might. Plus, in addition to any jars, the corpse is worth a lot of money, too. There definitely would be willing buyers out there for an authentic, mummified corpse from the Old West—particularly the body of an obvious victim of murder."

"That's so disgusting."

"People are messed up. Some people."

"Including whoever killed Samuel."

"And Barney. And whoever attacked Beatrice."

"So," Janelle reasoned, "after Kyla uncovered the corpse yesterday, Michaela came over here today to steal the corpse. Samuel tried to stop her, which forced her, in turn, to take the hatchet to him."

"But the corpse of Joseph Cannon is still there," Chuck countered. "She didn't take it. Besides which, your theory doesn't explain Barney's killing. Or how roughly Joseph Cannon's body was shoved aside, as if stealing it wasn't the primary objective."

"Maybe it all started with Barney. Had you ever talked with him about the consultation work you did on the repatriation of Esther and the other bodies?"

"I might have mentioned it in passing any number of times over the years. I honestly don't remember. There wouldn't have been any reason for me not to, though."

"How about Michaela? Could she have talked with Barney about your consulting work on the repatriation?"

"Sure. She knew all about it. Donald Cuthair recognized how ridiculous her idea was to hold a big, public event and make a spectacle out of the repatriation. He only consulted with me to make sure I didn't see it any differently. Even so, Michaela blamed me for putting the brakes on the event. All that was a long time ago, though."

"Everything was quiet all these years," Janelle reasoned, "until Ilona came along and stirred things up somehow."

"Maybe."

"I'm not ready to give her a pass. We know she heard about the canopic jars from the woman in Mancos and hired Southwest Archaeology Enterprises to help track them down. Michaela assigned Samuel to work with Ilona. The two of them hoped to find the jars in the alcove. Instead, Kyla found the body while Ilona and Samuel were on their way to the canyon, according to what they told you, which would have been about the same time Barney was killed in Durango."

"Or," Chuck said, "Ilona and Samuel were still in Durango when Kyla called to tell them she'd found the body, which somehow led them to break into our house and kill Barney." Chuck blew air through his lips. "The whole thing is just so far-fetched."

"Nothing I can think of makes any sense either."

"You seem to be stuck on Ilona, though."

"She's as logical a suspect to me as Michaela."

"Maybe Michaela's in on it with Ilona. Michaela is the most money-minded person I've ever met. She's been that way since the day she founded SAE."

"What if Ilona's the same? You don't really know what she's like."

"I do know what Jason is like, though. You do, too. We saw him throw those groceries at Audrey. I definitely could see him attacking Beatrice. I could see him attacking anyone, Samuel included."

Ahead, Clarence came to an abrupt halt at the foot of the slot leading to the canyon rim. He held up his hand for silence and stared up the fissure, the girls bunched behind him.

Chuck stopped with Janelle thirty feet from the cleft. Clarence whirled and herded the girls back along the base of the canyon wall toward Chuck and Janelle, his face white.

24

"Someone's coming," Clarence whispered urgently to Chuck and Janelle. "They're way up in the top of the crack. They weren't in sight yet, but I heard their feet on the rock."

Chuck pivoted and took the lead. Janelle, Clarence, and the girls followed him as he ran back down the canyon, his legs churning. Who was descending the slot into the canyon? He'd assumed Samuel's murderer or murderers had fled. But what if they'd run off at first, and now, with the benefit of hindsight and clearer heads, were returning to eliminate the evidence of their crime?

Or, what if Samuel's killer or killers had fled down Gunnel Canyon from the murder scene to Long Canyon, circled back to the end of the dirt road via the established trail, come upon Janelle's SUV and Clarence's sedan parked at the end of the road—and were now returning to Gunnel Canyon in search of the cars' occupants?

They had to hide, all five of them, somewhere in the narrow canyon.

His sneakers left deep gouges in the sandy soil as he sprinted along the base of the cliff. He glanced back. The others were leaving obvious prints in the sand as they ran, too.

For now, as they followed the same route trod by Samuel, Ilona, and Kyla over the last couple of days, their footprints were simply more among many. Beyond the alcove, however, their prints would clearly reveal the direction of their desperate flight.

Chuck scanned the route ahead as he ran, searching for a way to conceal their presence in the canyon bottom before they ventured beyond the alcove. He rounded a bend in the canyon, the others close behind. A pair of massive ponderosas grew close against the canyon wall fifty feet ahead. On the far side of the trees, an opening stretched from the wall of the canyon. Tufted grass, brown with autumn, filled the opening, which extended to a thicket of scrub oak. Beyond the oak thicket, the dirt-walled water drainage that funneled runoff down the gorge cut into the canyon floor. He sprinted past the two ponderosas and stopped at the edge of the grassy opening.

"We'll cross here," he whispered to the others when they reached him. "Take big steps. Everyone needs to go a different way across."

Janelle walked first through the grass away from the base of the cliff. She reached the stand of oak brush on the far side of the opening and turned to face the others as they imitated her, each taking big strides via a different route across the opening.

Chuck crossed last. He looked back from the shade of the spreading oak branches. Only moderate signs of their passage showed in the grass—broken stems and a couple of tufts crushed by their striding feet.

"That's the best we can do," he said softly. "They shouldn't notice. They'll be fixated on the alcove."

"Let's go," Rosie hissed, bouncing on her toes. "*Vamanos.* Hurry, hurry, hurry."

Taking Rosie's hand, Chuck slipped with her into the stand of scrub oak. They passed through the trees to the edge of the dirt-walled gully eroded down the middle of the otherwise flat floor of the canyon. The intermittent stream course, ten feet deep by fifteen feet wide, was dry now, weeks after the end of the summer thunderstorm season.

Chuck plunged with Rosie off the gully's crumbly edge. They dug their heels into the soil bank, half-walking, half-sliding to the bottom of the dry water course. Janelle, Clarence, and Carmelita followed, quietly descending the side of the defile. Chuck exhaled as they gathered on the pebble-strewn bottom of the narrow drainage, its walls rising several feet above their heads. They were out of sight of whoever was descending into the canyon. Provided their passage across the grassy opening went unnoticed, they were safe—for the time being, at least.

"We should be okay here," Chuck whispered.

Janelle scowled. "We're not the least bit okay here," she said softly but vehemently. "We're trapped."

"Not for long."

"What do you mean?"

"I'll head downstream until I'm even with the alcove. I'll keep watch until I see who's coming. If they're okay, we can join them and sound the alarm."

"And if they're not okay?"

"Then I'll . . . I'll . . ."

"That's what I thought." Janelle shook her head decisively. "The rest of us will not wait here while you go sneaking off alone."

"What, then?"

She put her thumbnail to her chin, frowning. "We can't wait around for someone else to sound the alarm. We're alone. We have no idea who or what we're facing. We have to get help headed our way."

At Janelle's side, Clarence nodded firmly. "What she says," he whispered.

"But we don't dare try to sneak back up the slot," Chuck said. "We'd be stuck in there if anyone came along, from below or above."

Clarence's breathing slowed. "Now that we're out of sight, I think the five of us shouldn't move around together very much," he said. "There's too much risk that we'll make noise as a group and give ourselves away." He put his hand to his chest. "But I could stay in this ditch and work my way up the canyon past the slot on my own. There's sure to be an easy way out at the head of the canyon."

Chuck frowned at him. "You barely made it down the slot to begin with. Do you really think you can find a place to climb out on your own somewhere farther up the canyon?"

Carmelita raised her hand. "I'll go, too," she said softly. "I'll get us out."

Clarence looked at Chuck. "If anyone can find us a way out of here, Carm can." He turned to Janelle. "We'll get to the rim and make the call."

Chuck nodded at Janelle.

She looked Carmelita in the eye. "You have to do as your uncle says."

Carmelita raised and lowered her chin resolutely.

"Be careful, Carm," Rosie whispered to her sister, her voice shaking.

"You, too," Carmelita replied.

She held out her fist and Rosie bumped it with her own.

Clarence and Carmelita departed up the walled gully, treading in silence on the sandy bottom of the drainage.

Chuck surveyed the rim of the defile above. He, Janelle, and Rosie were hidden from the person or persons Clarence had heard descending the slot from the canyon rim. They—whoever they were—must have reached the bottom of the cleft by now and almost certainly were headed for the alcove.

"You and Rosie wait here," Chuck whispered to Janelle. "I'll be right—"

She cut in. "We already went through this. We're coming with you."

"All right," he relented. "Follow me." He leaned down to Rosie. "Not a peep, okay?"

She circled her thumb and forefinger and nodded, her face grave.

* * *

Chuck's feet dug into the sand and pebbles lining the drainage bottom as he led Rosie and Janelle down the gully. Above the defile's dirt walls, the tops of the tallest ponderosas etched the sky.

Chuck stopped every couple hundred feet to climb the side of the gully and peer across the canyon floor. The first three times he peeked out, he saw only ponderosas and scrub oak rustling in the wind. The fourth time he looked, he spotted other movement as well.

On the far side of a dense thicket of scrub oak, visible only as a shadowy form, someone walked along the base of the cliff in the direction of the alcove.

Chuck froze, his eyes just above the floor of the canyon. Shielded by the screen of brushy trees, the person was unidentifiable.

Chuck slid back down the bank to Janelle and Rosie. "I spotted them," he whispered. "They're almost to the alcove."

"Them?" Janelle asked.

"One person. I can't tell who it is." He tilted his head down the drainage. "This way."

He scurried down the defile, trailed by Janelle and Rosie, until he judged their position to be even with the alcove. He dug his toes into the soil, climbing the dirt embankment once more, and slowly raised his head until his eyes were above the edge of the gully. As he'd calculated, he was looking directly at the mouth of the alcove. Widely spaced ponderosas stood between him and the foot of the cliff, affording him a good view of the recess.

He drew a startled breath at what he did not see in the cavern-like space.

25

The alcove itself appeared as it had when Chuck first had laid eyes on it yesterday with Rosie.

Dirt remained piled beside the depression in the alcove floor. But Samuel's mutilated body, which had lain beside the dirt pile just a short while ago, was gone. The bloodied hatchet was gone, too. The person Chuck had spied approaching the alcove from up the canyon moments ago was nowhere in sight, either.

Chuck slid back down to the bottom of the defile. Putting his mouth to Janelle's ear, he described the scene to her.

When he finished, she stepped back, searching his eyes.

"Samuel's body is gone," he repeated, whispering. "It's *gone.*"

"Do you think they could have been watching us?" she asked softly in reply. "What if, after we left, they came back, hid everything, and took off again? They'd have headed down the canyon, the opposite direction from the way we went."

"If they were watching us, I don't think they'd have allowed us to leave. Not after what we saw. They'd have tried to stop us."

"There were several of us, though. If there was only one of them, and they'd dropped the hatchet and were otherwise unarmed . . ."

"Even if you're right, they couldn't have hidden Samuel's body very well in just the last few minutes."

"Maybe they were buying themselves some time. Or maybe they're just insane, and there's less sense to what they're doing than we're giving them credit for."

"Insane is right, given what they did to Samuel." Chuck's thoughts turned to the person he'd spotted hiking down the canyon moments ago. "Whoever showed up just now must be in on it with them. They must have kept going, too, through the alcove and on down the canyon. It'd be easy to reach Long Canyon and circle back to the end of the road on the trail."

Janelle's jaw muscles twitched. "They'll get away."

"Not if Clarence and Carmelita call 911 in time. It's an hour's drive to the park exit."

"Carm," she said, her voice quavering. "*M'hija.*"

"She's with Clarence," Chuck told her. "Plus, they're going the other direction." He aimed a thumb over his shoulder at the alcove. "Away from all of this."

Rosie looked up at him. Tears glimmered in her eyes. He put his hand on her head and rocked her reassuringly. "It looks like we're in the clear down here in the canyon now," he said. He turned back to Janelle. "How about if we head over to the alcove to see if we can learn anything? Then we'll head back up to the rim, carefully."

"*And* find Carm and Clarence," Janelle said. Her gaze rose to the top of the gully. "You really think they're gone?"

"They're on the run, like you said. They have to be at this point."

Janelle raised and lowered her chin resolutely. "Okay."

Chuck scrambled back up the bank to eye level. The alcove remained empty, the canyon devoid of movement. He clambered out of the defile and helped Janelle and Rosie up to the floor of the canyon with him. He stole toward the alcove, bent double, with Janelle and Rosie close behind.

He was nearly to the recess when a scrabbling noise reached his ears. He stopped, shooting out a hand to halt Janelle and Rosie beside him.

The noise was coming from the depression in the floor of the alcove.

* * *

They were in full view, bathed in sunlight, at the mouth of the alcove. He searched the canyon floor around him, his eyes darting. A broken ponderosa branch the length and girth of a baseball bat lay beneath one of the trees. He hurried to it, picked it up, and tiptoed into the alcove, wielding the makeshift weapon in his hand.

The scratching noise continued in the depression. Someone, or some creature, was rooting around in the neck-deep cavity. Chuck raised the branch above his head, crept to the edge of the depression, and peeked in.

Kyla lay on her stomach at the bottom of the cavity, reaching her arm through the opening into the hidden chamber.

"Hey," Chuck said.

Kyla's body tensed. She yanked her arm out of the vault, tumbled backward, and cowered at the bottom of the depression.

"Jesus!" she exclaimed, her eyes on the club held aloft in Chuck's hand. "What the hell are you doing with that? Why are you here?"

"That's what I want to know about you."

"I'm doing exactly what I'm supposed to be doing."

Chuck lowered the branch. He stared at her as she continued.

"Samuel wanted me to help him make sure everything was—"

He raised his hand, silencing her, and scrutinized the floor of the alcove beside the depression where, thirty minutes ago, Samuel's dead body had lain in a pool of blood.

Marks in the dirt revealed that Samuel's body had been dragged around the edge of the cavity, out of the alcove, and on down the canyon. Someone had scattered dirt over the pool of blood that remained. The layer of dirt largely concealed the dark liquid. In a couple of places, however, blood seeped through the covering of dirt, black blotches saturating the brown soil.

"You don't know what's happened, do you?" Chuck asked Kyla.

"What don't I know?" she demanded from the bottom of the depression. "That someone moved the body? Of course, I've seen it. Somebody trashed the corpse. That's why I'm down here. I'm trying to figure out what they were up to." Her eyes narrowed as she looked up at Chuck. "It's you. You did it, didn't you?"

Chuck flicked the end of the branch, dismissing her accusation. "Samuel's dead," he told her.

Blood drained from her face. "Samuel? He's . . . he's *what*?"

"Someone killed him."

She scrambled out of the depression and gasped at the sight of Janelle and Rosie standing at the mouth of the alcove.

Rosie nodded at Kyla. "They cut him with an ax," she said.

Kyla whirled to Chuck. "I don't believe it."

"I wish it weren't true."

"I'm supposed to meet Samuel here. Instead of shutting down the dig, he said we needed to hurry up and finish it. He said Ilona has moved up her timetable, that she wants to get back to Europe as fast as she can."

"She does, does she?"

Chuck stepped over the hidden pool of blood. The metallic odor of the drying liquid rose into the air, stinging his nostrils. He trailed the drag marks made by Samuel's body past the depression and out of the alcove to a stand of scrub oak a hundred feet down the canyon. Kyla followed, stopping beside him at the edge of the thicket.

Samuel lay crumpled on the ground in the trees, half-hidden beneath broken oak branches and handfuls of fallen leaves that had been tossed over his body. Visible between the branches and leaves, his mouth, or what was left of it, hung open in silent terror.

A raven cawed, its hoarse cry carrying across the canyon from the opposite cliff. A squirrel chattered in the branches of a ponderosa towering high above the oak thicket. Chuck looked up through the fluttering oak leaves, catching sight of the squirrel as it leapt from one branch to another in the tall pine.

He dropped his eyes to Samuel's body. The deaths of Samuel and Barney were related. They had to be. Beyond that, what information did he have to go on?

One fact was reassuring: the killer or killers had abandoned the scenes of both murders, providing some small level of comfort as he stood unarmed in the bottom of the canyon with Janelle and Rosie.

Kyla put a hand to her mouth. She fell to her knees and vomited in the dirt beside Samuel's body. She wiped her mouth as she climbed back to her feet. "We have to get out of here," she said to Chuck. "It's not safe."

"This may be the safest place we could possibly be right now." He pointed past Samuel's body and on down Gunnel Canyon toward Long Canyon. "Whoever did this went that way. They'll be circling around and returning to the end of the road. The last thing we want to do is head back up there."

Janelle and Rosie approached the thicket. They stopped in the shade beneath the oak branches next to Chuck and Kyla. Janelle aimed a finger into the stand of scrub oak. The hatchet lay in the shadows where she pointed, abandoned next to Samuel's body.

"Unlike with Barney," Janelle said, "whoever did this didn't use a gun. And they left the hatchet behind."

"Two different murderers?" Chuck asked her.

"Different circumstances, anyway." A tremor entered her

209

voice. "Clarence and Carmelita don't know that whoever did this is headed for the end of the road. When they get out of the canyon and make the phone call, they may well head for the end of the road themselves."

Chuck shook. "You're right. We have to warn them."

A stick snapped behind him. "You're not going anywhere."

26

Chuck spun. Michaela McDermott stood at the base of the cliff on the far side of the recess.

He cursed. *Of course.*

He'd witnessed Michaela's greed all these years, her disregard for her employees, her dedication only to the ongoing growth of Southwest Archaeology Enterprises.

Michaela was all about making money. She was *only* about making money. It made perfect sense, then, that when presented with the biggest potential payoff of her career here in Gunnel Canyon, she'd crossed the line from greed-monger to murderer.

"*You*," Chuck growled at her.

Michaela wore a short-sleeved, plaid blouse, pressed slacks, and purple trail-running shoes.

Chuck edged Rosie behind him as a slender, long-limbed woman in a police uniform stepped to Michaela's side.

Chuck gawked at her. *Sandra.* How could she possibly be involved in Samuel's murder? How could he have been so utterly mistaken about her?

"What?" she asked in response to his look, her brow furrowed in what appeared to be innocent questioning.

He quaked. Was he wrong about Sandra? Did she not understand what Michaela was up to?

Sandra wore her service pistol at her waist. Michaela appeared to be unarmed.

Chuck glanced over his shoulder in the direction Samuel's killer or killers had departed after hiding Samuel's body just moments ago. He looked back at Michaela and Sandra, just arrived at the alcove from up the canyon.

The two of them couldn't possibly have dragged Samuel's body into the scrub oak thicket, made their way back up the canyon unseen, and returned here, to the alcove, all in just the last few minutes. Neither of them was Samuel's murderer.

But there was still Barney's murder to consider.

Sandra's sincere, one-word question was enough to convince Chuck of her innocence. But her handgun was belted at her waist, inches from Michaela. With a quick grab, the gun would be in Michaela's hands.

The owner of Southwest Archaeology Enterprises hadn't killed Samuel. But what if she had directed the act? What if Michaela somehow was responsible for Barney's death as well?

And what of Kyla? She claimed Samuel had summoned her to the alcove. But what if she was here on Michaela's orders, or the orders of someone else?

The Harvard fellow easily could have dragged Samuel's body into the thicket before returning to the depression in the floor of the alcove for a final search of the hidden chamber.

Chuck shot a sidelong glance at her. No telltale blood splattered her clothing. Could she possibly have remained clean while hacking Samuel to death? Had she changed her clothes afterward?

Chuck caught Sandra's eye and dipped his head, motioning her away from Michaela.

Sandra stepped sideways, putting space between herself and the SAE owner, and raised her hand to the butt of her gun.

"Two of your employees are dead," Chuck said to Michaela. "I don't think you killed them outright, but I do think your actions played a role in their deaths."

Michaela's eyes grew large. "What do you mean, *two* of my employees?"

"Samuel."

Sandra stared at the dirt-covered puddle of blood next to the depression in the floor of the alcove. "Oh, dear God," she said.

She hurried to the edge of the depression and looked into it.

"Where?" she demanded, turning to Chuck. "How?"

"The same as Joseph Cannon." He pointed behind him. "His body is back there in the trees."

Michaela blanched, her mouth falling open. "Samuel?" Her eyes brimmed with tears. "Please, God. No."

She and Sandra followed the drag marks to the oak thicket. They stood over Samuel's maimed body. Michaela moaned. Sandra spun, searching the canyon, her fingers now wrapped around the handle of her gun.

"It's just us," Chuck told her. "He, she, they—whoever it was—took off." He avoided looking at Kyla. "They went down the canyon."

Sandra's eyebrows rose. "They'll circle around to the road."

"We're thinking the same thing."

Releasing her gun, she pulled her phone from her pocket.

"That'll only work up on the rim," Chuck said. "Clarence and Carm are on their way to call for help. They should be out of the canyon by now."

Sandra's mouth fell open. "Carmelita? Your daughter?"

"We were just heading up to warn them when you showed up."

"We have to go," Sandra said. "Now." Shoving her phone back in her pocket, she charged back to the alcove and on up the canyon.

Chuck turned to Rosie. "How fast can you run?"

She pumped her fists at her sides. "Fast, fast, super fast."

"Stick with me."

Michaela approached from the oak thicket. Chuck looked at her and Kyla, then at Janelle. He sprinted across the floor of the alcove. Rosie fell in behind him. He looked back as he left the recess. Kyla and Michaela trailed Rosie. Janelle took up the rear, tracking the two women as he'd hoped.

He wove through the ponderosas along the base of the cliff, gripping the branch in his hand like an oversized relay baton. Ahead, Sandra settled into a ground-eating lope. He matched her pace, Rosie on his heels.

Sandra reached the bottom of the walled slot leading to the canyon rim. Chuck arrived with Rosie at the base of the cleft seconds later. Sandra was twenty feet up the slot and climbing fast. He dropped his makeshift club and clambered after her, jamming his fingers into cracks in the facing stone walls to haul himself upward.

Rosie panted as she climbed behind him. "Wait up," she called breathlessly.

He turned sideways in the cleft and reached a hand down to her. "You're doing great," he said as he pulled her up to him.

Above, Sandra gained headway on them.

Chuck climbed several more feet and again stopped to help Rosie.

From the top of the cleft, a gunshot rang out.

27

Sandra screamed and tumbled backward. She gripped her upper arm and pinballed down the narrow cleft, her head striking one wall of the slot, then the other.

Chuck leapt up the cleft toward Sandra. Her knee clipped a rocky outcrop and she cartwheeled head over heels straight at him. He caught her in his arms, the weight of her body propelling him backward. He wedged himself sideways in the cleft, halting their plunge but wrenching his shoulder and ripping the skin from his elbows in the process.

Rosie climbed toward them, panting.

"No!" Chuck cried to her. "Down! We've got to get out of here!"

A second shot rang out. The bullet struck the stone wall above them and ricocheted harmlessly out of the cleft. The shooter seemed to be firing blindly, from a concealed position.

Rosie hurried back down the slot. Michaela sprinted past the base of the cleft, in sight for less than a second as she fled on up the canyon. Kyla and Janelle appeared at the bottom of the slot. Janelle helped Rosie to the canyon floor and the two of them headed up the canyon after Michaela. Kyla scrambled up the walled slot to Sandra and Chuck.

Sandra moaned in Chuck's arms, her eyes closed. Her forehead was deeply bruised. Blood seeped between her fingers, still wrapped around her bicep.

Kyla slipped past Chuck, placing herself directly in the line of fire from above, and grasped Sandra's ankles. "Ready," she said, lifting.

A third gunshot rang out. This one was off target as well, zinging out of the cleft high above their heads. Kyla ducked but maintained her grip on Sandra's legs.

Chuck lifted Sandra in his arms, wincing as pain surged through his shoulder. He backed down the slot with Kyla holding Sandra's ankles and following.

He scanned the canyon floor from the foot of the cleft. Janelle, Rosie, and Michaela were nowhere in sight, but they'd headed up the canyon from the bottom of the slot.

He sped after them, hurrying backward along the base of the cliff with Sandra in his arms and Kyla at Sandra's legs. His heel struck a rock protruding from the sand and he stumbled, nearly falling. He caught himself and looked over his shoulder as he backed around a bulge in the cliff that marked a bend in the canyon. Beyond the bend, the top of the canyon wall was lined with boulders worn out of the soft sandstone of the mesa but not yet tumbled from a section of cliff that overhung the canyon floor. Beneath the overhang, across a stretch of bare sand, a small alcove opened at the base of the canyon wall, its roof no higher than Chuck's chest.

"In here," Janelle called from the shadowed recess.

Chuck backed across the sandy opening with Kyla, Sandra suspended between them. He lowered Sandra close to the ground and, ducking his head, peered into the alcove. The recess was a dozen feet deep and twenty feet long, resembling the small, roofed openings he and Rosie had encountered along the base of the Falls Creek escarpment. The ammonia-like scent of rodent droppings filled the air in the recess. Janelle crouched in the shadowed space next to Rosie, their heads inches from the roof.

Still ducking, Chuck backed into the recess. Kyla followed, gripping Sandra's legs. They lay Sandra on the dirt floor at the feet of Janelle and Rosie.

Michaela sat in near-darkness against the back wall, her legs drawn to her chest, her eyes big and round and unblinking.

Janelle probed Sandra's head and neck. Her fingers came away from the examination free of blood.

"Good," she commented.

She pressed two fingertips to Sandra's neck below the jawline.

"Steady. Strong."

Sandra continued to grasp her bloody upper arm with her fingers. Janelle pried them free one by one. Sandra opened her eyes and grimaced, her face twisting. Her eyes grew unfocused and fell closed once more.

Janelle looked at Chuck. "She must be concussed. It's good that she's at least showing signs of consciousness."

Sandra's eyes blinked open. "Thank you," she whispered to Janelle.

"No," Janelle said. "Thank *you*. You took one for the rest of us."

Sandra struggled to sit up. "The shooter . . ."

Janelle pressed her gently back to the ground. "You're okay now."

Sandra closed her eyes. Though shallow, her breaths were smooth and regular.

Chuck stared at the open stretch of canyon floor beyond the unprotected mouth of the alcove. They were not safe from the shooter here. He unsnapped the leather stay over the gun strapped at Sandra's waist and slipped the gun from its holster. Pivoting with the pistol in his hand, he swept the canyon floor with his eyes but spotted nothing.

Kyla crawled to Chuck's side. "What next?"

"I don't think the shooter will dare come down the slot," he told her. "It's too exposed. But someone needs to guard it just in case."

"I'm on it," Kyla said.

Her eyes went to the gun in Chuck's hand.

"Sorry." Even after her help with Sandra, he wasn't about to trust the weapon to her. "I still need to get out of the canyon. I'll have to be armed up there. But I dropped my club at the bottom of the slot."

Kyla huffed. "That'll have to do."

She left the alcove and disappeared back around the bend in the canyon toward the cleft.

Janelle locked eyes with Chuck. "You have to get up there. *Carm.*"

"She and Clarence will have gone to ground at the sound of the gunshots."

"Assuming they were still safe at that point."

Chuck tipped his head to her in acknowledgment. "I just need the answers to a couple of questions, so I'll know what I'm facing when I get up there."

He turned to Michaela.

She tightened her arms around her shins, tugging her knees tight to her upper body.

"You brought this on yourself," he told her. "On all of us."

Her face was drained of blood, her eyes haunted. She didn't respond.

"I need to know," he demanded. "The jars."

Michaela loosened her arms from around her legs, hands falling to her sides. "You know how it is," she said, her voice so soft the words were barely audible. "Each contract hardly covers the expenses of the one before it. It's a never-ending game of catchup."

"For you."

Her eyes went to the dirt floor. "Yes," she admitted. "For me."

"Your bids were always too low."

"That's how you win them." She dug her fingers into the dusty soil on either side of her. "That's how I made it work, for a long time."

"Your mansion on the hill, your penthouse office."

Michaela rotated her hands. Dirt trailed from her fingers. "All I ever did was stay a step ahead of the banks—until last year, when everything caught up with me." She curled her hands into fists. "I kept bidding lower, winning more contracts, hiring more people. Then lower. Lower. I had to get to a turnaround point. I *had* to."

"Who'd you sell your soul to, Michaela?"

She turned her face to the mouth of the recess, the sun-drenched canyon beyond. "I'd worked so hard, for so many years. I was going to lose it all, everything."

"Not your workers. You paid them next to nothing. They had nothing to lose."

"Ours is a labor of love," she said, her eyes coming back to Chuck and her voice growing stronger. "You know that as well as I do. Getting paid anything for what we do is a gift."

"What'd you do, Michaela?"

"I had to find a way out."

"Which Ilona provided."

Blood rose in Michaela's cheeks, forming matching red dots high on her cheekbones. "You have no idea how much money is sloshing around right now, looking for places to hide. It's pouring out of Russia, the Middle East, China. There are only so many London condos to buy, only so many Krugerrands. So the money turns to art . . ."

". . . and antiquities," Chuck finished for her. "Artifacts."

She nodded, her head falling so low her chin touched her chest.

"Ilona," Chuck urged.

Michaela raised her head. "She's not a crook, despite what you think."

"But she offered you access to crooks."

"You already know everything."

"I'm getting the idea."

"Ilona was the first to mention the canopic jars to me."

"They're real?"

Michaela nodded. "They exist."

"Whoa," Rosie breathed.

28

"There's a journal," Michaela said.

Chuck frowned. "A journal?"

"Joseph Cannon's. He was called Joey."

"The corpse."

"He's why I came out here today. Samuel called me before he . . . before . . ." Her voice faltered.

"Why is he dead, Michaela? Who killed him?"

"That's just it," she said plaintively. "I don't know."

"Who was shooting at us just now?"

"I don't know that either. It was supposed to be just Sandra and me. I called her after Samuel called me. I knew she'd want to see what he had to show us."

"Which was what?"

"Samuel felt, as I did, that the jars were the key to Barney's death." She swallowed, her eyes downcast. "When Ilona contacted me from Helsinki, I saw a way out. I would bend the rules just once. I was sure there would be enough jars for the scholars and for me, too."

"Enough for you to sell on the black market and get yourself out of debt," Chuck said, disgust filling his voice.

"Yes," Michaela admitted.

"Did Ilona know?"

"I'm sure she suspected. But this was a big opportunity for her, too. It was going to be so easy."

"You saw dollar signs. You invited Ilona to come to Mesa Verde. You'd grab the jars, divvy them between you, with nobody the wiser."

Michaela nodded, her jaw stiff. Then she shook her head. "It got out of control so fast. I figured I could handle Samuel, but he brought in Kyla without even asking me."

"Somebody else got wind of it, too."

She nodded again.

"Who?"

She looked at Sandra, sprawled on her back in the dirt. "I told you," she said, her gaze rising to Chuck and her voice breaking. "I don't know."

"Barney and Samuel are dead because of you. Sandra's lucky to be alive."

"And," Janelle said to Chuck, "Carm and Clarence are up on the canyon rim, unarmed."

"Right," he said to her. He turned back to Michaela. "What else?"

She wagged her head. "I'm sorry. I'm just so sorry."

"Sorry means nothing," he spat. He turned to Janelle. "I'll track Clarence and Carm to the head of the canyon. I'll make sure they're safe, and I'll make sure help is on the way. Then I'll come right back down here."

"You have to stay safe yourself."

He hefted Sandra's gun. "I've got this." He gripped Rosie's arm with his free hand. "Take care of your *mamá* for me, will you?"

"Yes, Daddy," she replied with a solemn nod.

He pressed the safety lever on Sandra's pistol, assuring it was engaged, and slipped the gun into his waistband at the small of his back. He crawled out of the alcove and raced up the canyon, staying close against the canyon wall to remain out of sight of anyone above.

As he approached the head of the canyon, the opposing cliff walls grew lower and closer together, rising less than twenty feet above his head and facing each other from little more than fifty feet apart. The dirt-walled gully in the middle of the canyon floor disappeared and two sets of footprints marked the sandy bottom of the narrowing ravine—the small prints of Carmelita's sneakers and Clarence's larger boot prints. Chuck followed the tracks up and out of the canyon, bypassing fallen boulders and lifting himself over waist-high ledges covered in windblown sand. Reaching the canyon rim, he scurried into the surrounding piñon-juniper forest.

He didn't call 911. The need to maintain silence was paramount. Besides, Clarence and Carmelita would have alerted the authorities by now.

A layer of dried needles covered the ground beneath the trees, the forest duff revealing no tracks to indicate the direction Clarence and Carmelita had gone when they'd left the canyon.

His back to the afternoon sun, Chuck headed east through the forest in the general direction of the parking spots at the end of the dirt road. He pulled the pistol from his waistband, clicked off its safety, and held the gun in front of him, peering around him, his head swiveling, as he slipped through the trees.

He placed each step with care, avoiding sticks that would snap noisily underfoot, and halted every minute or so to look and listen before resuming his stealthy advance.

After ten minutes of slow progress, he spotted a flash of sunlight off the window of a vehicle some fifty yards ahead. He stopped and waited, hoping for a sound, a sign of movement, anything that might guide his next action.

Seconds passed. A minute.

The breeze sighed through the branches. Sparrows chirped overhead.

He couldn't wait any longer. He took a steadying breath and advanced toward the vehicle, each step slower than the last. He extended the gun before him, scanning the forest ahead.

An older-model pickup truck, white, two-wheel drive, its rusted body squared at the corners and its frame set low to the ground, sat deep in the woods a hundred feet off the dirt road. Rather than in the graveled area at the end of the graded dirt road, the truck was parked in the forest well before the end of the dead-end road, out of sight of anyone driving past.

Chuck stole to the pickup. Its doors were locked. Inside, the truck's cracked dashboard was clear of items, the black vinyl seat empty. The bed of the truck, scratched and rusted, contained ranch implements—a hoe, a hard-tined rake, and a pair of shovels. All the implements were worn and dirt-encrusted from use. The forest floor around the vehicle, carpeted with piñon needles, was free of footprints.

Chuck put his hand on the hood of the truck. The white metal was cool to the touch; the pickup had been parked here for some time.

He turned a slow circle. No sound. No movement. Nothing.

He followed the twin impressions of the pickup's tires pressed into the needle-covered forest floor back to the dirt road. Remaining in the cover of the forest, he paralleled the road toward the turnaround and parking area at the road's end.

Ahead, sunlight flashed off the chrome and glass of a number of vehicles now parked at the end of the road. He ducked low and continued his slow, careful approach. He saw as he drew nearer that Janelle's mini SUV was parked beside Clarence's battered sedan. Another vehicle was now there as well, this one a luxurious German SUV, its pearl finish gleaming in the sun. The pricey sport utility vehicle had to be Michaela's, having brought her and Sandra there from Durango.

He tiptoed nearer. Samuel's black pickup truck sat beyond Michaela's SUV. Parked beside Samuel's truck was the lime-green subcompact that had been parked there yesterday—Kyla's rental car, no doubt.

The five cars at the end of the road accounted for everyone Chuck knew to be on Wetherill Mesa, which meant the shooter must have driven the old pickup hidden back up the road in the forest.

The fact that no more gunshots had sounded from the mesa top was a relief. But where was the shooter now? Why was the shooter's car still hidden in the trees? After the shot that wounded Sandra, the errant shots that followed seemed to have been a stalling tactic, after which the shooter should have retreated to the hidden truck and sped away.

And what of Carmelita and Clarence? Certainly, in the aftermath of the gunshots, they were hiding somewhere in the trees. Chuck willed them to remain hidden as he crept up to the cars parked at the end of the road.

He peered into each of the vehicles in turn. All were empty, their occupants scattered—Samuel dead, his mutilated body in Gunnel Canyon; Janelle, Rosie, Sandra, and Michaela concealed in the low-roofed alcove in the upper reaches of the canyon; Kyla guarding the base of the slot in the canyon wall; and Clarence and Carmelita hunkered somewhere in the forest atop the mesa.

Chuck straightened beside Samuel's truck. His best option at this point, he decided, was to return to the head of the slot leading into Gunnel Canyon, the shooter's last known location.

"Don't move," said a voice behind him.

29

He tightened his shoulders, preparing to spin with Sandra's pistol in his hand.

"I said *don't move*," commanded the voice, that of a female.

He froze.

"I'm warning you. Stay put."

The voice was rough like sandpaper—and familiar. It was that of Elizabeth Mantry, the woman from Mancos.

A circle of cold metal pressed against the back of Chuck's head. A hand reached past him and removed Sandra's pistol from his grip.

The gun disappeared behind him and the circle of metal left his skull.

"All right. Turn around. Slowly."

Chuck pivoted. Elizabeth faced him from several feet away. She had straw-colored hair, cut short, barely covering her ears. She wore faded jeans, leather boots, and a denim work shirt. Her muscled forearms extended from the rolled sleeves of her shirt. Her gray eyes glinted with malice. Blotches of dark red splattered her shirt and pants and the toes of her boots.

Elizabeth looked to be in her forties. She held a shiny carpentry nail in her left hand and Sandra's gun, its barrel trained on Chuck's stomach, in her right. The nail matched the one Chuck had retrieved from the park road yesterday, its head wide enough to have created the sensation of a gun barrel pressed against the back of his skull.

"Elizabeth Mantry," Chuck said.

"Chuck Bender," she responded.

"You hid here, behind the cars, waiting for me?"

She nodded, her head rocking as if on a spring. "I knew somebody would be coming. I figured it would be you."

"How do you know who I am?"

"From your picture on your website."

"You're a murderer."

She shrugged. "I'm my great-great-uncle's keeper."

"Joseph Cannon."

"Joey," she confirmed with another springy nod. "He was sixteen when he died. According to what he wrote, his little brother—my great-grandfather Carl—was jealous as all get-out when he rode off to go to work for Gustaf Nordenskiöld. But when Joey never returned, I'm sure Grandpa Carl realized how lucky he was to have been left behind."

"And now, a century later, you're killing others to avenge your uncle's death."

"The better way to say it would be that I recognized a unique opportunity to *take advantage* of my uncle's death."

"Joseph's journal," Chuck said. "Where'd you find it?" He had to keep her engaged. If she was speaking, she wasn't shooting.

"It's not really a journal. It's a packet of papers. I found them tucked away with my grandmother's things after she passed. Naturally, I was curious. They were notes Joey wrote about himself and his life on mismatched pieces of this and that. They gave a pretty clear picture of who he was—how much he hated the farm, his excitement at being hired by Nordenskiöld, and a final paragraph about how lucky he was to have been asked to perform a secret dig at the far western end of the mesa."

"The secret dig was aimed at finding canopic jars. You're still trying to find them a century later."

She nodded, her chin bouncing.

"Did he mention the jars in his notes?"

"Only the dig."

"How'd you learn about them?"

"From Ilona Koskinen. She got hold of me."

"She said it was *you* who contacted *her*."

Elizabeth's eyes darkened. "The little snake. That's a lie. She was going through Nordenskiöld's papers at her museum. No one in Finland had ever looked at them very closely before she went through them. They turned out to be quite informative."

"But Gustaf published his book, *The Cliff Dwellers of Mesa Verde*, after he returned from Europe. He finished it before tuberculosis killed him. It laid out all his findings and what he believed they revealed about Ancestral Puebloan culture. Surely, he'd have included in it any information he had about the existence of Ancestral Puebloan canopic jars."

"As it turns out, Gustaf didn't tell the whole story in *Cliff Dwellers*."

"You're referring to the secret dig, the one he assigned to your uncle."

Elizabeth's chin bobbed behind the outthrust gun. "He had good reason not to tell that part."

Chuck pictured the cleaved head of Joey Cannon, the young man's body hidden in the secret chamber in Gunnel Canyon all these years. Hidden, yes, but not forgotten. "Gustaf suspected what had become of your uncle, didn't he? He figured your uncle had been murdered, and he didn't want what had happened to Joey to come back to him in Europe."

"Impressive," Elizabeth said, ticking the barrel of Sandra's gun up and down. "That's why Nordenskiöld didn't include any mention of the jars in his book. I'm sure he planned to return to America to look for them, and to learn what had happened to Joey, too." She swung the nail through the air like a stubby wand. "But the tuberculosis took him instead."

"How do you know all this?"

"From Ilona. After Gustaf died, no one had much interest in his old papers. They were stored away in the national museum in Finland."

"Along with the remains of the eighteen Ancestral Puebloan people Gustaf shipped back from Mesa Verde."

Elizabeth aimed the nail's pointed end at Chuck, aligned with the barrel of the gun. "That was the worst of it, if you ask me. Those museum people clung to those corpses all those years like they were diamonds. It was pure, one-hundred-percent evil."

Chuck stared at the bloodstains on Elizabeth's clothing. *Evil?* He glanced away. "The one thing I don't get is the punctured tires," he said, looking at the nail in her hand. "What was that all about?"

"I had to make sure no one got away with the jars. I set the nails against the tires and waited in the trees until you and everyone else got back from the canyon yesterday. If any of you had come back with the jars, the nails would have stopped you long enough for me to come along and take what was rightfully mine. But every last one of you came back empty-handed."

"You almost killed my daughter and me."

"But I didn't, did I? Not yet." She twisted the nail back and forth in the air as if screwing its pointed end into Chuck's sternum. "Besides, I'm not looking to kill anyone. I'm just looking to finish what Uncle Joey started."

"To enrich yourself."

"That's what I'd expect you to think. And, yes, I do, in fact, deserve a little something for all the risks I've taken. That's what Samuel didn't understand. I told him to move away from the hole, but he wouldn't budge. I couldn't have that, of course. His hatchet was right there on the ground. He barely defended himself." She flexed her arm. "I've split firewood my whole life. Splitting him just came natural to me." Her lips turned down. "But, please, don't misunderstand me. My expenses will be covered with only a jar or two. The others will go to academia. They'll provide an incredible legacy for Uncle Joey."

"Except that the jars are gone. Long gone. They were taken decades ago."

"Oh, no." Elizabeth shook her head emphatically. "Oh, no, no, no. The circles are right there in the dust, fresh as a new-bloomed flower. Samuel tried to convince me the jars weren't there when they first opened the hole yesterday. But any fool could look at the circles and know he was lying. He took them for himself, and he came back today to cover his tracks. When I realized the lies he was telling me . . . well, put it this way: he got what he deserved. I had to hide when you came along with all your people. It was a goddamn circus there for a while, what with all your whimpering and carrying on. When you finally left, I pulled Samuel into the trees and threw some branches over him and hightailed it back here, lickety-split."

Chuck stared at Samuel's killer, resolve building in him. Regardless of the gun in Elizabeth's hand aimed at his gut, he would say what he wanted to say, what he *had* to say to her.

30

"Samuel was telling the truth. The jars weren't there when he and the others opened the chamber yesterday," Chuck said. "The circles in the dust looked fresh to you because the chamber was only opened once in the thousand years since it first was built by the Ancestral Puebloans and closed up with the jars inside it. The only time it was broken into was when the jars were stolen. That was in 1891, when your uncle was killed."

"How can you possibly know that?" Elizabeth demanded.

"By the tracks of the two insects, darkling beetles and European meat beetles, on the floor of the crypt. Darkling beetles like darkness. They'd have been attracted to the chamber when it first was constructed. The weight of the jars placed in the dust on the floor of the chamber would have obliterated their tracks, and any beetles left inside would have died away when the vault was sealed shut. That's why there are no tracks of darkling beetles across the circles indented in the dust—whereas the narrower tracks of the meat beetles pass right across the circles."

"Meaning what?" Elizabeth challenged.

"Meaning everything. European meat beetles are handy archaeological time stamps here in North America because they were introduced to this continent by Spanish explorers who came here in the 1500s. That was centuries after Ancestral Puebloans abandoned Mesa Verde, which means the tracks of the meat beetles in the chamber couldn't possibly have been left there at the time of its construction by the Ancestral Puebloans. When your uncle's corpse is analyzed, I'm sure remnants of dried jerky will be found in his pockets. European meat beetles lay their eggs in meat, most often beef. The beetles would have hatched from the dried meat after Joseph's death, and after the chamber was sealed back up with his body inside it. The beetles would have wandered around the closed chamber until they died, leaving their tracks behind. The fact that their tracks go right across the circles imprinted in the dust by the canopic jars proves the jars were removed from the chamber at the time of your uncle's murder in 1891, not yesterday by Samuel and the others."

The gun trembled in Elizabeth's hand. "But I . . . I . . ."

"And now," Chuck continued, attempting to ignore the shaking pistol, "I have a question for you. How was it that Gustaf came to know about the jars in the first place?"

Elizabeth blinked. The gun grew still in her grip. "A Ute medicine man told him about them. That's what he wrote in his notes, the ones Ilona studied. The story of the jars was passed down through generation after generation of Utes. The medicine man told Gustaf where the jars were hidden. 'It is time,' the old man said, according to what Gustaf wrote. Gustaf sent Joey to dig in the spot revealed by the medicine man. But the man must have told others, too. The Utes had been driven off their good bottomlands along the Mancos River and into the desert scrublands by white settlers like my ancestors. Ilona thinks the medicine man revealed the location of the jars to as many settlers as he could in an attempt to set them against each other."

"Which explains how your uncle wound up with his head cut in two and the jars stolen." Chuck looked Elizabeth in the eye. "The beetle tracks prove the jars were taken when your uncle was murdered. The fact that they're not in any museum or public collection proves they were sold on the black market to a private collector."

Elizabeth adjusted her grip on Sandra's gun. Her eyes grew hard and she bared her teeth. "It's you who will pay for this," she snarled. "For Uncle Joey, for my great-grandfather, for me."

She leveled the gun on Chuck's chest, her finger tightening around the trigger.

Movement flashed behind Elizabeth from the back of Samuel's truck. A stout tree branch slammed into Elizabeth's head. She toppled forward, reflexively pulling the trigger on her gun as its barrel sank.

The gun blast echoed through the forest and the bullet buried itself in the dirt at Chuck's feet with a muted *thwop*. Elizabeth landed facedown in front of him. Blood seeped from the top of her head. He reached down, tore the gun from her grasp, and stepped back, aiming the pistol at her prostrate form.

Behind Elizabeth, Kyla dropped the club-like ponderosa branch. "I waited as long as I could," she said.

"Too long," Chuck told her, his entire body shaking.

"I didn't want to have to do that."

"You know what she did to Samuel."

"She's crazy."

"She's a murderer."

"Two times over."

"I don't think so."

"What do you mean?"

"She killed Samuel with his hatchet. But Barney was shot. So was Sandra." Chuck waved Sandra's pistol at Elizabeth, sprawled on the ground. "If Elizabeth shot Barney yesterday and Sandra today, why didn't she have her gun with her just now? Why did she have to take Sandra's gun away from me to arm herself?"

He shuddered, his thoughts returning to Elizabeth's truck, hidden up the road in the forest. There had been *two* shovels, not one, among the hand tools in the bed of the truck, both of them encrusted with dirt.

He looked from Elizabeth's unmoving form to Kyla. The Harvard student no longer stood guard at the cleft leading to the floor of the canyon—where Janelle and Rosie hid in the alcove with Sandra and Michaela. "You left the slot."

"I waited, but nothing was happening," Kyla said. "It was obvious the shooter was gone, so I climbed up to the rim and came this way. I figured you might need some help. Turns out I was right." She pointed at Elizabeth. "I saw her take the gun from you while I was sneaking up through the trees."

"Thank you," Chuck said to her.

He sprinted for Gunnel Canyon.

31

Chuck raced through the forest with Sandra's gun in his hand. He was convinced Clarence and Carmelita were safe; the sound of the gunshot fired by Elizabeth was sure to keep them in hiding. But Janelle and Rosie were defenseless in the alcove in the bottom of the canyon with Sandra and Michaela.

The sandstone shelf at the edge of Gunnel Canyon appeared ahead through the trees. He slowed, approaching the canyon rim with caution.

By safely passing this way just a short time ago, Kyla had proved that the shooter had abandoned the head of the slot leading to the bottom of the canyon. But where had the shooter gone?

Chuck licked his lips, his heart pounding.

Rather than descend the slot toward a potential ambush, the shooter must have departed in search of another way into the canyon—presumably taking the more circuitous route via the canyon's head, where the imposing cliff walls petered away. Chuck—and Clarence and Carmelita before him—would have climbed out of the head of the canyon before the shooter's descent into the gorge via the same route.

Chuck sped up, charging along the canyon rim and plunging down the slot.

As he exited the bottom of the cleft, the high-pitched *ping* of a small-caliber gunshot sounded from up the canyon where Janelle and Rosie waited in the alcove.

* * *

Fear choked him as he raced up the canyon along the base of the cliff.

"No more!" Janelle's voice commanded from out of sight ahead.

Chuck dug his feet into the earth, halting where the cliff wall pressed outward, the recess and Janelle beyond.

"That's *enough*," Janelle said, her voice raw and powerful. "You shot Michaela. You got your revenge."

Silence followed her words.

Chuck crept forward. He poked his head from behind the extended segment of rock, gaining a view of the alcove and the open section of canyon floor leading to it.

Janelle stood in front of the shadowed opening, facing Chuck, her back to the alcove and the overhanging cliff above it. Michaela lay on her side, curled into a ball, in the sand at Janelle's feet. Michaela's neck was slack, her head drooping to the ground.

Audrey stood in front of Janelle and Michaela, her back to Chuck, a small, dark pistol in her hand, its barrel trained on Janelle.

Chuck swallowed, his throat parched. He was too distant to reliably target Audrey with a shot from Sandra's handgun. But the only way to get closer required crossing the open ground in front of the alcove. If Audrey heard him approaching before he got within range, he would place Janelle in even greater danger.

"You got what you wanted," Janelle said to Audrey. "You're done now." She held out her hand, palm up. "Give me the gun."

Audrey shook her head. She tilted her pistol downward, aiming it at Michaela's unmoving form on the ground. "I'm not even sure I hit her."

Janelle kept her eyes on Audrey. "What do you mean? She's dead. She's not moving."

Audrey raised her gun to Janelle. "She got what she deserved."

"And you got what you wanted."

"You have no idea what I wanted," Audrey growled. "What I've wanted for a long time. What *we* wanted."

"We?"

"Elizabeth and me. She got in touch with Barney after she heard from Ilona in Finland. She hired him to do an archaeological survey of her family's land for some extra cash. After she got to know him, she brought up what she really wanted—to follow up on Joey Cannon's disappearance and find the jars. Barney told me how much they were worth. That was when I got involved. How could I not? We were still on the hook for Jason's college loans. We were behind on the mortgage, the car payments, the credit cards. And Michaela was paying Barney next to nothing, like always."

Audrey addressed Michaela, on the ground. "I made him ask you for a raise. Just a little one. But you told him there were plenty of younger archaeologists, just out of school, who would love to have his job." Her voice rose as she cursed Michaela's unmoving body. "You *bitch*, you."

She returned her attention to Janelle. "That was it for me. I called Elizabeth and told her I would do whatever she needed. I told her I would make sure Barney did whatever she needed him to do, too."

"Was it her idea to break into Chuck's study?"

"No, that was mine. There were so many places to consider, and time was so short. Ilona already had arrived from Finland. While she and Samuel dug over here in the canyon, I convinced Elizabeth we should check the south alcove in Falls Creek. Everybody knows that's where they reburied Esther and the rest of the mummies. I figured mummies and canopic jars naturally would go together. But we dug and dug, and hacked and hacked at the back wall, and came up with nothing. Zero. Zilch. Elizabeth was furious. I had to find something to calm her down, so I told her about Chuck's files. I knew there'd be all sorts of ideas in them for where we could look next."

Audrey wiggled her pistol. "I never should have brought this with us. It's just a little thing we keep around the house for self-defense. I hardly even know how to use it."

"What about the postcard?"

"I spotted it in one of Chuck's folders and took it. Elizabeth was so mad about the time we wasted in Falls Creek. I wanted to prove to her my idea had been a good one. One look at Esther and you just knew the jars had to be buried with her."

"But Barney was holding the card when he . . . when you . . ."

"We'd agreed that we wouldn't take anything, that we would just go through the files for ideas. We left everything lying around on the floor to make it look like a break-in."

"But you took the card."

"I couldn't resist. Just to show Elizabeth, that's all. But when Barney saw it, he ripped it out of my hand. He insisted we had to return it. We were already out in the alley by then. I was freaking out. I tried to get it back from him so we could get out of there, but he wouldn't let go. He wouldn't listen to me." Her voice grew hard. "All his years of work, for nothing. Why couldn't he have provided for me? For our family? But he had to work for peanuts, and me and Jason, we paid the price. We're *still* paying the price."

Her shoulders slumped.

"I pulled the gun out of my pocket. I hadn't told him I was bringing it. I hadn't really thought anything about it, just that it would be good to have along. I pointed it at him, told him to give me the postcard. 'Give it to me!' I said to him. 'Give . . . it . . . to . . . me!'"

Tears streamed down Audrey's face.

"He backed away from me. He told me, 'No.' *No*? He'd never stood up to me that way before, not once, not *ever*. I wouldn't have it. Not from him, not from anyone. I squeezed the trigger. A little red dot showed up in the middle of his shirt. And the surprise in his eyes? Oh, God. I pulled the trigger again and again. His eyes got dimmer each time. Finally, he fell over. His head smacked the pavement. That's how I knew he was gone. I was going to grab the card from his hand. But it was just a scrap of paper, it meant nothing." She drew a shaky breath. "I ran to the end of the alley. Then, I remembered to slow down. I stuck the gun in my pocket and walked across town, calm as could be, and waited for the police to come knocking on the door."

"What about Beatrice?" Janelle asked.

"Beatrice?"

"Don't play dumb with me."

"Okay, okay," Audrey said. "She called me, supposedly to tell me how sorry she was about Barney."

"That sounds like something she'd do."

"Maybe to you. But I'd only met her once or twice, when Barney and I stopped by your place. And now she calls me up out of the blue to tell me how bad she feels for me? I wasn't having any of it." Audrey's voice grew sharp. "I was plenty suspicious, believe you me. Why wouldn't I be? I went over there to have a little talk with her, and she just kept right on asking me all sorts of questions."

"That's how she is. She's a talker."

"Yeah, well, too much for my liking. When she asked if Barney had ever worked at Mesa Verde, she must've seen something in my eyes. She said she was going back to the kitchen to make some tea. But I could tell she was nervous. She was shaking from head to toe. I followed her back there and caught her sending a text on her phone. I told her to give it to me, just so I could see who she was texting. I must've shoved her. I don't remember. The next thing I knew, she was on the floor and all I could think was to get out of there."

"I'm sure she didn't see you and Barney at our house," Janelle said evenly, "because she didn't say anything to me or Chuck. You just thought she saw something, which is good. That means what you did to her was an accident. Barney wouldn't want you to—"

"Barney?" Audrey snapped. "*Barney*? How dare you try to tell me what my husband would or would not want me to do." She tightened her grip on the gun.

Chuck tightened his fingers around Sandra's pistol as well. Audrey was making no move to stand down. He had to act.

He stepped around the outcrop in the canyon wall and snuck forward, treading silently through the sand in full view of Janelle—and Audrey, if she happened to catch sight of him in her peripheral vision.

Janelle lifted her finger, drawing Audrey's attention. "I'm sorry. I didn't mean to speak for Barney," she said. She pointed at Audrey's pistol. "I only know there's nothing to be gained from any more of that."

Chuck stole closer.

Janelle held Audrey's gaze. "I'm asking you, for the sake of our children, yours and mine—for Jason, and for Rosie and Carmelita—to do what, deep down, you know is right."

Chuck was twenty feet from Audrey now. Close enough.

Audrey's pistol shook. "I won't hurt Rosie. I won't hurt Carm. You have my word on that. But I won't let anyone stop me from protecting myself and my dear Jason. Not you. Not anyone."

The gun grew still in her grip in clear preparation for firing.

"Audrey!" Chuck barked from behind her.

She spun, swinging her gun with her.

The deep-throated *whomp-whomp-whomp* of an approaching helicopter filled the canyon, the beat of the rotors reverberating off the cliff walls.

Audrey glanced up, tracking the sound. She stiffened, staring up at a boulder the size of a small car plummeting off the overhanging cliff, straight at her. She threw herself backward to the ground. The rock struck the earth with a resounding *thump* where she'd stood a millisecond before.

Clarence and Carmelita peered down from the edge of the cliff. Audrey raised her gun from where she lay in the sand, aiming up at them. They ducked back, out of her line of fire.

Janelle leapt past the fallen boulder and chopped her hand down on Audrey's gun arm, wrestling for control of the pistol.

The gun fired and Audrey screeched, letting go of the pistol and grasping her ankle with both hands.

Janelle took the gun and backed away, aiming it at Audrey's chest.

Audrey looked up at Janelle, her face pale. Blood streamed from her wounded lower leg. "Help me," she whimpered. "Please, help me."

The helicopter appeared above the rim of the canyon and roared across the band of sky visible between the canyon walls.

Janelle glanced at Sandra's pistol in Chuck's hand, trained on Audrey. She set Audrey's handgun in the sand and knelt next to Michaela.

Michaela's eyes popped open. "Audrey was right," she said to Janelle. "She missed." She sat up and turned to Chuck. "I was convinced you had to be in on all this, what with the postcard from your study, and Barney's killing in your backyard," she said. "I was wrong."

Chuck glanced at her while keeping the gun trained on Audrey. "You were wrong."

"I'm sorry."

He waved off her apology with his free hand.

Rosie charged out of the alcove. "Daddy!" she cried, wrapping her arms around him.

"It's okay, *m'hija*," he said, pulling her close with one arm. "Your *mamá* took care of things. So did your uncle and sister."

Rosie craned her head toward the top of the cliff. Clarence and Carmelita grinned down at her.

Rosie waved to her big sister. "Good work, *hermana*," she called.

EPILOGUE

One Week Later

Chuck turned ears of sweet corn on the grill in the backyard using metal tongs. He set the tongs aside and zipped his fleece pullover to his chin.

The sun was below the horizon, the October air chilly in the deepening evening shade behind the house.

Janelle shouldered open the back door and descended the steps carrying an earthenware serving bowl in one hand and a platter of griddle-heated tortillas in the other. She wore jeans and a lightweight down coat. The sugary smell of the grilled corn mixed in the air with the peppery scent of the homemade tomatillo salsa in the serving bowl.

Janelle set the bowl and platter on the weathered picnic table beside the grill. Chuck dipped his finger into the salsa. She slapped his wrist. "Quit that," she said, smiling.

He licked his finger. "Mmmm," he exclaimed, his eyes closed. "*Excelente.*"

"Of course it's *excelente.* It's my *mamá's* recipe."

Rosie left the house carrying a platter of sides in individual bowls—grated cheese, sour cream, cilantro, diced onions, sliced black olives, and chopped leafy greens. Carmelita followed with a pot of stewed pinto beans and a plate of sautéed red and yellow peppers still steaming from the skillet.

Both girls wore shorts. Goosebumps stood out on their bare legs. They did, however, wear long-sleeved fleece tops in a bow to the cool evening.

Clarence came out last, in loose jeans and a baggy sweatshirt. He grasped a pair of locally brewed Ska Pinstripe ales in one beefy hand and a third bottle of Pinstripe in the other.

He leaned his broad backside against the screen door, pressing it closed behind him, and raised the bottles in the air. "Come and get 'em," he said, descending the steps to the yard.

Chuck and Janelle took a bottle each. The three of them clinked the glass tops together.

"Cheers," said Chuck.

"Right back at you, *jefe*," Clarence replied.

Janelle took a deep swallow. "Mmmm," she moaned, her eyes closed, imitating Chuck a moment ago. "*Excelente.*" She shot him a teasing grin, her dark eyes crinkling, before announcing, "Fajita time, *familia mia*, while everything's hot."

Carmelita aimed a finger at the bottle in Clarence's hand as she joined him at the table. "Only one," she told him. "You know that, right?"

"*Jesu Cristo*," Clarence muttered, settling on the bench seat beside her. "What are you, my drill sergeant?"

Carmelita nodded curtly. "I'm your fearless leader."

Chuck caught her eye. "Instead of ruling the world, is your latest plan just to rule your uncle?"

"I'm *starting* with him," she said. "I'll expand from there." She addressed the others. "Uncle Clarence is neglecting to mention that it was him who asked me to be his coach. We started with fifty SkySteps, up and down. We're increasing it by ten steps every day. We did ninety this afternoon, plus a mile run on the Grid trail."

"You can call it running if you want," said Clarence. "I call it stumbling." He looked around the table. "I've only lost two pounds so far."

"It's only been five days," Carmelita countered. "Besides . . ."

She scowled at the bottle of beer in his hand, her brow constricting above her pixie nose.

He tucked the bottle behind his back. "Don't nobody get between me and my *cerveza*."

She poked her finger into his belly. "That much is obvious."

"I know, I know," he admitted. "That's why I asked you to be my coach."

Chuck stacked a platter with the roasted ears of corn.

"All things in moderation," he said, sending the corn around the table and sitting down. "Isn't that right?"

"*Sí*," said Clarence.

"Just like me," Rosie said. "I'm a moderate dancer now."

Chuck hid his smile. "*Modern* dancer. You're a modern dancer now."

"That's what I said. Modern. I love my lessons. My teacher has a big booty, just like me. She says it's bootyful."

Chuck exchanged a glance with Janelle, who'd agreed with his idea to sign Rosie up for lessons.

Rosie continued. "Carm can climb around on the roof at the rock gym all she wants. I'm staying on the ground from now on, and spinning and spinning and spinning. Dancing is the most fun *ever*."

Carmelita rolled her eyes. "You've only had one lesson so far."

"That's all I needed to know how much I love it. Daddy was right. It's the perfect thing for me. It lets me move my bootyful body all around and around." She shook her shoulders and dipped her head in time to a silent beat.

"Yo, *bambina*!" Clarence exclaimed. "You show 'em, girl."

He raised his hand and she slapped it from across the table.

"I'm grooooovin' now," she sang out, still rocking in her seat.

Clarence shimmied along with her. "Just so's you don't get yourself a booty as big as mine."

"My teacher said I'm perfect-sized for dancing."

"She's right," Janelle said, passing the platter of tortillas. "Like your daddy said, it's all about moderation."

They filled their tortillas and buttered and salted their corn.

Rosie took a bite of her fajita. "I'm so happy to be home," she said, chewing.

"Me, too," said Carmelita.

Chuck and Janelle had worried about how Rosie and Carmelita would handle returning to the house, but the girls had slept through their first night back and every night since.

"Me, three," said Clarence.

Rosie giggled. "You don't live here, Uncle Clarence."

"Oh, but I could. Maybe I'll move in and kick you out of your bedroom. You'd have to sleep with Carm in her room." He looked at Rosie, his face set. "That'd be okay with you to not have your own room anymore, wouldn't it?"

Rosie looked from Clarence to Janelle, her eyes growing large and round. "He wouldn't ever do that, would he, *Mamá*?"

"No, *m'hija*," Janelle assured her. "Believe me, Chuck . . . your daddy . . . couldn't put up with your uncle staying with us for more than twenty-four hours. Neither could our refrigerator. You know why, don't you?"

Rosie smiled, a piece of cilantro flagging one of her front teeth. "Because it would be empty!"

"We'd starve to death," Janelle agreed with a definitive nod.

"Just a minute, there," Clarence warned. "I'm on a diet now. Carm's holding my feet to the fire."

"Is a diet that includes beer *really* a diet?" Janelle asked him.

"In moderation. I get to drink beer in moderation."

"Just one at each meal," Carmelita confirmed. She narrowed her eyes at her uncle. "Not including breakfast, *verdad*?"

He sighed. "*Verdad. Dos cervezas cada día*, one at lunch and one at dinner, that's all."

Beatrice appeared in her kitchen window above the fence at the side of the yard. They waved to her from the table.

She opened the window. "Brrr," she called. "It's pretty cold out there, isn't it?"

"It's not hot," Janelle agreed. "But it's not as cold as it's gonna be in a few weeks."

Carmelita set her fajita on her plate. "How are you feeling, Beatrice?"

"I'm doing fine, sweet pea, thanks for asking," she replied. "Everybody always tells me how hard-headed I am. Turns out they're right." She cackled and closed the window with a parting wave.

Pasta Alfredo appeared in the study window next to the picnic table. The cat crouched on the inside ledge and looked out at them, her tail wrapped around her bunched feet.

"Aww," said Rosie, eyeing the cat. "She looks so sad and lonely in there."

"She's barely five feet away from us," Chuck said. "Besides, you know the rule."

"She's a full-time inside kitty," Rosie intoned, "so she doesn't eat all the birds."

Chuck looked across the table at Carmelita. "Maybe when you move on from Clarence and you're the supreme ruler of all the world, you could make everyone else keep their cats indoors, too."

Carmelita jutted her jaw. "Sure," she said. "I could do that."

Chuck looked past Pasta Alfredo at the framed picture of Janelle and the girls facing out from where he'd rehung it on the far wall when he'd cleaned up the study.

Rosie followed Chuck's gaze into the room. "I wish Audrey would've died when she shot herself, instead of just hitting herself in the leg."

"You don't have to worry about her," Chuck said. "They'll keep her locked up for a long, long time. Probably forever."

Carmelita wiped her mouth with her napkin. "They're going to give Joseph Cannon's body back to his family, aren't they?"

"Yes. To all the Cannons—except Elizabeth—for reburial in the family cemetery on the old Cannon farm."

Rosie rubbed a dribble of grease from her chin with the back of her hand. "Elizabeth will be in jail for a long time, too, just like Audrey, won't she?" she asked Chuck.

"That's the plan."

"But I don't have to be a witness in court or anything. That's what you promised."

"Sandra says there will be more than enough witnesses without you and Carmelita having to be involved. Sandra herself for one, your *mamá* for another." He reached out to Janelle and squeezed her hand. "You were amazing, *cariña*. You stood up to Audrey. You saved everybody—Sandra, Michaela, Rosie. No wonder you got the call from Mark Chapman yesterday offering you the full-time position."

Janelle's face flushed. "I can't wait to get started," she said. "But someone's going to have to keep an eye on things around here when I'm working." She tilted her head at Carmelita and Rosie. "And by 'things,' I mean these two." She held Chuck's gaze. "Nights, weekends, holidays—it's all going to be up to you."

"Good," Chuck said. He looked at the girls. "Okay with you?"

Carmelita nodded. "I'll let you know when you screw up."

"I'm sure you will."

Rosie clapped her hands. "The first thing I want to do is go find the jars with you."

"The canopic jars?" He sighed. "That's easier said than done. There's plenty of evidence that they exist. But for now, at least, they're gone. Maybe they're still being held in somebody's private collection after all these years, or maybe they were destroyed a long time ago. We just don't know."

"That stinks," said Rosie.

"I'm going to write a paper about them. I'll lay out everything we've learned so far. Who knows, maybe somebody will read it and come forward. There are so many priceless objects in so many private collections all around the world—artifacts that have been handed down from generation to generation, until the people who have them don't even know what they've got."

"They're ass—"

"Rosalita!" Janelle scolded before Rosie completed the word.

Risking Janelle's wrath, Chuck said, "They're the descendants of assholes, anyway. Every now and then, though, people do the right thing and return artifacts their predecessors bought illegally. When they do that, they make the world a better place."

"Do you think it'll happen with the jars?" Rosie asked.

"We can always hope."

"Plus," she said, "maybe there are more jars out there somewhere, still in the ground, waiting to be discovered."

"Along with lots of other stuff, too."

She smiled. "That's why I'm going to be an archaeologist when I grow up—just like you, Daddy."

ACKNOWLEDGMENTS

This book and the National Park Mystery Series would not exist without the support of a team of people to whom I am greatly indebted.

My early readers of *Mesa Verde Victim* provided invaluable wisdom and advice. They include my wife Sue, Margaret Mizushima, Roger Johns, Chuck Greaves, John Peel, Kevin Graham, Lyle Balenquah, and Lt. Pat Downs of the La Plata County Sheriff's Department.

The editorial team at Torrey House Press is simply the best. Thanks to Kirsten Johanna Allen, Anne Terashima, Rachel Davis, and Kathleen Metcalf.

A shoutout to the many award-winning and bestselling mystery authors who have lent their names to mine in the form of thoughtful, enthusiastic quotes that have helped the National Park Mystery Series find increasing success.

And, as always, to the independent booksellers keeping books and reading alive in communities large and small across America, my enduring gratitude.

FURTHER READING

Though *Mesa Verde Victim* is fiction through and through, it is based on the true history of the Ancestral Puebloan culture, which thrived across the Four Corners region a thousand years ago, and the study and plunder of the culture's surviving artifacts and grave sites over the last century and a half.

In working to get the factual portions of the story right, I leaned heavily on the late-1800s writings of Gustaf Nordenskiold and the more recent work of Judith and David Reynolds, including Nordenskiold's *The Cliff Dwellers of the Mesa Verde, Southwestern Colorado* and the Reynolds' *Nordenskiold of Mesa Verde: A Biography*.

I learned a great deal from Florence and Robert Lister's evocative books chronicling the history of archaeological discovery in the Four Corners. Particularly informative for *Mesa Verde Victim* were the Listers' *Earl Morris & Southwestern Archaeology*, and Florence Lister's *Prehistory in Peril: The Worst and the Best of Durango Archaeology*, and *Pot Luck: Adventures in Archaeology*.

ABOUT SCOTT GRAHAM

Scott Graham is the author of eleven books, including the National Park Mystery Series from Torrey House Press, and *Extreme Kids,* winner of the National Outdoor Book Award. Graham is an avid outdoorsman who enjoys mountaineering, skiing, backpacking, mountain climbing, and whitewater rafting with his wife, who is an emergency physician, and their two sons. He lives in Durango, Colorado.

TORREY HOUSE PRESS

Voices for the Land

The economy is a wholly owned subsidiary of the environment, not the other way around.
　　　　　　　—Senator Gaylord Nelson, founder of Earth Day

Torrey House Press is an independent nonprofit publisher promoting environmental conservation through literature. We believe that culture is changed through conversation and that lively, contemporary literature is the cutting edge of social change. We strive to identify exceptional writers, nurture their work, and engage the widest possible audience; to publish diverse voices with transformative stories that illuminate important facets of our ever-changing planet; to develop literary resources for the conservation movement, educating and entertaining readers, inspiring action.

Visit www.torreyhouse.org for reading group discussion guides, author interviews, and more.

As a 501(c)(3) nonprofit publisher, our work is made possible by the generous donations of readers like you. Join the Torrey House Press family and give today at www.torreyhouse.org/give.

Torrey House Press is supported by the National Endowment for the Arts, Back of Beyond Books, The King's English Bookshop, Wasatch Global, Jeff and Heather Adams, Stephen Strom, Diana Allison, Kirtly Parker Jones, Kitty Swenson, Jerome Cooney and Laura Storjohann, Heidi Dexter and David Gens, Robert Aagard and Camille Bailey Aagard, Kathleen and Peter Metcalf, Rose Chilcoat and Mark Franklin, Stirling Adams and Kif Augustine, Charlie Quimby and Susan Cushman, Doug and Donaree Neville, the Barker Foundation, the Sam and Diane Stewart Family Foundation, the Jeffrey S. and Helen H. Cardon Foundation, Utah Division of Arts & Museums, and Salt Lake County Zoo, Arts & Parks. Our thanks to individual donors, subscribers, and the Torrey House Press board of directors for their valued support.

Join the Torrey House Press family and give today at www.torreyhouse.org/give.

CANYONLANDS CARNAGE

A National Park Mystery
by Scott Graham

Coming next in the National Park Mystery series

TORREY HOUSE PRESS

SALT LAKE CITY • TORREY

1

Chuck Bender snugged the straps of his personal flotation device tight around his chest. He thrust his feet against the whitewater raft's round aluminum foot bar, straightening his legs and pressing his hips into the low captain's chair positioned at the center of the raft.

Counterweighted oars extended through bronze oarlocks from the sides of the big, rubber boat into the calm water of the Colorado River. He lifted the oars out of the river. Droplets sparkled in the midday sun as they streamed off the oar blades and back into the brown, silt-laden water.

Clarence Ortega, Chuck's brother-in-law, sat in the front of the raft on an oversized plastic cooler strapped with inch-wide webbing to the raft's metal frame. The heavyset young man, twenty years Chuck's junior, gripped the nylon straps affixed to the cooler, his fingers curled around the loops of webbing at his sides. He stared downstream, where bursts of water spouted into the air from a rapid three hundred feet ahead.

The churning whitewater was the first of Cataract Canyon's two dozen unforgiving rapids over the course of fourteen torturous miles in the heart of southeastern Utah's remote Canyonlands National Park. The roar of the roiling whitewater nearly drowned out Chuck's words as he leaned forward and said to Clarence, "We're all set. Hold on tight and we'll be through this first one in a heartbeat."

"It's my heart I'm worried about," Clarence replied over his shoulder. He bent forward over the cooler, his back and neck stiff. "Look at that," he said as he peered ahead. "The water's shooting straight up into the air. *Jesu Cristo.*" He turned his ear to the whitewater. "You didn't tell me it would be this loud."

Chuck dipped an oar into the river and gave it a tug, spinning the raft a few degrees to keep it aligned with the flow of the river, straight downstream. "Loud doesn't necessarily mean terrifying."

"I'm way more than terrified, *jefe.* I'm scared to freakin' death. That *rapido* sounds like some sort of crazed beast that's been let loose and is looking to swallow us whole."

"That's what twenty-three-thousand cubic feet of water sounds like when it plunges through a rapid."

"Plunges is right," Clarence said, his voice shaking.

Chuck looked downriver past Clarence's hunched frame. They would enter the whitewater in less than a minute, last in a procession of eight boats—two hardshell kayaks and half a dozen inflatable rafts—on a two-week river journey, coined the Waters of the Southwest Expedition. The kayaks led the way. The rafts followed, lined a hundred feet apart in the center of the river.

Seated in their highly maneuverable playboats, one lime green, the other electric yellow, the group's two safety kayakers dug their dual-bladed paddles into the water, powering toward the head of the rapid. The kayakers, Liza and Conch, would run the rapid first and station themselves at its bottom, ready to rescue any expedition members tossed from the rafts by the force of the surging waves.

Liza and Conch were guides for Colorado River Adventures, the outfitter for the expedition, as were the captains of all the rafts except the one at the end of the line, which was helmed by Chuck.

The expedition's lead inflatable boats were a pair of fourteen-foot-long paddle rafts—small, lightweight watercraft carrying no gear, only passengers. Three paddlers lined each side of the rafts, six to a boat. The paddlers hugged the rafts' air-filled side thwarts with their legs like rodeo riders atop saddle broncs. Five paddlers in each boat held paddles aloft, ready to dig them into the water at the command of the captains positioned at the back right corners of the two rafts.

Unlike the paddlers' upraised paddles, the captains' paddles were held blade-deep in the water beside them. The captains swung the paddle blades back and forth in the current, using their blades as rudders to align the lightweight boats directly downstream as they approached the stretch of turbulent water.

Three sixteen-foot-long passenger rafts followed the two paddle rafts. Seated at the midpoint of their boats, the passenger-raft captains gripped stout, fiberglass-shafted oars in their sun-bronzed hands. Four expedition members rode in each raft, one at each corner—save for the last of the three boats. The final passenger raft, captained by Tamara Fisher, head guide on the trip for CRA, lacked a passenger at its right rear corner, opposite Joseph Conway, senior engineer for the US Bureau of Reclamation Department of Water Planning, who was stationed at the left rear corner of the raft.

The expedition members at the front of the passenger rafts held paddles, set to stroke through the rapid to aid their captains. Those at the rear corners, like Joseph, were tasked merely with clinging to the rafts to avoid being thrown into the frothing water as the boats heaved and bucked through the turbulence.

Chuck captained the expedition's so-called gear barge at the end of the procession. He'd been hired to serve as the expedition's naturalist and historian, offering mini-lectures along the way about the Colorado River's geology, plant and animal life, and, his specialty, the basin's human history, particularly that of an archaeological nature. Clarence was the expedition's unpaid swamper, performing all manner of grunt work—setting up and taking down the group's portable toilet, putting up and stowing tents and cots for more senior expedition members, and washing dishes and chopping vegetables during meal preparation and cleanup in the camp kitchen—in return for his free trip down the river.

The gear raft was eighteen feet long and half again as wide, its inflated tubes more than two feet in diameter. The gargantuan boat carried the group's camping and kitchen gear—sturdy tables, collapsible chairs, cooking supplies, steel fuel tanks, aluminum dry boxes stuffed with food and drinks, and two coffin-sized plastic coolers filled with meat, cheese, and produce.

All told, the gear raft and its load, strapped fore and aft and along the sides of the boat, weighed more than three-quarters of a ton. Given its immense size and weight, the raft had been challenging for Chuck to steer the last five days. Even the slightest of breezes sweeping across the river knocked the boat off course during the initial, sixty-mile, flatwater portion of the journey. He knew the massive raft would be infinitely more challenging to manage in the first Cataract rapid just ahead and in the rest of the canyon's rapids as well—a fact that, for reasons of selfish pride, he had yet to share with Clarence.

The current slowed where the river pooled before it poured over the lip of the rapid. The procession tightened in the sluggish water, the space between the boats diminishing to fifty feet.

Chuck's gaze was drawn to the unoccupied rear corner of the passenger raft directly ahead. He shivered despite the blazing desert heat of the late-May day. The spot should have been occupied by Ralph Hycum, the esteemed professor emeritus of water policy from the University of Nevada, Las Vegas School of Law. Ralph had been a co-leader of the Waters of the Southwest Expedition, which was comprised of professors, scientists, politicians, water activists, and government officials voyaging together down the river through Canyonlands National Park to experience the park's magnificent red-rock landscape by day, and, around the campfire each night, to debate and seek consensus regarding the contentious regulations for water allocation in the arid American West.

Chuck hadn't known Ralph before the start of the expedition. But he'd grown close to the retired UNLV law professor over the first three days of the journey. He'd enjoyed discussing with the professor the vagaries of the West's convoluted water laws late into the evening hours—until two nights ago, when Ralph had died in his tent of an apparent heart attack. Ralph's body had been airlifted out of the canyon the next morning by an emergency helicopter summoned via satellite phone by Chandler Coswell. Chandler had co-organized the trip along with Ralph and was now the expedition's sole leader.

Ralph's death had cast far less of a pall over the trip than Chuck had anticipated—until he'd reminded himself that the group comprised the West's top field experts on water use and conservation, and that the expedition members therefore were seasoned outdoors people familiar with the risks associated with wilderness travel. Like Chuck, they doubtless had lost numerous friends over the years to whitewater drownings, mountaineering accidents, avalanches, rockfalls, and the like. To die as Ralph had, in a tent in the backcountry of natural causes after a long and fruitful life, likely was the dream of just about every member of the expedition.

After dinner the last two nights, Ralph's closest friends had told stories of past river journeys they'd taken with the professor. The trips had ranged from the desolate Yarlung Zangbo River, deep in the Tibetan Himalaya, to the crowded Hudson River, teeming with water traffic in New York City, and had included numerous journeys down the Southwest's magnificent, cliff-walled desert rivers, similar to the Waters of the Southwest Expedition through Cataract Canyon. At the end of the tales, the group members hoisted their drinks—cans of beer, tumblers of whiskey, mugs of herbal tea—in hearty toasts to Ralph.

Chuck looked away from the empty spot at the back of the passenger raft formerly occupied by Ralph Hycum. He gazed instead at the horizon line extending flat as a straight rule from one side of the river to the other at the top of the upcoming stretch of whitewater. He'd spent the last several weeks studying online videos of rafts navigating Cataract Canyon's rapids, committing to memory the moves he'd be required to make with the heavy, unwieldy gear boat in order to successfully navigate each stretch of whitewater.

Cataract Canyon's twenty-four rapids were spaced so closely together that they were named simply by number in downstream order, from Rapid 1 to 21, except for the canyon's three most notorious stretches of whitewater—named, appropriately, Big Drop One, Big Drop Two, and, most challenging of all, Big Drop Three. The final three punishing rapids would come one after the other in quick succession tomorrow over the course of a steeply descending mile at the end of the canyon.

Ahead, Liza and Conch dropped into Rapid 1. First the safety kayakers' boats, then their bodies, then their helmeted heads disappeared from view as they slipped over the horizon line and downward into the whitewater beyond.

The lead paddle raft reached the top of the rapid seconds after the safety kayakers. At the boat captain's shouted command of "All ahead full," the paddlers in the raft dug their paddles into the water in unison, as they'd practiced on the calm stretch of river over the preceding days. In response, the raft seemed to almost leap over the horizon line and on out of sight after the kayakers. The second paddle raft plunged into the rapid close behind the first.

Clarence said something unintelligible as he faced downstream in front of Chuck.

The rapid was less than three hundred feet away now, its deep-throated growl growing louder with each passing second.

"What's that?" Chuck asked, raising his voice to be heard over the thundering whitewater.

Clarence turned his head and raised his voice as well. "I said, there are a lot of forces at work."

Chuck looked from Clarence to the geysers of water spurting out of the rapid above the horizon line. He grimaced. He didn't need this right now.

"The rapid has so much power, so much force," Clarence continued. "It's got me thinking."

The roar of the whitewater was loud as a jet engine in Chuck's ears. The first of the three passenger rafts crested the horizon line and dropped into the maelstrom, following the kayakers and paddle rafts.

"Thinking about what, for Christ's sake?" Chuck shouted.

"Ralph didn't look that old, in his early seventies maybe, and he supposedly was in good health." Clarence faced forward again and hunkered over the cooler, gripping the straps at his sides.

"So?"

"So," Clarence yelled, "I've been picking up on some stuff—forces, like I said—that I hadn't mentioned to you." The wind whipped off the rapid, moist and cool in the desert heat, carrying the words back to Chuck. "Ralph was too young, too healthy. Seeing this rapid and the forces involved, it's got me convinced that what I've been thinking is right: no way did Ralph die a natural death."

2

Chuck gaped at the back of Clarence's helmeted head. "What the hell are you saying, Clarence?"

"I mean, consider the odds," Clarence hollered.

"You really think—?"

Clarence nodded. "I do. The force of this first rapid made me realize I needed to say something."

Chuck oared backward, slowing the gear boat to add space between it and the remaining two passenger rafts still in sight above the rapid. He gritted his teeth. "Now is not the time, Clarence. In fact, it's the very worst time."

"Sorry, *jefe*," Clarence shouted back. "I just had to say it."

Chuck huffed. They were seconds from dropping into the rapid. He had no choice but to focus on the task at hand.

The rapids in Cataract Canyon formed where house-sized boulders were flushed by flash floods into the river from side canyons. The boulders congregated in invisible piles beneath the surface, roiling the water above. The least threatening of the canyon's rapids were those composed solely of standing waves. Thanks to their constant downstream flow, standing waves offered relatively safe, rollercoaster-like fun as rafts reared up and over them while passengers whooped and hollered in delight.

In contrast, waves known as "holes" formed in the steepest, toughest rapids. Holes were waves that fell backward onto themselves, creating dangerous, recirculating pits in the middle of whitewater runs. To enter a hole in a raft was to risk flipping and flinging passengers into the maw of the hole, where they could be trapped beneath the flipped boat or sucked deep beneath the surface of the water until they drowned.

Numerous holes lurked in the rapids of Cataract Canyon. Indeed, the most treacherous of the canyon's rapids featured more than one hole, requiring captains to oar their boats back and forth across the river in the midst of seething whitewater to bypass them.

Rapid 1 was challenging but not necessarily death defying, rated Class IV on the Class I through V scale of whitewater difficulty. It featured only one hole, but the hole was situated in the very center of the river at the base of the rapid's entry tongue, making it difficult to avoid.

Ahead of the gear raft, the second and third passenger rafts dropped out of sight over the horizon line one behind the other. The gear boat, with Chuck in the captain's seat, was now fifty feet from the top of the rapid. He pushed forward with his oars once, twice, three times. The sour smell of perspiration rose from his armpits, blotting out the sweet, pungent scent of the desert, as he shoved the oars hard away from his chest, adding speed to the raft for use as momentum during the upcoming whitewater run.

The raft crested the horizon line, at which point the four-hundred-yard stretch of whitewater that was Rapid 1 came into view. Chuck surveyed the scene before him, noting first the kayaks and paddle rafts bobbing through the boisterous tail waves at the bottom of the rapid a quarter mile downstream. As he watched, the kayakers peeled off, one to each side of the river, while the paddle rafts coasted through the gradually diminishing waves where the rapid ended and the calm water of the river resumed.

Upstream from the lead kayaks and paddle rafts, two of the three passenger rafts already were successfully below the Rapid 1 hole. The two rafts bounded through the monstrous standing waves in the heart of the rapid. The paddlers at the front corners of the boats dug their paddles into the river while the guides, seated in the center of the boats, strained at their oars. Behind the guides, the expedition members at the back corners of the boats lay on their stomachs, clinging to nylon straps to remain aboard.

The third and final passenger raft, just ahead of the gear boat, floated down the center of the rapid's entry tongue. Tamara pushed forward with her oars while her front paddlers stroked with their paddles, the head guide and her paddlers working as a team to complete the lateral move required to break their boat out of the V-shaped tongue before reaching the hole.

Had the water level been lower, Chuck would have positioned the gear boat to enter Rapid 1 at the edge of the river. He then would have oared the raft away from the Rapid 1 hole from the side of the river. This time of year, however, the river was swollen with snowmelt from the Colorado and Wyoming mountains to the north, making the current so powerful that raft captains who hugged the edge of the river at the head of Rapid 1 would not be able to reliably break their boats through the compressing waves of the rapid's entry tongue and avoid the hole at the tongue's bottom. Instead, those who entered the side of the Rapid 1 tongue at high water levels risked having their boats typewritered—that is, swept by the tongue's powerful side waves into the center of the river and on into the hole, which lurked at the base of the entry tongue like a dark, menacing entrance to the underworld.

When the river was high, as now, the required move to avoid the Rapid 1 hole was first to crest the horizon line in the center of the river with speed gained from initial oar strokes, then to use that speed as momentum, along with more speed and resultant momentum gained from additional oar strokes as the raft floated down the smooth entry tongue, directing the boat across the current with enough force to break through the tongue's compressing waves before reaching the hole.

As Chuck looked on, Tamara—continuing to shove forward with her oars while her paddlers dug into the water with their paddle blades—punched her raft nose-first out of the tongue and away from the hole.

The gear raft, with Chuck at the oars, dropped over the horizon line and began its descent down the Rapid 1 tongue. The oversized thwarts of the massive boat rode so high above the river that any paddlers stationed at the boat's front corners would not have been able to reach the water with their paddles. It was up to Chuck alone to power the raft out of the entry tongue before reaching the hole.

The current picked up speed. He performed a quick push-pull maneuver with his oars, spinning the big raft until its stern faced three-quarters downstream. Seated with his back to the hole, he reached far forward with his oars, his arms fully extended, and dropped the oar blades into water. He pulled backward, enlisting his shoulder and back muscles to apply far more power to the stroke than he could have with a forward push.

His first pull on the oars would initiate the process of sending the raft sideways across the tongue. Several more pulls on the oars, as the raft coursed down the tongue, would, in theory, result in enough momentum for the raft to punch backward through the tongue's lateral waves above the hole.

If Chuck's backward-stroking attempt to break out of the tongue failed, he still would have a few precious seconds to spin the raft forward and strike the hole's breaking wave head on. Nine times out of ten, a raft that entered a hole nose-first would break through the hole and float on downstream unscathed. The key was to never, ever enter a hole sideways, because the narrower side-to-side width of an oval-shaped raft meant floating into a hole in that position, as opposed to lengthwise, increased the odds of flipping exponentially.

Chuck heaved backward on his oars, initiating his first stroke in the center of the rapid's entry tongue. The thick oar shafts bowed where they passed through the oarlocks at the sides of the raft, transferring the power of his stroke to the oar blades. The blades began their forward sweep through the water. He pulled harder, applying every last bit of his strength to the stroke. In response, the oar shafts bowed another inch—at which point, the right oarlock snapped in two.

The freed oar straightened with a vibrating *zing* and skittered sideways across the raft's side thwart. The oarlock's U-shaped top remained wrapped around the oar handle, while the bottom half of the oarlock poked from the head of the oar tower at Chuck's side, its sheered bronze shaft glinting in the sun.

Chuck stared at the spot where a second ago his oar had been secured to the oar tower. His heart rose, pounding, into his throat.

Oarlocks were purposefully fashioned from soft metal. As such, they were designed to break when rafts struck immoveable objects like rocks or cliff walls. But all oarlocks were built to withstand many times more force than any human could possibly apply to them. Yet the gear boat's right oarlock had failed when Chuck had pulled hard against it—leaving him and Clarence in dire condition.

The raft sped down the middle of the tongue, straight for the hole. There wasn't enough time before the boat reached the hole for Chuck to replace the sheered oarlock or to jury-rig a loop of webbing around the oar tower and return the loosed oar to partial service. Instead, he had only the left oar to work with. He released the right oar, grabbed the left oar handle with both hands, and pulled, pivoting the raft until it faced downstream. Thirty feet ahead, at the bottom of the tongue, the hole's backward-cresting wave surged ten feet into the air.

Beside Chuck, the unsecured right oar slid off the thwart and its blade dove into the water. The force of the current against the blade pinwheeled the oar's heavy shaft above the water's surface. The shaft swung across the front of the boat like a pendulum, and the O-shaped iron counterweight, bolted below the handle, struck the side of Clarence's helmet with a violent blow.

"Clarence!" Chuck cried out, too late.

Clarence collapsed across the cooler, his head cradled in his hands. The raft pivoted around the pinwheeling oar until the big boat floated sideways in the current. Chuck dug the left oar into the water and yanked in desperation, but the raft floated into the hole sideways before he could reorient the boat to again face it downstream.

The raft rode sidelong up the face of the wave until it was nearly vertical. Clarence tumbled off the cooler. His big body slammed into a square metal storage box strapped to the raft frame. Chuck toppled out of the captain's seat. As he fell, the handle of the left oar, still secured in its oarlock, struck his ribcage a bruising blow. He wrapped his arms around the left oar tower, clinging to the boat as water poured over the thwarts from all sides.

The raft's forward motion up the wave halted. Still sideways, the boat slid back down the face of the wave into the heart of the hole. The water gushing over the thwarts swept Clarence out of the boat. He disappeared in an instant beneath the surface of the river.

The raft reached the bottom of the hole and stuck there. The madly recirculating water at the base of the wave suctioned the lower thwart, trapping the boat, while the collapsing top of the wave shoved the upper thwart so far over that the boat's massive load of gear hung in the air directly above Chuck's head.

Before the raft flipped entirely, the water sluicing over the thwarts ripped Chuck's arms free of the oar tower and swept him out of the boat. He plunged into the swirling center of the hole. Like Clarence before him, he immediately was sucked beneath the surface of the water. The river closed over him, reducing his world to bubbling quiet and murky darkness.